"If we were working together, it would go something like that," Nick said cautiously.

"Seems to me that we're both working toward the same goal. We both want to know what Gray stole. Why not work together?" Alex added in his own mind, silently, *And it would have the added benefit of me keeping an eye on you until I figure out just what your role in all of this is.*

Nick nodded readily enough and said a shade too enthusiastically, "That's not a half-bad idea."

Alex snorted to himself. Nick had obviously had the exact same thought—that by running around together, he could keep an eye on Alex, too.

If Nick had, in fact, been pulling a one-man surveillance op for the past week, he had to be dead tired. Which made the fight he'd put up when they met that much more impressive. Alex made a mental note never to tangle with this man in a dark alley when he was fully rested.

Dear Reader,

Often books are written far in advance and at different times of the year from when they're published or when the story takes place. I was fortunate enough to get to write this story during the holidays, and it was so much fun to really dig into holiday cheer, blast holiday music, decorate my home to the max and explain to my family that I *had* to do it to put me in the proper mood to write this book. Look out, hubby, when I have to write my next Christmas story in July!

Another reason this book was so much fun to write was because what's better than one hot, sexy, smart, funny hero in a story? Two of them! Of course, as much fun as a holiday love story was to play with, I did have to put the suspense in Harlequin Romantic Suspense, too. With the help of my heroes, Nick and Alex, we cooked up a really exciting, holiday-themed plot that the two of them got to unravel, with plenty of thrills, chills and danger along the way.

I hope this story gives you all the feels it gave me as I wrote it. Happy holidays, and may your season of hope be filled with as much laughter, love, family and friends as Nick and Alex's.

Warmly,

Cindy

HIS CHRISTMAS GUARDIAN

Cindy Dees

HARLEQUIN

ROMANTIC SUSPENSE

HARLEQUIN®
ROMANTIC SUSPENSE™

Recycling programs
for this product may
not exist in your area.

ISBN-13: 978-1-335-73812-7

His Christmas Guardian

Harlequin Enterprises ULC
22 Adelaide St. West, 41st Floor
Toronto, Ontario M5H 4E3, Canada
www.Harlequin.com

Printed in U.S.A.

New York Times and USA TODAY bestselling author **Cindy Dees** is the author of more than fifty novels. She draws upon her experience as a US Air Force pilot to write romantic suspense. She's a two-time winner of the prestigious RITA® Award for romance fiction, a two-time winner of the RT Reviewers' Choice Best Book Award for Romantic Suspense and an RT Book Reviews Career Achievement Award nominee. She loves to hear from readers at www.cindydees.com.

Books by Cindy Dees

Harlequin Romantic Suspense

Runaway Ranch

Navy SEAL's Deadly Secret
The Cowboy's Deadly Reunion
Her SEAL Bodyguard
His Christmas Guardian

Colton 911: Chicago

Colton 911: Desperate Ransom

Mission Medusa

Special Forces: The Recruit
Special Forces: The Spy
Special Forces: The Operator

Code: Warrior SEALs

Undercover with a SEAL
Her Secret Spy
Her Mission with a SEAL
Navy SEAL Cop

Visit the Author Profile page at Harlequin.com for more titles.

Chapter 1

Nicholas Kane straightened the bow tie at his neck. It wasn't often he wore a tuxedo in his line of work, James Bond movies notwithstanding. The fact of the matter was that being a black operative for a shadowy, government intelligence agency had very little to do with glamour and a whole lot to do with, well, shadows.

Tonight, the man he was following, code-named Gray, was supposed to visit an expensive auction house in New York City and a private preview of the paintings and other objets d'art coming up for sale in several days' time. Hence, Nick's monkey suit.

His quarry, tall, burly and mostly bald, was not hard to spot stepping out of a black limousine and heading for the front door. Nick watched the man's second bodyguard scan up and down the street and move inside behind the main bodyguard and the principal.

He supposed it was odd that the only name he knew

the man by was Gray, in spite of Nick having worked for the spymaster for the past four years. He figured Gray had gone by so many aliases over time that the guy had just gotten lazy about coming up with new names for himself.

The limousine pulled away from the curb. Its driver would be the third member of Gray's personal security team.

Now. This was his window to slip into the auction house unspotted. While the driver parked, nobody on Gray's team would be watching the street. In two minutes or so, the driver would come back on foot and take up an unobtrusive position somewhere down the block and report on anyone suspicious who went inside the building.

Nick knew the protocol. He'd been Gray's driver more times than he could count.

He slipped out of the alley and crossed the street quickly, jaywalking to take advantage of a break in the steady stream of yellow cabs that were the lifeblood flowing through the asphalt veins of New York City.

He slowed as he approached the converted warehouse that had been turned into one of the city's most exclusive art galleries and auction venues. The brick box of a building was ugly, but the worst of its ugliness was hidden behind festive holiday lights and a huge garland of pine boughs around the front door. He knew from casing the joint earlier today that this place was, at its core, a large and very-well-secured vault. Even a guy like him would have a hard time breaking into it, let alone getting out with any of the art consignments inside it.

"Invitation?" a bored bouncer-type murmured as he reached the glass front door. Only by looking closely could Nick spot the spiderweb of steel wire embedded in the glass itself.

He reached inside his tuxedo jacket to pull out the engraved invitation, which he handed to the security guard.

"Have a good evening, Mr. Clark."

Nick had no idea where the Medusas had obtained the invitation for him, nor who the real Mr. Clark was. He was just glad the women special operators had been willing and able to help him out on short notice. They'd obviously pulled strings or called in a favor. That was how it worked in his world. It was all about who you knew. Who owed you. Who would help you out in a pinch.

Just inside the front door loomed a Christmas tree at least twelve feet tall, twinkling with lights. It was lavishly decorated in gold, silver and a creamy champagne color, all very stylish and very elegant. Two large, dim, glass-walled galleries opened off to the left and right. They were crowded with men in black tuxes and women in long gowns, all of them dripping with wealth.

Bare branches, painted white, wrapped in strands of white Christmas lights and hung with tiny red glass balls, were artfully placed all around the room. Somewhere, a harpist was plucking stripped-down versions of Christmas carols, and the air smelled of sugar cookies and… Was that the scent of hot cocoa? For just a second, Nick flashed back to his grandmother's kitchen at Christmas, helping her decorate cookies with colored sugar and sprinkles.

This place was far too chic to succumb to an actual festive air, but he appreciated the nod to the holidays. He didn't often get to celebrate them in his line of work. Sadly, evil stopped for no date on any calendar.

Downward-pointing spotlights hung on tracks across the ceilings of the galleries, creating isolated pools of brilliant radiance in the darkness. Each column of light illuminated its own treasure, some bit of color and shine created by an old master, a painting or sculpture, a piece of exquisite porcelain or jewelry.

Nick wandered into the left-hand room, keeping an eye out for Gray.

He snagged a flute of champagne off a waiter's tray and paused in front of a small painting. It was plain and mostly brown, a scene of a Dutch kitchen dominated by a fireplace and a huge iron kettle. A discreet, typed card beside the painting described it as a seventeenth century work in the style of Vermeer. It went on to say that it was possibly an unsigned study by Maria Vermeer.

Nick rolled his eyes. He was no great art expert, but even he knew that no paintings had ever been proven to be the work of Vermeer's eldest daughter. Rumors had long persisted that several surviving paintings attributed to her father were actually her work, but none had ever been proven to be hers. Obviously, the auction house was trying to drive up the price of the ugly little painting by invoking Vermeer's name. He wished them luck with their endeavor.

There.

He caught a glimpse of Gray in the gallery across the hall. Nick cast his gaze down at the Limoges porcelain vase on a stand in front of him but in no other way moved. Gray's bodyguards would be men fully as trained and observant as he himself was. No sense whipping around to stare at his subject or turning his back abruptly on the man and tipping off his security team.

After a moment more of staring at the pale gold vase with its delicate, hand-painted spray of wildflowers, he moved to his left to study a painting. The painting itself didn't interest him. But, if he unfocused his eyes, he was able to watch Gray peripherally while appearing to stare directly at the blurry colors of the art.

Gray was leaving the other display room. He was in conversation with a man who Nick recognized as one of the owners of the gallery, and the two of them headed up the welded steel staircase rising from the middle of the ground floor.

Nick swore under his breath. Should he follow Gray upstairs and not lose sight of him, or should he hold his position down here and not risk exposing himself to Gray's men?

He compromised and headed back toward what would be a staging area for employees. Nick would lay odds there were more stairs back there, somewhere. He went through a set of swinging doors marked Employees Only and found himself in a commercial kitchen.

The place was busy, bustling with waiters coming and going, returning trays of empty glasses, picking up new trays of champagne and lifting platters of canapés. Nick blended in with the flow of waiters, moving with them through the kitchen, only peeling off to the side when he spotted the treads of stairs tucked in the corner.

He jogged up them quickly and silently. His dress shoes had custom-made soles that looked like regular shoe leather but were softer, quieter rubber.

The entire second floor of the warehouse was a single, open gallery. Paintings hung all around the space, and display stands in the middle held all manner of art objects.

The crowd was much thinner up here. As Nick slipped into the room and browsed a half dozen paintings, he noted immediately that the expected sale-price ranges on the works up here were significantly higher than those of the pieces downstairs. This was where the heavy hitters in art collection would be shopping.

Nick spent several minutes cruising the entire floor but

never spotted Gray or his companion. Swearing under his breath, he headed for the back stairs once more.

Up or down? If he chose wrong, he stood to lose the elusive Gray altogether. It had taken him a week to find out the man was doing some sort of business with this gallery, and it had been more luck than skill that he'd gotten the tip. How long would it take him to pick up the trail again, especially if the guy left New York?

Maybe never. The man hadn't been a spymaster for decades without being killed for nothing. Gray was paranoid bordering on obsessive about his personal security.

Nick made a decision and jogged up the stairs.

The third floor was also a single, spacious gallery. However, this one had a half dozen security guards posted around the space. They all stood stoically still, hands crossed in front of their belt buckles, statue-like. But he wasn't fooled for a second. Their gazes roved constantly, taking in everyone and everything in the room.

If the second floor was for exclusive collectors, the third floor held offerings for only the most serious and wealthy of them. Nick turned to stare sightlessly at the first painting he came to, a modern thing that was mostly geometric shapes. Expected price: one to three million dollars. *Well, okay, then.*

He turned to study a square white-and-blue vase that the typed card beside it identified as a Ming Dynasty piece. Expected price: two million.

Of more interest to him: the glass case protecting the Ming vase made for a decent impromptu mirror. By moving slightly to one side, Nick could scan the whole gallery in the reflection on the glass.

No more than twenty customers strolled around in here, and it only took him a few seconds to spot Gray and the gallery owner standing beside an exhibit in the middle of the room, just at the top of the main staircase. A gold statue of some kind was displayed in the case the two men were studying. In fact, most of the people in the room were clustered around the same piece.

As Nick moved to another display case, this one holding a pair of gaudy earrings, he watched the reflections of Gray and the gallery owner as they headed for the stairs and disappeared from sight.

Nick debated racing down the back stairs to follow them, but given how observant the gallery guards were, he dared not be so obvious. Instead, he drifted toward the front of the room to take a look at the gold piece everyone seemed so interested in.

It was about a foot tall, a statue of a man on a horse. The horse half reared, its mane and tail flowing artfully around its body. The rider wore billowing Middle Eastern–style robes and a turban on his head, and brandished a curved sword. The man's eyes were emeralds, his clothing and saddle studded with rubies and tiny pearls. The craftsmanship of the statue itself was spectacular. The stallion's mane blew in an invisible wind, his nostrils flared, and tension quivered in his muscular haunches.

Interested, Nick read the accompanying card. The statue dated to roughly the time of the Third Crusade—1189–1192. Weight—nearly three pounds. Made of gold and assorted precious gems. *Origin: Persian. Provenance: unknown.* Possibly a piece from a nativity scene, possibly one of the Three Wise Men. *Estimated sale price: six to ten million dollars.*

Ho. Lee. Cow. For a dude on a horse?

Of course, if the piece was solid gold… He did the math fast. At current prices, that was nearly four million dollars' worth, just in the meltdown value of the gold itself.

With a mental lurch, he realized he'd gotten distracted.

Gray was getting away from him. This time he used the main stairs to leave the gallery. He descended swiftly but was careful to keep his whole demeanor relaxed. Casual. Nothing that would draw attention.

Why was Gray interested in a ten-million-dollar gold statue? Surely the man didn't have that kind of money lying around. Gray was a spy, not a billionaire, after all.

Sure, most people in covert operations squirreled away money over the years. They weren't home to spend their paychecks, which tended to stack up in checking accounts, and it was ops normal to skim a bit here and there from operational cash that passed through their hands to various informants and dealers in stolen goods and information. But ten million bucks? No spy could steal that much over the course of one career and not get caught. Not unless they had a very, very profitable side gig going.

Which was, of course, the entire reason he was trailing Gray in the first place.

As he rounded the turn in the steel staircase to head for the ground floor, he spied Gray, flanked by his two dangerous-looking bodyguards, heading out the front door.

Swearing, Nick hustled the rest of the way down the stairs. He had no choice but to race outside right now or risk losing Gray.

A limousine was parked out front, its passenger door open, and his quarry was just climbing inside.

Nick jammed his hand into his coat pocket, and he palmed the device inside. Moving fast, he went down the steps, across the sidewalk, and toward the back of the limo. The security guard standing beside the limo stiffened.

But without even looking in the guard's direction, Nick hustled past the vehicle, sliding between it and an

SUV that had just pulled up to the front of the gallery. As he did so, he touched the limo's taillight briefly, as if bracing himself against the vehicle to keep his tux from rubbing on it.

Then he darted out into traffic and ran across the street. He made it to the far sidewalk without being hit by a taxi, and he strode off in the opposite direction from the limo. Without looking back, he turned the corner.

Stopping now would be an amateur move. He'd planted a tracker inside the rim of the taillight, and he knew to let the device do its job. He walked for another block, doubled back briefly, reversed directions and dodged around another corner, and doubled back again.

Nope. He wasn't being followed.

Finally, he let out a sigh of relief. He paused in the darkened alcove of a closed store and pulled out his cell. The tracker app on his phone popped up, and a red dot was superimposed on a street map of Upper Manhattan. Bingo. The tracker was live and on the move—

The black shape of a man came at him swiftly and silently.

Nick dropped his phone and threw up his hands just in time to block what would have been a lethal blow to the side of his head. Trained hand-to-hand fighter that he was, he stepped forward, closer to the attacker, to cut off the guy's range. While short punches were still painful, they were less dangerous than full-on roundhouses, where a man could really put weight and momentum behind his fist. That and moving in close took kicks out of the equation.

Of course, moving in close meant he couldn't kick or punch effectively, either. Which was why he lowered his head and charged the assailant with the intent to wrap his arms around the guy and immobilize him that way.

Except at the last instant, the attacker sidestepped with blinding speed, stuck out a foot and gave Nick a mighty shove.

He had superb balance, however, and knew not to overextend his weight too far forward when jumping at someone. Hence, Nick was able to catch his balance and right himself without face-planting on the sidewalk. But it was a close thing.

He whipped around to face his attacker, who had settled into a fighting stance.

Nick did the same. He studied his opponent. The guy was close in height to him. Maybe not quite as muscular. But he already knew the guy was wicked fast. And the man's stance shouted of being a skilled fighter.

He wasn't gonna lie. If this fight weren't probably to the death or at least serious injury, he would relish getting to spar with a guy like this, who seemed evenly matched with him.

Without warning, the attacker lunged, feinting left and coming in on the right. Nick matched the move, dodging a blindingly fast, low hook kick at the last second, before the man knocked his foot out from under him. Dang, that guy was fast.

Nick jumped back, eyeing his opponent cautiously. He needed to go on the offensive, and fast, or he was going to be in real trouble against this guy. He charged forward, and instead of trying anything tricky, actually barreled straight ahead into him.

His attacker had already sussed out that he, too, was no amateur in unarmed combat, and had expected him to do something fancy at the end of the straight-on lunge. Instead of bracing for impact, the assailant had remained balanced on the balls of his feet, ready to jump to one side or the other.

Which meant Nick's extra twenty pounds on the other man had its desired effect. The attacker staggered back, barely managing to stay on his feet as Nick delivered a flurry of fast punches that forced the guy to parry frantically.

Nick pressed his advantage, keeping up a barrage of fast slaps, jabs and low kicks. The assailant fell back, retreating down the dark sidewalk.

He seriously wanted to know who this guy was. Nick hadn't spotted him interacting with the other members of Gray's security team. He must've been some sort of overwatch guy, posted to stand off at a distance and observe Gray's movements going into and coming out of the gallery.

That was a new operational procedure for Gray, and Nick wanted to question his attacker about what other changes Gray had made recently. Given that Nick and the Medusas had recently taken an entire team of Gray's operatives into custody, it made sense that the spymaster, in the interest of paranoia and self-preservation, had changed things up.

Nick stalked after the man. Any second now, the guy was going to turn and run. If he didn't miss his guess, he would have about six strides to catch up to his would-be assailant and tackle him before the other man's superior speed took over and he darted out of range.

The guy jumped.

But not away from Nick. *Toward him.*

Nick threw up his hands to ward off a pair of lightning-quick jabs to his face that would've broken his nose if either connected. Dang, this guy was fast. Like…*fast.*

The man jumped again, sliding past Nick's left shoulder with such speed he barely saw the move. He started to spin to face the attacker, but too slowly.

An arm went around his neck from behind. The man's chest plastered against his back, and one of the guy's legs went between Nick's knees.

Not good. *Not good.*

That stance was the first part of bracing oneself to yank a target's head sharply to one side, the goal being to break the target's neck.

Frantically, Nick did the only thing he could. He threw his left hand backward over his shoulder as far as it would go and grabbed a handful of the attacker's hair at the back of the man's head. He hoped he had a solid enough grip on the guy's hair to give a violent yank of his own.

At the same time, Nick tensed all the muscles in his neck and shoulders as hard as he could in what was surely a futile effort to protect his spine from breaking when this guy tried to kill him.

Contrary to television depictions, it took a hell of a lot of strength to snap a person's neck, particularly a fit, strong adult male's. But, if a person knew the right technique and knew how much force to apply, it worked about as fast and effectively as it did on TV. It was a nearly instant kill.

He felt the guy's entire body tense against his back.

Here it came.

He was going to die.

Chapter 2

Alexander Creed was stunned when his opponent whipped a hand backward and grabbed a big fistful of his hair like that. He felt the power in the guy's arm. This dude could undoubtedly yank hard enough to wrench his head around awkwardly to the side. Maybe the guy would only sprain his neck something fierce. But maybe the guy would kill him.

They were at an impasse. They each had a lethal hold on the other. One wrong twitch by either of them, and their opponent would make a good-faith effort to snap their neck.

He didn't want to kill this guy. He wanted to talk to him. Find out why he'd been following Harlan Gray.

Alex grunted in the big man's ear, "I'll let go if you'll let go."

"Why should I?" the man choked out from under Alex's forearm across his throat.

"Because the alternative is for me to break your neck," he snapped. Surely, this man knew that. The guy had shown himself to be a hard-core fighter with serious training in the past sixty seconds.

"I'll break yours first."

"Maybe. But I've got you in a better hold. I will definitely break yours. You *might* manage to break mine. I'm willing to take that chance."

The man plastered against the front of his body was perfectly still for a moment more. Alex could actually feel the wheels turning in the dude's brain, calculating the odds.

The man's painful grip on his hair released.

Alex breathed a sigh of relief. He let go with his left arm, keeping his right arm across the guy's throat for an extra moment. Long enough to jam his left hand in his coat pocket and grab the metal objects inside.

He let go of his target's neck, and the man—predictably—spun around to face him. As he did so, Alex reached out fast and slapped a handcuff down on the top of the guy's left wrist. Then, as the guy jolted, Alex slammed his own right wrist into the other bracelet.

"What the hell is that for?" the man growled, staring down at their handcuffed wrists.

He shrugged. "I don't feel like chasing you across half of Manhattan. And now you're not getting away from me until we have a conversation."

"Indeed," his prisoner said darkly. "I'm looking forward to speaking with you, as well."

"Shall we take this conversation off the street?" Alex asked rather more politely than he was feeling toward this walking, talking, pain in the ass.

"Oh, yeah," the prisoner agreed with way too much enthusiasm. The guy thought that once they were alone they were going to have round two of their previous matchup, did he?

Not if he could help it. The prisoner had been ridiculously strong and nearly as fast as he was. It was the closest he'd come to losing a hand-to-hand fight in years. And he didn't like the sensation one bit. He was used to being in total control of everything and everyone around him, thank you very much.

Alex murmured, "I have a place not far from here. Truce until we get there?"

The guy looked grumpy about it but nodded once, tersely. There was a jerk on his wrist as the prisoner bent down to scoop up his cell phone off the sidewalk.

"This way." Alex took off, moving briskly in the same direction his target had been traveling before they'd fought.

They walked in silence for several minutes, winding along small side streets that were mostly deserted at this time of night. Here and there, window frames were lit with Christmas lights. As they reached a major thoroughfare, some business was broadcasting holiday carols through a tinny speaker, and huge lit snowflakes hung from the streetlamps. As they waited at a traffic light to cross the intersection, a fat snowflake drifted down to the ground in front of them. Several more wafted past, floating gently.

His prisoner shook their joined wrists a little and asked lightly, "Do you always walk around Manhattan handcuffed to other men? Doesn't that draw a wee bit of negative attention?"

Alex shrugged. "I haven't seen anyone tonight appear to notice, let alone care."

The other guy huffed. "Sometimes, I hate this city."

"Just because folks here aren't freaked out by a little kink doesn't make it a bad place."

The prisoner shot him a sharp look. "You're into handcuffs and bondage, are you?"

Alex snorted. "Not me. I'm not paid to have such preferences. I'm paid to be a straight-arrow type." This guy had no idea how straight an arrow. He had no choice in the matter. In his line of work, even the slightest deviation from complete and utter self-discipline was intolerable to his employers.

Alex muttered, "If you're worried about what other people will think, we can always hold hands. That'll hide the bracelets."

His prisoner's eyes lit with…something. Interest? Amusement? Challenge?

"Fine." The guy grabbed his hand firmly as the light changed, shocking Alex to his toes. The man's was hard and callused. But then, so was his. They made a good pair. Holding hands firmly, they walked quickly across the multiple lanes of traffic.

They strode away from the brightly lit avenue behind them and into residential side streets. They stopped in front of an aged brick building, and Alex used a key to let them into the lobby, dominated by a fluffy Christmas tree hung with a motley assortment of ornaments. The tenants in the building apparently each brought down an ornament to put on the tree, and the result was an eclectic and colorful collection of decorations.

A pair of elevators took up the wall opposite the tree and mailboxes. Alex pushed the up button between the elevators, and miracle of miracles, one of them was already down there. The doors slid open with that alarming hitch in their action that they always had.

"Looks pretty rickety," the prisoner said skeptically.

"I'm okay with walking up. I'm in reasonably good shape."

He snorted. The man was in significantly better than "reasonable" shape. When he'd had his arm around the guy's neck, it had felt as if he was hugging a lion, one made of pure, honed steel.

"Scared of elevators, are you?" Alex asked lightly.

"Very little in this world scares me," the guy responded quietly. There was no braggadocio in the man's comment, just a simple statement of fact.

As he'd thought. This guy was totally one of Gray's operatives. Aloud, he commented, "It would be a long climb. We're heading for one of the top floors."

They stepped into the elevator and the doors closed partway, stuck a little, then shut the rest of the way. The lift lurched into motion with the faint sound of a gear grinding somewhere nearby.

He pushed the button for the twentieth floor and then looked over at his prisoner in the decent light of the elevator. Strong features were partially obscured by shaggy dark brown hair in need of a trim. The man's face was clean-shaven, but his jaw looked pink and vaguely irritated as if he'd recently taken off a beard.

His earlier assessment had not been wrong. The guy was muscular from head to toe. Not the flashy bulk of a weight lifter, but the hard, functional muscle of a man whose life depended on his strength. He would expect no less of one of Gray's hirelings, of course. But still. The man was an impressive physical specimen. Enough so that a frisson of interest—personal interest—skittered down his spine.

No. This was work. He had a job to do, and no matter how hot the guy handcuffed to his wrist might be, nothing was going to get in the way of his focus.

Still, a little voice whispered in the back of his mind, *this one was hard not to notice in* that *way.*

His employer didn't care in the least if he was gay, but his employer would care very much if he ever let a personal attraction to anyone get in the way of his job.

The elevator dinged, and the doors slid open. He stepped to the front of the conveyance, along with his prisoner, and noted that they simultaneously paused just inside it and looked up and down the hallway before exiting.

No doubt about it. This guy was an operator like him. Maybe not exactly like him—he was, after all, the one who got sent out to fix problems caused by other operators—but definitely similar in skills and abilities.

They reached the door of his crash pad, and he unlocked it to let them inside.

A tiny bathroom on the left and a walk-in closet on the right formed a short hallway. Beyond that was a single, sparsely furnished room, with a kitchenette backing up to the bathroom, a sofa on the left wall, a TV on the right wall and a mattress on the floor under the window. A banged-up table and two chairs took up the corner beside the closet.

But the dingy space also had a state-of-the-art security system with motion sensors, pressure pads under the stained carpet, infrared sensors and a silent alarm, currently linked to his phone, which—on cue—was vibrating in his pocket to warn him of an intruder.

"I have to reach into my pants pocket," he informed his prisoner.

The man nodded and let his left arm go loose so Alex could reach into his pocket with his right hand and pull out his phone. Thank goodness the guy didn't make any snarky comment about asking if he needed help reaching into his pants. If there was one thing he couldn't abide in this world, it was people with no sense of taste or decorum.

The man was cooperative and followed Alex's hand with his own so Alex could type the security code into the phone to disable the alarm system.

"We good?" the guy asked.

"We're good," Alex replied. "No machine gun will pop out of the wall now and mow us down."

"Gee. I rather prefer laser beams that cut intruders in half," his prisoner said dryly.

"You a James Bond fan?" Alex asked.

"Aren't you?"

The answer to that was obvious. Every spy, ever, was a fan. Even if they wouldn't admit it to another living soul. The cool gadgets alone were envy-worthy.

The prisoner's unshackled hand snaked out fast, reaching for their joined wrists. Before Alex could brace himself to fight, the guy had jammed a small handcuff key into the lock and popped the bracelets open.

Alex stared, shocked, at the empty bracelet now dangling from the bracelet still on his wrist. The bastard had a master cuff key on his key ring. He could've unlocked the handcuffs at any moment during the entire time they'd walked across the city to this place. The *entire* time. But instead, the prisoner had dared him to hold hands. What could it mean?

He looked up at his former prisoner, one eyebrow arched in silent question.

The guy shrugged, replying as if he thought Alex was silently asking why he hadn't unlocked himself sooner, "I wanted to see where you would take me."

"Why did you care where I was taking you?" Alex blurted.

"Because I do, in fact, have questions for you. Several of them."

This was new. Usually, he was the interrogator while the other guy fidgeted nervously, awaiting his judgment with fear and trepidation. His attention perked up considerably as he regarded the man standing before him.

Alex's brows slammed together. "I'm the one in charge here. You're my prisoner, not the other way around."

The man held up his naked left wrist. "Was your prisoner. Past tense."

Alex scowled as he unlooped the bracelet from around his wrist and stowed the handcuffs in his back pocket. If nothing else, this unpredictable guy was certainly proving to be interesting. "Nonetheless, I'm questioning you."

"Nope. I'm questioning you," the other man shot back.

Alex glared. "I won the fight."

"You did not! I also had you in a head grip that would've broken your neck. We fought to a stalemate."

"Did not."

"Wanna go again?" the other guy asked aggressively.

"Not particularly," Alex answered honestly. "You're not half bad at handling yourself."

"I could say the same of you," the man admitted grudgingly.

Coming from this accomplished fighter, he would take that as a high compliment indeed.

"We seem to be at an impasse," Alex said grimly. "Again."

At least the guy hadn't bolted out of here already or tried to kill him the moment they stepped inside the crash pad. Maybe they could find a civilized way out of this… whatever this was.

There was a thought. Having one of his jobs actually be civilized. He got so tired of tracking down and killing people, one after another in an endless stream of death. Every single person he tracked always turned out to be corrupt. Why couldn't just one of them turn out to be a good guy? Before he'd gotten into this business, he'd had no idea that finding just one honest man would be such an impossible task.

He stared at his guest, and his guest stared back in what appeared to be frustration. The man's eyes were dark in the relatively dim lighting of the apartment, and Alex guessed they were brown. Either that or the guy was wearing contact lenses. He would need better light to know for sure.

"Tell you what," the man said. "How about I ask you a question, and then you ask me a question?"

Alex considered the suggestion briefly. If nothing else, he might be able to figure out who this guy was based on what he wanted to know. "Fine. But I'll go first."

The man shrugged.

"Who are you?" Alex demanded.

"I'm just a guy. Who are you?"

"That wasn't what I meant. What's your name?" Alex clarified.

"Bob. Call me Bob."

"Right. And I'm Santa Claus," Alex replied dryly.

If the guy wasn't going to cooperate, he had other tools at his disposal to identify him. To that end, he pulled out his cell phone and pretended to read a message on it. As soon as he had his camera app opened, though, he whipped the phone up, pointed it at the guy and snapped a fast picture.

As *Bob* lunged toward him, Alex hit the send button.

"Too late," Alex announced, snatching the phone away from the man's grasping fingers.

"Who did you send that to?" the guy ground out.

"To my employer."

The fellow swore under his breath. "Do you work for Gray?"

"That's two questions," Alex objected. "I only agreed to you asking one question."

The guy visibly vibrated with tension. "*Do you work for Gray?*"

Alex was startled. "You should know, since you work for him."

He watched as the guy's dark eyebrows slammed together, and he blurted, "Not anymore, I don't."

Okay, that was not the response he'd expected. "Explain."

"How do you know who Gray is?" *Bob* asked.

"Nope. Not gonna answer that."

"Then, I'm not saying another word to you."

Alex sighed. This was the problem in dealing with covert operators. None of them trusted anybody. "Fine. Why don't you take a seat? The facial recognition request I sent will be back in a few minutes, and then I'll know who you are anyway."

"Not bloody likely," *Bob* muttered.

Fascinating. The guy didn't think his face was in facial-recognition databases, did he? Too bad he didn't know Alex had access to the classified database the government kept of *everyone*'s faces—the *really* classified database.

His guest lounged on the sofa, taking up way more than half of it as he threw a muscular arm across the back of the cushions and propped one ankle on top of the other knee.

Manspreading much? Alex rolled his eyes at the subtle posturing. Whatever. He was neither awed nor intimidated by such tactics. He took out men like this one every day.

Rather than compete for real estate on the couch, Alex

pulled out one of the kitchen chairs and sat down on it. He studied "Bob," who studied him back intently.

The guy really was good-looking, in spite of that awful haircut that hid half his face and the hint of a dark five-o'clock shadow that hid the rest. Although that was probably the point. The man had rugged features, a square jaw and a nose that either had a slight hawk bump to it or had been broken before. It was a masculine face and sexier than ought to be legal. In fact, the whole man oozed sex appeal.

Not that he was looking, of course.

If the guy didn't work so hard to hide it from view, it would be a highly memorable face. Which in their line of work was a bad thing. Spies needed to be able to slide in and slide out of places without being noticed.

Take himself, for example. He'd completely mastered the art of being blandly unremarkable. He kept his light brown hair in a boring haircut, he made sure never to get too pale or too darkly tanned, his eyes were an indeterminate color somewhere between green and blue, and he always wore exactly the kind of clothes a middle-aged dad would wear in whatever place he was working in. He even knew how to stoop just enough to look tired all the time and how to move to disguise how fit and athletic he actually was.

Silence stretched out between them until it, too, became a competition. Privately, Alex was amused. He could and did go days at a time without speaking to another human being. This guy was going to lose in a battle of who could be quiet the longest.

As he watched his guest, though, he did note the steady, observant way the man's dark eyes took in everything around him, never staying still, flicking from one point of interest to another. And any time Alex even shifted his weight the slightest bit, that penetrating gaze snapped back to him, alert and wary.

He might look relaxed sprawled across the sofa, but Alex didn't miss the way "Bob's" body was coiled, poised to spring at any moment. Definitely a lion in human clothing. A hungry, restless one, on the hunt.

Alex's cell phone buzzed silently, and he picked it up off the table. A message scrolled across the screen. His identification request was complete. He tapped the button to download the file associated with this man's face, and it opened on his screen.

He read aloud, "'Name—Nicholas Kane. Current location—unknown. Current status—inactive, on personal leave of absence. Last assignment—Sunny Creek, Montana. Employer—'" A pause. "Ah. Interesting." Alex looked up. "What on earth is in Sunny Creek, Montana, that would be of interest to a CIA Special Operations Group guy like you?"

Chapter 3

Shock rolled through Nick as the man across the room from him started reading out classified information about him. Accurate, *highly* classified information that in the hands of the wrong person could get him killed in a New York minute. Which was not amusing, given that he was actually in New York at the moment.

He surged up off the sofa and across the room. His would-be captor made it to his feet before Nick was on him, but Nick had jumped behind him and had him by the throat before the man could do much but gurgle.

It wasn't so much fun now that the shoe was on the other foot, was it? He tightened his grip hard enough to cut off most of his oxygen. He didn't sever so much air that the fellow passed out or died but enough that he didn't have enough fuel for his muscles to launch a counterattack.

"Who. Are. You?" he gritted out into the guy's ear.

"Let me go…and I'll…tell you," his target rasped.

This time he was pressed up against the guy from back of the neck to knees. He felt his lithe strength and got a brief impression of an otter—strong, fast and slippery. Nearly impossible to restrain.

Except he was having no trouble holding him in his grasp.

Suspicion that his captive was intentionally not fighting him rolled through him. Nick frowned. Should he reciprocate with a modicum of trust?

Maybe some cautious mistrust…as opposed to outright hostility…was called for. Slowly, carefully, he loosened his arm from around his target's neck. He let go altogether, and the man stepped away from him equally carefully, making no sudden moves.

A vague impression of missing the feel of the man's torso pressed back against his shocked him into momentary stillness.

He stared at his host. The medium brown hair in a neat cut, medium eyes somewhere between blue and green, medium height, medium build—everything about the man screamed, *Don't look at me. Nothing to see here. Move along.*

Although that was the point, he supposed. This man was clearly some sort of black ops guy, himself, and they were all trained to be inconspicuous and fade into the woodwork in any environment. They were all chameleons.

The guy held out both hands, well away from his sides, in plain sight and said soberly, "I think maybe you and I do need to talk, for real."

Nick leaned a hip against the kitchen counter behind him, his casual stance belying his readiness to attack or defend himself again, if need be. "You go first."

"You and me, Nicholas. We work for more or less the same people."

"How much more and how much less?" he snapped. "And call me Nick. Nobody calls me by my real name."

"Okay, Nick. We work for the same company. Different department."

Nick highly doubted that. As a training officer, he knew pretty much everyone in the Special Operations Group, and he'd never seen this guy, let alone worked with him. And nobody else in the agency would have the skill and experience to go toe-to-toe with him except another SOG guy. There were government covert operatives, and then there were the guys like him, the best of the best, the ones assigned to do the tasks nobody else would even think about trying.

The guy continued, "I'm investigating a colleague of yours."

"Who? Why?" Nick exclaimed.

"We received intel that someone you work with might have absconded with something they shouldn't have on a job."

Nick didn't, by the slightest bat of an eyelash or flinch of a muscle, give away his shock at those words. Indeed, the team he usually ran with *had* stolen something a while back while running a covert operation in a tiny near-Asian nation called Zagastan.

He hadn't gone on the mission. Instead, he'd been sent on a solo job that turned out to be a wild-goose chase. At the time, he'd been damned suspicious of why he'd been diverted to a bust operation at the last minute, too. It had smelled to him as if his teammates had gotten rid of him because they knew he would never go along with whatever they'd planned to do on that mission.

As it turned out, they had not been wrong. He would

never condone theft nor the murder of US military members totally uninvolved in their operation. And his teammates had done both.

"Who exactly are you investigating?" Nick asked cautiously. It dawned on him with a jolt that this man could be investigating *him*. After all, he'd been a member of the same team that had committed the crimes. Plus, this guy probably didn't know the rest of his team was quietly in custody already, captured by him and the Medusas, and being held at a black ops site that didn't exist on any map, anywhere.

The man stared at him hard. Nick stared back. He didn't care if they got into another pissing contest to see who could be silent the longest. In his military career, he'd been a sniper, and he could lie perfectly still and silent in a hide for days on end.

The other guy surprised him by actually answering, "I'm investigating Harlan Gray."

"Harlan? Is that the rest of his name?" Nick blurted.

The man in front of him shrugged. "It's as good as any other name."

Nick was staggered. This guy knew that the name, Harlan Gray, was an alias? Only a handful of people on the planet even knew Gray was alive, let alone knew what handle the bastard was operating under at the current time.

Nick figured his ex-boss went through a whole new identity every few years. Gray undoubtedly scrubbed every trace of his previous persona before assuming the next one. In fact, Nick was terrified that, after his larcenous teammates' recent disappearance, Gray would erase this version of himself and disappear, *again*, never to be found.

Nick had been lying on a beach once when Gray had

walked up to him, and in the bright sunlight, looking up from that odd angle, he'd seen the thin white lines of plastic surgery scars under the man's chin. He suspected every time Gray changed his name, he also changed his appearance.

"What did Harlan steal?" Nick had been dying to know that ever since he'd heard about the theft.

A real-time-photo intel analyst had been observing a SEAL operation raiding a terrorist's compound in Zagastan. She'd been using drone cameras hovering above the compound to provide intel to the SEAL team on the ground, and she'd spotted his teammates exiting the rear of the clustered buildings, carrying a large wooden crate among the four of them. She'd described it as looking very heavy.

The way Nick figured it, his teammates had used the SEAL raid to distract the bad guys, slipped in the back way when nobody was looking and moved in to steal whatever had been in that crate. Then, while the SEALs were still mopping up, they slipped out the way they'd come.

The photo intel analyst had also described a man *exactly* matching Gray's description breaking into the remote surveillance facility she'd been working at that night. Allegedly, he'd held her at gunpoint and had stolen the entire computer tower at her workstation. It would've held the only video images downloaded from the drone she'd been using to observe the operation. By taking that CPU, Gray had successfully stolen all evidence of his operatives' theft. So it was only the woman's word against Gray's to say that anything had gone down at all.

Thing was, she had no reason to lie. And her description of the man who'd stolen the computer and video of the theft was so spot-on Gray that he'd never doubted her story for a second. Not to mention, after that night, Gray and his teammates had been hell-bent on finding and killing the woman.

That alone would've convinced him she was telling the truth.

Of course, Gray and company hadn't counted on the woman being more than a simple photo intel analyst. It had turned out she was also a fully trained special operator in her own right.

Gray had ordered him, along with his teammates to search for her. Nick had made an excuse to leave his team to conduct his own hunt for the woman. Interestingly, his colleagues hadn't objected—at all—when he'd proposed going off by himself to track down a few obscure leads on the woman they were hunting.

He'd done it because he wanted to hear firsthand why his teammates had cut him out of that mission and what she'd seen that had the lot of them so hot and bothered to kill her and silence her for good. His fellow operatives had agreed to the plan because they wanted to get rid of him.

He'd found the woman…and found out the hard way that she belonged to an all-female team of Special Forces soldiers who called themselves the Medusas. An apt name. They were as dangerous as any snake-haired goddess.

The Medusas had set a trap for him and captured him. It had taken a while to establish that they were working toward the same objective, but eventually, he'd told them why he'd been tracking her, and they had asked him to help them set up an ambush for his teammates.

It had pained him to help take down a group of men he'd run with for almost four years and thought of as closer than brothers. But they'd crossed the line with the theft and subsequent murder of three marines. They had to be taken out. Better by him than by some total stranger, he supposed. A stranger like the man standing in front of him now.

There was a code of honor among operators. You didn't throw your buddies under the bus, but you also didn't ask them to cover up crimes for you. His teammates had broken that code. In every way they could've betrayed his trust, they had. It still stung. A lot.

At least the Medusas had agreed to his request that his part in capturing his buddies not be revealed to them. Indeed, his former team had been led to believe that he'd escaped the trap in which the rest of them had been captured. For their benefit—and for Gray's—the Medusas were continuing to keep up a ruse of hunting him.

He had no idea if his ex-teammates bought the story or not. One thing he did know for sure: he wasn't interested in finding out if Gray bought the tale or not.

"My turn to ask a few questions," the man in front of him said.

Nick noted that the guy had pointedly not answered the burning question of what, exactly, his teammates had stolen. Maybe he didn't know. Or maybe he just wasn't telling.

"What were you doing for Harlan Gray earlier tonight?" the man asked abruptly.

"Nothing," Nick said. "I was following him."

"Why?"

"No comment."

The man sighed. "Look. I get it. You're an operator. I'm an operator. We don't trust our own mothers. But if you don't start giving me some real answers, and soon, I'm going to have to take you into custody. And then things will go sideways for you very fast."

"Why's that?"

"Because I have permission from my superiors to take whatever action I deem necessary to do my job. *Whatever* action I deem necessary."

"Who are your superiors?" Nick snapped.

"The same as yours. Only I report to someone significantly higher up the food chain than you do. Which means you'll get no protection from your bosses regarding what I do to you."

Nick frowned. The guy hadn't said that as a brag. If anything, the answer had been given with a reluctance that rang of truth. "Why would you take me into custody? I wasn't involved in the theft. I didn't know anything about it."

"You know about it now," the man accused. "For all I know, you were the front man stateside who arranged for the stolen item to slip into the United States undetected."

"You think whatever they took is here?" Nick blurted, alarmed. Privately, he was panicked that Gray and his teammates had gotten their hands on a small nuclear device. It would explain the weight of that crate and why they were willing to kill to protect the secret of its existence.

What he couldn't for the life of him figure out was why Gray and the others would want something like that. In the four years he'd worked as one of Gray's personal bodyguards, the man had never once hinted at having any beef with the United States government or the American people.

Gray struck him as more the greedy type. The man liked his creature comforts and was accustomed to a luxurious lifestyle. And, Gray wasn't getting any younger. It was hard to tell his age, but Nick though he had to be approaching sixty. Which was ancient in the world of covert operations.

"I'm certain whatever they stole is here," the man in front of him said grimly. "In New York."

Aww, hell. If they did have a nuke, did that mean it was in the city? Not good.

The prospect concerned Nick enough that he was willing to take a chance and actually answer the worried-looking man in front of him. "I was following Gray because I'm trying to figure out what he and my former teammates stole and to understand why they all turned on me. Why did they cut me out of their mission to steal whatever they stole? And why did they conceal the theft from me?"

"So you're mad you didn't get to participate in the theft?" the other man asked ominously.

What was the deal with him? All of a sudden, the man's entire body had dropped into readiness for violence, relaxed but coiled to erupt into hostility at a moment's notice.

Alarm exploded in Nick's gut. He didn't know who this guy was, but no doubt about it, he was extremely dangerous. Lethal. The guy had gone from calm to cobra in the blink of an eye. Frankly, it was damned disconcerting.

Very carefully, Nick said, "I would never steal anything my superiors didn't specifically order me to take. In answer to your question, no, I'm not mad I didn't get to help steal whatever they stole. I'm angry that they stole anything, apparently off the books, and that they did it behind my back. I'm furious that they betrayed me. I'm here in New York in an effort to clean up whatever mess they've made and right the wrong they've done."

The man studied him intently for several long seconds.

His body uncoiled slightly, and Nick slowly released the breath he realized he'd been holding.

"How do you know your teammates cut you out of a theft and are concealing it from you?" the man asked.

Nick shrugged. "Given your presence, I'm gonna go ahead and say it's obvious that whatever Gray and my team stole was *not* a sanctioned theft by the government. As for how I figured that out in the first place, call it intuition.

"First, I got sent on a bogus mission by myself, which made me conveniently not available to go on the op where they stole whatever they stole. Second, they abruptly started excluding me from conversations. Went silent when I walked into rooms with them. Third, they started sending me out on solo ops way below my pay grade to handle, as if they were trying to get rid of me while they dealt with something else. Fourth, Gray abruptly ordered us to hunt and kill some photo intel analyst in *the US military*. I find it damned weird to be ordered to hunt one of our own. And fifth, the guys on my team started acting…jumpy…around me."

"If you are telling the truth, it does sound as if they were hiding something from you," the man replied soberly.

Nick responded, "If you and I are, indeed, in the same line of work, then you know what I'm talking about. Guys like us, we get feelings about people. My gut is yelling at me that my teammates have done something really bad behind my back."

"Yes, but why should *I* trust your gut?" the other man asked.

Nick shrugged. "It's no secret I'm gay. I expect it was in that dossier on me you showed off by pulling up just now."

The man shrugged back. "It was in there. What of it?"

"I grew up in a family where to come out would have been a death sentence. My father was a violent man with a violent temper, a houseful of weapons and very specific ideas about what my sexual orientation should be. I learned very young to read other people and their intentions. My life depended on it. Which is to say, I'm not wrong about my team. They did something illegal, and they're hiding it from me."

"Any guess as to what they stole?"

"None. That's why I'm following Gray. I'm trying to figure out what they grabbed and do whatever I can to mitigate any damage they've caused."

"What makes you so sure he's in on it?"

"He broke into a military communications facility and stole the only evidence of the theft at gunpoint. Sounds to me as if he's in on it, wouldn't you say?"

"You know about that incident? How?" The guy sounded genuinely surprised.

"Gray sent me and the rest of the team across the country to track down the intel analyst he took the equipment from. He didn't tell me why he wanted her found and eliminated, of course. I had to learn that directly from her once I found her."

"Gray specifically told you to kill her?" the man asked with interest.

Nick sighed. "Gray rarely gives a direct kill order. He knows better than to legally expose himself like that. He specifically told us to call the rest of the team if one of us found her. Then we were to converge on her and do whatever was necessary to silence her about what she saw. The implication was clear that we would take her down—kill her—together."

"Interesting. He wanted you to have blood on your hands, too?"

Nick jolted. He hadn't thought of it like that before. He'd been too wrapped up in the guilt of leading his team into the Medusa's ambush to clock that Gray had been trying to get him to commit a crime, too, one that would force him to remain silent about his teammates' crimes.

Nick said heavily, "I found the intel analyst in Montana. In answer to your earlier question, that's what was in Sunny Creek. Or rather, who was in Sunny Creek." He added bitterly, "The other guys always did call me too much of a Boy Scout to work with them. They knew I wouldn't murder an innocent American soldier who was just doing her job any more than I would've gone along with stealing something off the books."

The man pursed his lips, as if he agreed with their assessment of him being too much of a Boy Scout for his line of work.

"Hey. I serve my country. I follow any legal orders I'm given, and I've killed more than a few bad guys in my day. But I'm not a random criminal."

"That's good," the other man said seriously. "Because I'm the guy who takes out the random criminals in our ranks."

"Come again?" Nick asked sharply.

"I'm a fixer. And I've been assigned to fix the problem of Gray and his rogue team. You can call me Alex, by the way."

"You got a last name, Alex?"

"Creed. I'm Alexander Creed."

Holy shit. He'd heard that name before. Whispered in tones of respect and fear. Creed was a legendary assassin within the special operations community. His nickname in the Middle East, where he'd spent years working for Uncle Sam, was *Almawt*. It meant very simply *Death*.

In the American intelligence world, he had an even more ominous name. *The Judge*.

"You're the Judge?"

Alex rolled his eyes. "I hate that name."

"But you're him? You're the guy who's sent out to judge other spies and then execute the sentence you impose upon them?"

"I don't impose anything. I investigate allegations against operators. And, when I'm certain of the facts of the situation, I take appropriate action to contain the situation—and contain the operator."

"The way I hear it, you kill them." Nick stated it as a fact, rather than a question.

"I don't always kill the people I investigate. Only the most heinous of criminals are sanctioned to death."

Nick snorted. "Yes, but you're only sent after the most heinous of criminals, aren't you?"

Alex shrugged. "The people I investigate shouldn't have gone rogue. They made their choice, and I make my judgment."

He couldn't argue with that. Especially since it was exactly the same reason he was in New York now. His teammates and his boss had gone rogue. He wanted to know what they'd done, and when he found out, he planned to take action to rectify the situation. Maybe not action as extreme as the Judge might take, but he needed to fix the problem. It had happened on his watch, and he bore some responsibility for not stopping his team from doing whatever they'd done.

A shocking thought made him blurt, "Are you investigating me?"

"I wouldn't be talking with you like this if I was."

Not reassuring.

Nick studied Alex intently. He didn't for a second believe that Creed was the guy's actual name. Men like them didn't really even have names. They drifted from one legend to the next, never using any details from their real lives. After a while, they'd dealt in lies for so long that they had no real lives left to hide anymore. They were ghosts, wandering through the world without ever leaving any trace of anything substantial about themselves behind.

He found the man fascinating. How could he not? Alex was not only handsome but smart and fully as skilled as anyone he'd ever worked with—but definitely not trustworthy.

He didn't believe for a second that Alex was telling him the truth, the whole truth and nothing but the truth. If Creed was the Judge, he would totally be investigating Nick. It might not be the formal investigation he'd been sent out to do, but the man would watch every operative he came across for signs of corruption.

Heck, this guy might not even be the real Judge. It was entirely possible Alex worked for Gray, and that this entire encounter was an elaborate ruse to get him to reveal how much he knew about the spymaster's involvement in the theft. This could just as easily be a test of loyalty by his ex-boss to find out if Nick was willing to turn him in to the few authorities who had jurisdiction over Gray and his team.

Nope. He didn't trust Alexander Creed as far as he could throw him.

Chapter 4

Alex studied Nick's body language with a certain wry amusement. He didn't expect the man to take him at face value, and from the way Nick's expression was shuttered and blank, it was clear Nick didn't believe his story of being a fixer for Uncle Sam.

The ironic bit was that it was the God's honest truth. However, the act of telling the truth had apparently made Nick utterly doubt it. Not that it was any skin off his nose if the guy believed him or not. He still had a job to do, and at the end of the day, he would get it done with or without Nick's help. And God protect the man if he got in the way of the job.

"How did you spot me tonight, *Alex*?"

His lips pursed a little at the special emphasis on his name. Yes, he was fully aware that Nick didn't trust it to be his name. But then, he doubted Nicholas Kane was on this guy's birth certificate, either.

And they were back to square one, neither of them believing a blessed thing the other one said. For example, he had no reason whatsoever to credit the whole story about Nick being a Boy Scout and Gray and his teammates not trusting him.

It was much more likely that Gray had assigned Nick to pretend to leave the team, to follow Gray from afar and then pick off anyone who attempted to follow him. It was the sort of game within a game Harlan Gray was known for.

"Earth to Alex. Come in, please."

"Excuse me?"

"You zoned out on me there for a sec. So, tell me. How did you spot me tonight?"

"Oh, that. You planted something on the taillight of Gray's limousine. That was what caught my attention. It made me curious. I assume it was a tracking device of some kind?"

Nick shrugged. But that wasn't a denial.

"Perhaps you should check in with your tracking device? See where Gray went? I'd love to know where he's staying," Alex said pleasantly.

"Won't matter," Nick replied. "He never stays in the same place twice. Wherever he goes tonight, he won't go back there again."

That fit with what he knew of Gray. Men like him had more enemies than they could count, and the only way they stayed alive was by taking caution to absurd extremes. Of course, he was the exact same way. Minus the new digs every night. Doing that was more expensive than his personal resources would allow for.

But it did beg the question of how Gray was affording such a lavish spymaster lifestyle. He wasn't doing it on his government salary alone. That was for sure. And the man's dossier said nothing about inheriting family wealth or holding investments that would account for the money his life took.

Sure, it was a known thing that most spies put away emergency cash over the years. They skimmed a little here and there, took side jobs or the occasional bribe for themselves. He wouldn't blink twice at an operative doing that, and he certainly wouldn't kill an operative for building a nest egg for their retirement. After all, the vast majority of them were emphatically not pure as the driven snow, ethically. They couldn't be and continue to do their jobs for long. Espionage was a dirty business no matter how one sliced it.

The men and women he killed were the ones who went fully off the rails, who committed violent criminal acts without permission from the government. Those who killed innocents, caused national security threats and who betrayed their country to its enemies. Assuming the thing Gray and his men had stolen turned out not to be a security threat to the US, he was less concerned about the theft than he was about them murdering three American marines. For that alone, he was prepared to kill Gray and his team without prejudice.

It was Alex's turn to ask a question. "Any idea what Gray was doing in that art gallery this evening?"

Nick surprised him by answering, "Yes, actually. He met up with one of the owners of the place and they went up to the third floor. They took a long look at a small gold statue. Then Gray left."

"Any idea what the statue was?"

Nick frowned. "The card beside it said it might be a piece from a nativity scene."

"Nativity? As in Baby Jesus in a manger?"

"I guess. The card said it might depict one of the Three Wise Men."

"What did it look like?" Alex asked, curious.

"It was pretty. About yea tall." Nick held his hands vertically about a foot apart. "Whole thing was made of gold. It was a statue of a guy sitting on a horse that was half-rearing. It had a bunch of jewels and little pearls on it, too. The card said the sale price is estimated at six to ten million bucks."

Alex whistled low. "Did Gray look at any other pieces while he was in the gallery?"

"Not that I saw. I wasn't doing a tight tail on him, mind you. So I didn't have him in sight every minute. But he wasn't there long enough to browse much."

He murmured, "I wouldn't want to try a tight tail on him. Not with his bodyguards."

"Gee. Thanks. I used to be one of those guys, and I trained most of his current protection team, so I'm gonna take that as a compliment."

Alex rolled his eyes, and Nick grinned. His teeth were white and straight, and impudent dimples flashed in his cheeks. The man had *dimples*. Dammit. He was a sucker for dimples.

Particularly when their owner was a smart operator and hot. So hot.

"How did you pick up Gray's trail, anyway?" Alex asked belatedly.

"The last time I talked with the guys on my team before they were…apprehended…one of them commented out of the blue that he'd never been to the Big Apple at Christmas and he'd heard it was pretty."

Alex frowned. "It could've just been a random comment."

"Nah. Burt's a stone-cold killer. Definitely not the

kind of guy who's into holiday cheer. Also, one of the other guys glanced over at me and back at Burt significantly as if to signal him to shut up and not say anything more in front of me."

"Fair enough." Then something else hit him. "What do you mean by 'apprehended'?"

"The four guys who stole the crate? I lured them into an ambush. With the help of a military team, we captured three of them and killed the fourth guy."

Alex blinked, startled. This man had already done 80 percent of his job for him? Cool. All that was left now, then, was for him to finish investigating Gray and kill him.

Nick was speaking. "…got to New York City, I got lucky. I texted a guy who was brought in for some training with me about a year back. He was being groomed to take a spot on the personal security team. At any rate, he didn't answer my text, but his phone pinged as being in Manhattan. I tracked it to a restaurant and spotted Gray having supper there. I've been on his tail ever since. At least, until you knocked me off him."

"In other words," Alex said, "we need to hightail it over to wherever Gray is bunking down tonight and pick him up before he leaves in the morning."

"If we were working together, it would go something like that," Nick said cautiously.

"Seems to me we're both working toward the same goal. We both want to know what Gray stole. Why not cooperate?" Alex added in his own mind, *And it would have the added benefit of me keeping an eye on you until I figure out just what your role in all of this is.*

Nick nodded readily enough and said a shade too enthusiastically, "That's not a half-bad idea."

Alex snorted to himself. Nick had obviously had the

exact same thought—that by running around together, he could keep an eye on Alex, too.

If Nick had, in fact, been pulling a one-man surveillance op for the past week, he had to be dead tired. With nobody to trade off shifts with him, he'd undoubtedly been operating on only short catnaps and practically no sleep for seven days. Which made the fight he'd put up when they met that much more impressive. He made a mental note never to tangle with this man in a dark alley when he was fully rested.

Playing on Nick's fatigue, Alex said easily, "You know as well as I do that two of us teaming up will make the job exponentially easier. We'll both get some rest, we can put up a more effective perimeter around the target and we can run handoff tails. If one of us gets spotted, the other one can take over. It's a win-win for both of us."

Nick huffed. But Alex had seen the man's eyes flicker when he mentioned getting some rest. Nick was running on empty. A frisson of worry for his companion startled him. Exhausted operators made mistakes. Sometimes fatal ones. The idea of Nick dying made him feel faintly nauseated. No doubt about it. Nick needed a partner, and soon.

A partner like him. Someone who could pull his weight, keep up with a top-flight operator and not get in his way. The kind of partner he would want if he ever worked with other agents.

Alex waited him out, not pressuring him to accept the plan. If Nick was anything like him, the harder someone pushed him, the harder he would push back.

"Fine," Nick said abruptly. "We work together to find out what Gray stole and what he's up to now."

That went beyond the scope of Alex's mandate to investigate only the theft, but he was okay with the notion of finding out what Gray was doing in New York. One thing he did know from his mission in-brief, the US government had not sent Gray here. Whatever he was doing in town, he was doing it for himself. Which made Alex fairly certain this junket was somehow related to last spring's theft.

Aloud, Alex said, "Let me grab some gear, and then we can head out and pick up Gray's trail again."

"Sure."

He headed to the safe house's well-stocked closet for the spy in need and pulled out a rucksack that was already stuffed with all the supplies and tools he required to set up a moving surveillance operation. "Do you have a kit?" he asked Nick over his shoulder.

"Not really. I've been having to do everything on the fly."

Impressive. And exhausting. Sure, guys like them could improvise everything from disguises to weapons to surveillance gear anywhere they found themselves, but that didn't mean it was easy. And doing it while also maintaining contact with a wily and suspicious target? Suffice it to say, Nick must be better than most spies at his job.

Alex pulled another backpack out of the closet. "This isn't specifically a surveillance kit, but it's got stuff in it you'll find useful." He started to unzip the pack, saying, "Let me just remove the firearm—"

"Leave it. If we accidentally tangle with Gray's guys, we'll need all the firepower we can get."

He looked up at Nick and studied him long and hard. Did he dare arm a man he didn't trust at all?

It was totally a test. Nick knew they didn't trust each other. He was pushing to see what reaction he would provoke. Thing was, the guy undoubtedly was armed already. One more pistol wouldn't make a difference.

Alex's gaze narrowed, but he said easily, "Sure. No problem."

He rezipped the second backpack and then tossed it to Nick. Surreptitiously, he slid the box of ammo he'd just palmed from Nick's supplies and tucked it into his own bag, which he slung over his shoulder.

"Let's go hunting, shall we?" Alex said lightly.

Nick nodded and flashed another one of those dimpled, killer grins of his. "Lead on."

"You're the guy with the tracking device. You lead the way."

They headed downstairs, and Alex wasn't surprised when Nick headed for a major street. It was what he would do. Sure enough, Nick hailed a cab and didn't have too much trouble getting one at this late hour on a big thoroughfare. It was drunk o'clock for cabbies and a lucrative time of night.

Yet again, he was startled by how similarly they seemed to operate. They thought alike. They *were* alike. Which was exceedingly weird. For most of his life, he'd felt completely alone. Different. Yet here was another person with so much in common with him.

They headed toward SoHo and were let out on a street corner bracketed by trendy bars. A small crowd of patrons stood outside, waiting for cabs and rideshares. Their cab was snatched up the second they climbed out of it.

Alex noted that Nick immediately pasted on a smile and matched his physical movements to those of the people around him, casual, loose, a little drunk. But then, he was doing the same.

A very wasted woman startled Alex by stepping in front of him and draping her arms around his shoulders.

She mumbled something about wondering why such a hot guy was going home alone. Usually, women didn't take much notice of him. Must be the booze talking.

He stiffened reflexively, relieved he hadn't snapped her neck reflexively, too.

Nick stunned him, however, by moving over to the woman and gently untangling her arms from around his neck. "Sorry, honey. The pretty guy is taken."

The clear implication was that Nick was the significant other.

He didn't stiffen when Nick casually looped his arm across Alex's shoulders and used his free arm to move the drunk woman aside. If anything, he found himself leaning in against his handsome partner. They continued on through the crowd.

Alex put his arm around Nick's waist, registering that it was hard and lean, slabbed in muscle. The heat of Nick's body permeated his clothing until his entire left side tingled. As they walked, the outsides of their thighs brushed together lightly.

With each step, Alex's breath came a little shorter and a little faster. He was surrounded by the masculine smell of Nick's aftershave, the feel of his powerful body. The man's sex appeal washed over him like a hot sauna, leaving him panting and starting to sweat.

They passed through the crowd and came out of it onto a relatively deserted stretch of sidewalk. Nick's arm lifted off his shoulder, and he turned Nick's waist loose. The night air felt cold against his skin where Nick's heat had just been.

"The signal is stationary. About two blocks that way and one block over," Nick said low, showing him a map view of the nearby area with a red dot parked a few blocks in front of them. Quickly, Alex memorized the layout of the streets and the location of that ping.

"Split up and look for a vantage point?" Alex murmured.

"You'll need my cell number."

Alex pulled out his phone and they traded each other's contact information. It was weirdly intimate touching their display faces to each other in mimicry of a kiss.

Nick cleared his throat gruffly. "Okay, then. Call me when you find a good spot, and I'll do the same."

Alex peeled off at the next corner, turning left, and Nick turned to the right. Whether or not he would ever see Nick again was the main question. He gave it about even odds that the guy would bolt and flee New York at the first opportunity. Which was too bad. The spy was hot.

Work, my man. Work. You're here to nail Harlan Gray, not Nick. He smirked at his own double entendre until the lust from walking past the bar swept over him once more. Okay, so he wouldn't be averse to nailing Nick. After they'd apprehended and dealt with Gray.

He walked fast until he reached the narrow street Gray's hidey-hole was on. He crossed the road, being careful not to even glance in the direction of the safe house Gray was inside. Once out of sight of it, he doubled back, working his way down a fetid alley, made marginally less gross by the thin layer of snow.

Ah, Christmas in the city.

He eased his way to the end of the alley and snaked a tiny camera around the corner on a flexible handle. He scanned the street—bland, residential, lined with beige apartment blocks, mostly in the five-to-ten-story-tall range. He counted rows of windows on Gray's building.

Eight stories tall. One of Gray's men would undoubtedly be out there, but Alex doubted he could spot the guy if he was half as good as Nick.

Alex scanned the rooftops around him, looking for one across the street and taller than the building Gray's ping had come from. Two structures down on his left was a ten-story affair that looked to have a brick wall around its flat roof. It would be a cold, wet night up there, but it should be a good spot to watch Gray from.

He backed down the alley a ways and texted Nick.

I've got a place to watch the front from.

Nick texted back.

There's nothing behind the building that'll work for a hide, and I've got one of Gray's guys moving around back here anyway, patrolling.

He's probably trying to stay warm.

He's successfully blocking me from setting up any kind of surveillance back here.

Alex simply texted back.

Join me. I'll text you my location.

He waited for several agonizingly long seconds and then Nick replied.

Coming.

Really? Joy and shock flooded Alex's belly in equal measure.

What was up with that? This was a freaking job. He had no time for a personal life. Even if Nick had made a point of telling him he was gay. Which (a) he hadn't had to do, which made the fact that he'd done it very interesting, and (b) had been in his dossier, anyway.

Alex backed all the way down the alley to the far end and quickly texted Nick his location. It didn't take long for a dark shadow to loom beside him. Dang. He hadn't seen Nick coming, let alone heard him.

Silently, they moved to the rear of the tall building Alex had picked out. He gestured for Nick to open the door and watched with interest as Nick methodically checked for alarms, disabled the standard fire-exit alarm on the rear alley door and picked the lock.

Nick cracked the door open, and when nothing happened, swept it aside and bowed ironically, gesturing for Alex to go first.

He rolled his eyes and headed inside. They were in a stairwell, and Alex headed up it, counting floors as he went. He moved steadily but quickly, certain that Nick would not only keep up but also not be winded by the fast climb.

They moved in perfect sync, kind of like they seemed to do everything. His steps were silent; Nick's steps were silent. His breath was deep and regular: Nick's breath was deep and regular. He paused at each stairwell to make sure the fire door was closed; Nick did the same. If they'd been dancing together, they couldn't have moved in any more perfect harmony.

They reached the top of the stairs, and this time, Nick gestured for Alex to go through the exercise of disarming the door alarm. Amused at how they continued to test each other, he unlocked it quickly and swept the door open for Nick, as well.

Nick slid left, his back against the wall beside the stairwell, so Alex slid right. The roof was flat, with only waist-high heating and cooling units and a rain-water collector on tall steel legs. They made their way across the roof, clearing behind each piece of equipment they came to, crouching as they approached the front edge.

They were alone up here. He was vaguely surprised that Gray hadn't posted a man on this roof to provide overwatch on the building Gray was sleeping in. Huh. So there were limits to the man's resources after all. Good to know.

Whoever had designed this structure had, most obligingly for him and Nick, built narrow drainage cracks into the brick wall skirting the roof. It made the job of running his little camera on its flexible handle through a slit and pointing it down at Gray's building a piece of cake.

Nick dug around in his pack and came up with a second miniature surveillance camera. He ran his through the drainage about three feet over from the one Alex was using.

They observed the building and the surrounding street for several minutes. Finally, Alex spotted the tiniest shift of movement about fifty feet from the front door of the target building. He breathed, "Got him. Gray's guy is under that tree behind the white delivery van."

Nick shifted his weight, tilting his camera that way. He watched for nearly a minute before breathing back, "Good catch. He's well hidden down there."

It started to snow again, and a flake hit Alex wetly on the face. This was going to get real uncomfortable real fast unless they protected themselves from the elements. To that end, he murmured, "There are Mylar blankets in our packs. How about we spread one to lie on and cover ourselves with the other one?"

"Sounds good," Nick replied, already hunting for the palm-sized bundle of thin, heat-reflective polymer.

Alex helped Nick spread out the first blanket, trying to minimize the crinkling sound it made as they unfolded it. The waterproof material reflected their body heat back at them as they stretched out on it, lying on their stomachs. Nick pulled the second Mylar sheet over himself and passed Alex the corner of it.

When they had it positioned over them both, black side up and reflective silver side down, facing them, they tucked the edges under their outside feet and hips. They left the top loose so they could move their arms and shift position to scan up and down the street.

In a matter of seconds, Alex felt Nick's body heat seeping through his warm clothing. As if that wasn't distraction enough, the guy really did smell good. The expensive cologne scent from their embrace while passing by that bar wafted to him once more. Man. That stuff was lethal.

Before they'd left the apartment, Nick had stripped out of his tuxedo shirt and jacket and had borrowed a black thermal turtleneck from him. But the scent of the cologne still clung to him.

Alex wasn't the kind of guy who typically found perfume intoxicating, but the alchemy of cologne and Nick's body chemistry did make his head spin a little.

Nick shifted to look left, and his shoulder rubbed up against Alex's. The bulge of heavy muscle against Alex's own shoulder was distinct, even through the arctic hiking coats with their layers of high-tech insulation, borrowed from the supply closet.

"Clear," Nick breathed.

Alex leaned in against Nick to point his camera in the

other direction, vividly aware of how his whole left side pressed up against Nick's. Again.

And again, it made his breath hitch and his concentration scatter. The man was all muscle and bone, and none of it was soft. *Brawn, thy name is Nicholas Kane.*

That man was far too distracting. Alex shook his head. He had a job to do up here, and he didn't need to be thinking about how sexy Nick was, for crying out loud.

He had to force himself to focus on the quiet street below. He divided it into one-building-wide chunks and cleared the sections of street one by one. Finally, he was able to say with confidence, "Clear."

He felt Nick's nod and noted with some shock that Nick made no move to pull away from him and put even an inch or two of distance between them. Well, then. Personally, he was in no rush to move away from the hunky warmth of Nick, either.

He whispered, "I got a full night's sleep last night. Why don't you catch a nap, and I'll keep an eye on things?"

Nick exhaled in relief. "Thanks, man. After a week of this, I'm wiped out. Wake me in about two hours, and I'll be good to go for a while so you can nap. I've gone longer with less sleep before."

Alex would bet he had. They both had.

In the span of perhaps three breaths, Nick's whole body relaxed against his. The guy had passed out, practically before he finished closing his eyes. Yeah. He was exhausted, all right. Apparently, he hadn't been lying about tailing Gray by himself for the past week.

Alex set up a routine of scanning left, scanning right, then scanning Gray's safe house up and down. The ping from Nick's phone told them Gray was in an interior room on this side of the building but not which floor he was on.

But they didn't need that info. They would watch the outside man, and when he left his post, they would know Gray was getting ready to move.

In the meantime, he relished the feeling of Nick's body against his left side. Was it creepy to enjoy the feel of the man even though he himself was dead to the world? Maybe, but he enjoyed it anyway. It wasn't as if he ever got any human contact in his line of work.

Idly, he tried to remember the last time he'd gone on vacation. His grandfather's funeral probably didn't count as an actual getaway, but that had been almost three years ago and was his most recent break of any kind. No wonder he'd been getting nasty emails from the Human Resources Department pestering him to take a few days off.

As he lay there, watching the stillness and silence of the street below, a few lazy snowflakes drifted down, creating a magical atmosphere. Was it weird that he was relieved that Nick's story about tracking his ex-boss was starting to look true? Nick hadn't taken off when they'd separated earlier. He could've, and Alex would've never found him again, mostly likely.

Privately, he was starting to root for Nick to be one of the good ones. How long had it been since he'd encountered an honest man? They were few and far between in his line of work. He hadn't realized how cynical he'd become somewhere along the way until just now, when he desperately wished for Nick to be fully the good guy he claimed to be.

He never got emotionally invested in any of the people he investigated. They were just a job to him. A decision to be made. Good or bad. Right or wrong. He really wanted *not* to have to take down this man. And not only because he was skilled enough to be darned hard to eliminate.

To be honest, he was enjoying the human companionship, even if the man could be infuriatingly distrustful. But then, so was he. It was shockingly pleasant to operate on a mission with an equal. He was even enjoying arguing with Nick. He'd known in a distant, intellectual way that he was lonely, but he'd had no idea how alone he'd been until Nick had blasted into his isolation.

He let Nick sleep for closer to four hours than two. At about the three-hour point, Nick entered a REM cycle, his body twitching faintly against Alex's and his eyeballs moving around a lot underneath his closed lids. Alex waited until the dream had completely abated before finally waking Nick. A sure way to feel like crap was to be woken from a deep, intense dream.

Nick's eyes snapped open as Alex laid his hand lightly over his mouth. He nodded once, and Alex jolted as Nick's lips moved against his palm. He lifted his hand away sharply. It burned where Nick's mouth had touched it.

"What time is it?" Nick mumbled.

"A little after four a.m."

"You should've woken me. I said two hours—"

"You were beat, and you hit a REM cycle. Given your recent sleep deprivation, I judged it more important for you to finish the REM cycle than for me to wake you exactly on time. Besides, nothing's happening below. What time of day does Gray usually move?"

"Varies. But he's not an early bird. You still have time to catch a nap."

Alex nodded, startled. He wasn't used to anyone else paying the least bit of attention to his well-being. It was… nice. Weird. But nice. "I think I will. Thanks."

Chapter 5

Nick lay in the dark as snow drifted down gently around them, listening to the quiet sound of Alex breathing beside him. This night had certainly taken a turn he'd never seen coming. He didn't know what to make of Alexander Creed.

The man was definitely very, very good at his job. Nick's own level of good—which was a rather high bar, if he did say so, himself. He was smart, self-contained, and confident in his abilities. And he was laser focused on figuring out what Harlan Gray was up to. At least they had that in common.

Of course, they also had in common the way their breath hitched every time they touched each other. When he'd grabbed Alex's hand hours ago as they walked across town handcuffed together, he'd heard the man's gasp. Which had been a good thing because it had masked the sound of his own gasp.

And then there'd been that arm-in-arm thing at the club. When that woman had rushed Alex, he hadn't even thought twice. He'd just flung himself forward to get her off him. He hadn't exactly claimed possession of the guy in so many words…but that was exactly what he'd done. And Alex hadn't freaked out.

Was it possible? Was Alex gay like him?

Normally, he had great gaydar. But then, his job required him to be expert at reading body language and subliminal signals. Of course, he was good at picking up little clues and hints that a guy was gay. But Alex was so self-controlled, so closed off, so freaking hard to read, that he couldn't tell. At all. Which was frustrating as heck.

They also had in common the fact that they'd both had a moment with their arm around the other one's neck, with every opportunity to break it. *And neither of them had done so.*

He was no murderer, but he got the distinct impression that violence was a routine part of Alex's job. There was a certain detachment, a certain weariness of the soul about the man that spoke of having seen a lot of death and having dealt out a lot of death.

While Nick had eliminated plenty of people in his career, most of them had been in kill-or-be-killed situations that he didn't carry away a large burden of guilt from. Even in his days as a sniper, he'd operated with the sure and certain knowledge that every person he was assigned to take out was a very, *very* bad person.

But if Alex was telling the truth, if he was a fixer for the US government, that meant he was executing sanctions against his own kind. Other spies, soldiers and covert operators who'd gone off the rails in one way or another and had to be stopped. And most of the time, that meant killing them.

Rough job.

He wouldn't want to do it.

Heck, he wasn't sure he *could* do it, even if he was asked to. The only reason he'd been able to stomach betraying his teammates to the Medusas was because the women had promised not to kill anyone they didn't have to. Vince Spinelli had been the lone man from his team to die the night of the Medusa ambush, and only because Vince had put a knife to a guy's throat and tried to kill him.

Alex shifted a little in his sleep, turning slightly toward him and snuggling a little closer. The man's whipcord strength was apparent, even in the total relaxation of sleep, as Nick registered lean, hard muscle everywhere their bodies touched.

Alex was younger than he'd expected. The way he heard it, the Judge had been operating for a number of years. Before his current gig, he'd allegedly worked undercover with some of the baddest dudes on the planet and walked away alive. And with the deep respect, and fear even, of said dudes.

He would've expected Creed to be a big, impressive, charismatic dude who owned every room he walked into. Nick definitely wouldn't have expected this quiet, unassuming, average-looking guy to be one of the most dangerous men on the planet, feared by both bad guys and good guys alike.

But then, he knew better than most not to judge books by their covers. It was why he was still alive. He was cautious and careful and never assumed anything about anybody. In the parts of the world he'd operated in, old men, women, even children, were often his enemies, armed, dangerous and out to kill men like him.

It was warm sandwiched between the Mylar tarps, and were they not watching one of the other most dangerous men on the planet, Nick would really be enjoying lying out here in the snow and silence cuddled up with the man beside him.

It was shocking how much alike he and Alex were. They both were used to working solo, distrusted each other completely but were reluctant to kill each other. And they had this mission in common.

Nick scanned the street below as the first dull gray light of dawn began to creep across the city under the scudding snow clouds. It continued to snow lightly, but a breeze picked up, and the gentle, lazy flakes of last night turned into slanting needles of cold against his skin.

Seven o'clock came and went, and the traffic below picked up considerably. He was just about to wake up Alex to ask for help keeping track of everyone moving below when he suddenly became aware of Alex staring up at him.

Nick pulled his eye off the camera viewfinder to look down at his companion. "G'morning, sleepyhead."

Alex frowned. "You should've woken me earlier."

"I was just about to, anyway. It's getting busy on the street, and I can't watch everyone."

Alex rolled away, and something deep and lonely in Nick's gut protested at the loss of that warm, relaxed presence against his right side. Slipping out from under the Mylar tarp, Alex took up a position a few more drainage slits down the wall to get a better angle on the south end of the street. Nick concentrated on the pedestrians heading north.

A gray-haired woman emerged from Gray's building, and he studied her intently, watching everything about the way she moved. How confident was the set of her shoulders? How controlled was the way she gazed around? Did her clothing and purse match her age? Did she move like an athlete or a slightly creaky middle-aged person?

Nothing about her set off any alarms in his head. Either she was just some lady going out to get breakfast or go to work, or she was a better actress than he was an operator.

A man came out of the building and turned left, and Alex murmured that he had him in sight. Nick scanned his half of the street intently. He had yet to see the guy parked under the tree move from his post. He must have a good disguise going down there, because nobody passing by him was even sparing him a second glance.

If he had to guess, Gray's man was dressed as a homeless person and was probably bundled up to the top of his head, such that nobody could see his face. It was what he would've done in the same situation.

Alex murmured, "Should one of us go around behind the building to spot Gray if he egresses that way?"

Nick was oddly reluctant to leave but nodded. "I'll go. I scouted it last night, so I know the lay of the land back there."

Alex nodded. "Have a bite to eat before you go. I'm betting that if you haven't slept in a week, you probably haven't eaten in a week, either."

He scowled. "You're not wrong, but I don't need a mommy."

"You do need calories," Alex retorted.

Nick grudgingly took the protein bar Alex held out to him. He noticed Alex was holding out his other hand and glanced down at two pills in the guy's palm.

"Stim pills," Alex said.

"Amphetamines?" he asked skeptically.

"Nope. Just caffeine."

"Cool." He'd popped the pills and washed them down with a swig from a water bottle before it dawned on him that he'd casually taken a pair of unidentified pills from a man he didn't trust.

Huh. Maybe he did trust Alex after all. At least a little bit.

"Are there earbuds in these kits?" Nick asked.

"I think so," Alex replied.

They both poked around in their packs and came up with small charger cases holding wireless earbuds.

As Nick linked the earbuds to his phone and poked them in his ears, Alex called his cell. Nick accepted and Alex murmured, "How do you hear me?"

"Five by five. How about me?" Nick responded.

"Loud and clear."

Now that they could talk freely without having to pull out their phones, he nodded to Alex, shouldered his backpack and, crouching low, made his way across the roof to the stairwell.

The rear of the building Gray had spent the night in opened up onto an alley that a bunch of other buildings also backed up to. It was a long, brick-walled canyon with only dumpsters for cover. And he had no doubt that long before Gray stepped out here, every last dumpster up and down the block would be checked in, under and behind by Gray's men.

Pulling the hood of his borrowed coat up over his head, he hiked down the alley briskly, searching as he went for a building whose rear exit had some sort of window in it.

He finally spotted one, farther down than he liked

from Gray's building, but beggars couldn't be choosers. He marked which building it was and then turned out of the alley. He walked up the street toward the front of the building he'd chosen.

"Is that you I see coming toward me?" Alex asked in surprise.

"Yes," he replied without moving his lips. He turned into his target building and was lucky to time jogging up the front steps with someone coming out the front door. He didn't have to stand there and try to get someone to buzz the lock, which would surely have drawn the attention of Gray's "homeless man" down the street.

The resident opened the door, and Nick held it politely for the elderly man.

"Aww, look at you, being all Boy Scout-y," Alex teased.

As Nick headed for the back of the building, he told Alex succinctly what he could do with his comment.

He heard laughter in Alex's voice as he replied, "What was that? You're breaking up."

"Stuff it," he bit out.

"You wish."

Startled, he wasn't sure how to reply. His fellow operators on Gray's team had never flirted with him. Ever. They were aggressively straight as a group, in fact. He'd always wondered how insecure they all were about their masculinity and which ones of the others were secretly gay, too. Statistically, he was not the only gay man among them. But nobody had been willing to talk about it. Ever. It had actually been super annoying to him.

"I'm sorry—" Alex started.

He cut off the apology quickly. "No need to apologize. No offense taken. In fact, I was just thinking about how irritating it was that my old team always tiptoed around saying anything that might be construed as sounding gay. It came off as being ultra-homophobic."

"Well, if it makes you feel better, you and I bat for the same team," Alex said lightly.

But Nick heard the strain in his voice. He wasn't used to being open about being gay, was he? Goodness knew, he'd never caught even a hint of a rumor that the Judge might be gay.

Aloud, Nick commented, "Yeah, I already figured that, but thanks for confirming."

"How did you know?" Alex blurted.

He'd arrived at the back door, and Nick peered out the long, narrow glass insert in the fire exit. The view down the alley was not great. Maybe he could cut away some of the weather stripping at the bottom of the door and slip his minicamera out the hole he made.

Belatedly, he answered Alex's question. "My dude. The way you reacted when I held your hand when we were handcuffed together—hot move, by the way. Most straight men would go board stiff if I grabbed their hand and wouldn't know what to do for a second or two. But you were as relaxed as could be about it."

"I was not relaxed about it!" Alex exclaimed under his breath.

"Okay, fair. You definitely felt the…whatever it was… between us. And it threw you for a loop. But not an 'oh, shit, I'm straight and holding another man's hand' loop. It was more of an 'oh, shit, this guy is hot and I'm not sure I want to kill him anymore' loop that I threw you for."

He pulled out his pocketknife and used its tip to start digging at the black weather stripping at the bottom right-hand corner of the fire exit, where there was already a small gap letting in a prick of light.

Alex said slowly, "You may be more observant than I gave you credit for."

"Gee. Thanks. Do you think maybe someday I might have a future in the intelligence business?"

Alex laughed, a barely audible gust of humor in Nick's ear.

Nick enlarged the hole enough to slip the minicam through it, and he sat down on the floor in front of the fire exit. He could be here awhile, crouching over the tubular end of the camera with its attached viewfinder, so he might as well get comfortable. And, barring a fire in this building, he wasn't likely to be disturbed anytime soon. He pressed his eye to the rubber cup and looked out.

It was disorienting getting a mouse's-eye view of the alley. Or, since this was New York City, maybe a rat's-eye view would be more accurate. He tilted the camera up slightly. There. Now he had a clearer sightline down the alley. If Gray and his men left their hide by the back exit, he would see them.

"So, Alex, when did you figure out you were gay?"

"About the time all the boys started getting interested in girls, I figured out girls didn't do anything for me. It probably took another year or two after that for me to realize that when I woke in the morning super, um, uncomfortable, I usually had been dreaming about a boy and not a girl."

"So that would have made you, what? Twelve or thirteen?"

"Something like that. What about you? When did you know?" Alex asked.

"Later for me. I was told over and over when I was a kid that gay people should all die. So, I fought it pretty hard. I was a junior in high school when I got really drunk at a party and another gay kid in my school pulled me into a closet and made out with me. I swore to him I was just drunk, straight and curious. He laughed in my face and gave me my first blow job."

"You said your dad would've killed you if he found out. Does he know now?"

"Oh yeah. When I finished SEAL training and went live on the teams, I thought I might finally be manly enough to please him and went home for a visit. He got more drunk than usual and called me…things. I told him he was exactly right, I was gay, and furthermore, he could kiss my ass."

Nick felt more than heard Alex's wince before he asked quietly, "How did that go over with him?"

"He tried to kill me. When he attacked, I put him down on the floor in a choke hold in about two seconds and very calmly told him that if he ever touched me again, I would kill him and no one would ever find the body."

"Um, wow. That's too bad."

Nick sighed. "I knew better than to rise to his bait. But he'd said so much hurtful, stupid crap to me over the years about the queer community that I snapped. I'm not proud of it. I was a SEAL, for crying out loud. I knew how to control my emotions. I never let people get to me like that."

"He was your father. That's different."

Nick pulled his eye away from the viewfinder to pinch the bridge of his nose for a moment. "Yeah. I found that out the hard way."

Silence fell between them. He went back to watching the alley.

Nick asked heavily, "Does your family know?"

"Yep. They claim they don't care, love me, are proud of me, and have never been anything but supportive."

"Lucky bastard," Nick murmured. "Wait a minute. They claim they're okay with it? What does that mean?"

"Ah, you are perceptive aren't you, grasshopper?" Alex murmured.

"You gonna dodge my question, or are you gonna answer it?"

Alex sighed. "It means my family said all the right things. But I found out later they weren't as okay with it as they said they were. My parents caught blowback from their church and apparently were rather negative about it to their friends and pastor. Behind my back, of course."

"That sucks," Nick said with feeling. At least his parents had been openly hostile to him and hadn't been two-faced about it. Plus, it didn't take a rocket scientist to notice that Alex was the kind of man who would despise being lied to. He wasn't the Judge for nothing.

"What about your mother?" Alex asked. "What does she think about you being gay?"

"She loved me but feared my dad. She was caught in the middle."

"You say that in the past tense. Has she passed away?"

"Nope. She's alive. But after I attacked my old man, she sided with him. Hasn't spoken to me since. I think I scared her. I mean, they knew I was a SEAL, but they didn't really know what that meant. It had never dawned on them that I was actually capable of killing."

Alex snorted. "Duh." Then, soberly, "I'm sorry. That sucks, too."

Nick sighed. At least Alex knew precisely what it meant to have been a SEAL and what he was capable of. And the guy had still snuggled up against him in his sleep.

Chapter 6

"I've got movement from our homeless guy," Alex said low. "He's going inside the building."

Nick murmured in his ear, "They're getting ready to move. They'll send a couple of guys out to watch the street and maybe put a sniper in a window. Then they'll bring around a vehicle and load up Gray."

"Same limo as last night?" Alex asked.

"No way. New place, new car, every day."

"Bummer. That tracker was handy."

Nick grumbled, "Yeah, and it's exactly why they change cars all the time."

"Okay," Alex reported. "I've got a guy deploying out onto the street. He's heading north. Have you got any movement behind the building?"

"Nega— Crap!" Nick bit out.

"What?"

"A car just raced down the alley." He watched it, reporting tersely, "It has stopped in front of Gray's building. Two men just sped fast out of the building and are getting in the vehicle. And, it's on the move again. Heading north. Dammit, they're turning left. Away from you." The whole stop had taken no more than five seconds.

"Did you see Gray get in the vehicle?" Alex asked tersely.

"I didn't see the faces of the two men who got in the SUV."

"What about their heights and builds? Could one of them have been him?" Alex asked. "Or were they decoys?"

"Possibly. I've never seen the team do anything like that before. Gray always stays in places with covered or underground parking. He moves to vehicles unseen. He doesn't go outside to get into cars."

"New safety protocol?" Alex suggested.

"Well, one thing we know for sure," Nick muttered. "If he's still inside the building, he's down at least three bodyguards. A driver for the vehicle, and the two guys who jumped in the car."

"Did you get a license plate number?"

Nick snorted. "As if. Magically, the plate was completely covered. I couldn't tell you if it was taped over or coated in mud. But either way, it was completely obscured."

"Of course it was. Like magic." A pause, then Alex mused aloud, "How do we tell if Gray's still inside the building or not?"

"How ballsy do you feel like being?" Nick asked.

"What do you have in mind?"

"I can approach the team. The guys know me. I trained most of them. I can ask to speak to Gray. Tell him I need to report in on the ambush that got the rest of my team caught."

"Yes, but won't he ask where you've been the past few months?"

"I'll tell him I had to go to ground. That I couldn't risk approaching him until I knew for sure I was in the clear."

Alex considered. "What if he doesn't believe you? You'd be walking into a death trap."

"We all have to die sometime."

Alex scowled. Nick was the first person with whom he'd made any kind of personal connection with in years. Literally years. He really didn't want to see the man throw away his life. Not to mention, death wishes were not good things for active operators to run around with. When they got back to the safe house—if they made it back to the safe house—he and Nick were going to have a little conversation about the whole prepared-to-throw-away-his-life thing.

Alex asked, with a sense of desperation that surprised himself, "How would you even figure out which unit Gray stayed in last night? Even if the apartments are huge, the building has to have at least three or four dozen condos."

"Call it intuition. I can feel Gray and his guys."

"What exactly do they feel like?" Alex asked dryly.

"They make the back of my neck crawl. As if a scorpion is walking across my skin, and all I can do is be perfectly still and pray it doesn't sting me."

"Spoken like a man who's done a sniper mission or two in a desert environment."

Nick grunted. "Obviously, you've pulled the same sort of mission."

Obviously.

"Let me come with you," Alex said. "I can at least lay

down covering fire for you if you have to beat a hasty retreat."

"That's not how Gray's team works," Nick said grimly. "Nobody gets away from them once they decide to detain or kill a target. There's no sense getting us both killed. If they take me out, at least you'll be able to finish the mission alone."

There was nothing Alex could say to that. He was the exact same way. Once he locked in on a target, that was it. He didn't stop or give up until he succeeded in executing his orders.

"Thanks for the offer to come along, but your presence would only raise red flags," Nick said. "I may be able to get close without freaking them out."

"I don't like this."

"I don't like it, either. But you tell me what better option we have."

Alex sighed. "I've got nothing. How are you going in?"

"I'll enter through the underground parking garage. It exits into this alley."

It sounded as if Nick was moving around as he spoke into his microphone. Alex heard a zipper and then faint scratching sounds. Nick was probably packing up his surveillance gear and disabling the fire alarm on the exit to the alley.

Nick said low, "I'm moving out."

"Update me as you can," Alex replied.

Nick didn't reply.

If waiting up here for the past seven hours had tested his patience, waiting for the next few minutes nearly killed Alex. Which shocked him. He could sit in a surveillance hide for days on end without ever getting twitchy. But two minutes of worrying about his new partner, and he was a hot mess.

What if he'd been spotted? What if he'd been shot? Oh, man. Should he go down there and check on Nick? Stage a rescue—

"I'm in the garage. Limo in sight. Gonna retrieve my tracker," Nick breathed.

Oh, thank goodness. Nick wasn't dead.

Alex tried to picture the scene in the parking garage. A dark, low-ceilinged space of tilting concrete ramps smelling of oil and exhaust fumes. Nick, gliding through the shadows, using pillars and vehicles for cover, making his way toward the limo. A pause to check for Gray's people. Then a low, slow approach to the back end of the limousine—

Nick swore quietly in his ear. "It's not here."

Alex didn't transmit it, but he swore, as well. Gray knew someone was on to him. Which would explain the change in security procedures and abrupt departure. Assuming Gray had actually left in that fast-moving car in the alley.

"Going inside," Nick breathed.

Alex couldn't help himself. He replied, "Be careful."

"Aww. You like having a partner?" Nick teased under his breath. "Or do you just like me?"

He liked having *this* partner. Not that he was about to admit it to Nick. No way was he feeding the guy's ego any more fodder.

Instead, he drawled, "Obviously, I prefer not working solo on a surveillance op. I mean, I get to sit back and watch the show while you stick your neck out. This is great. I'm just kicking back, up here on the roof, my feet propped on a rail, eating a power bar."

Nick laughed quietly. "Asshole."

Alex grinned. "Right back atcha."

Alex heard the distinctive ding of an elevator, and Nick

said, "I'll try the third floor. Gray won't use the first or second floors—too easy to access. And he won't use the top two floors. They're too exposed to an aerial attack. Which leaves me four floors to search."

"You're not going to actually search apartments, are you?" Alex asked in quick alarm.

"Relax, Grandma. I'm just gonna walk the halls and wait for a scorpion to walk across my neck."

"I'm the hottest grandma you've ever met," Alex retorted.

"No lie, my friend. No lie."

Welp. That silenced Alex but good. Nick thought he was hot, huh? What was he supposed to do with that? Ignore the attraction simmering between them and just do the job? Take a break from all of this at some point and explore whatever it was crackling and sparking between them?

The elevator dinged again, and Alex pictured Nick checking the hallway, then moving out of the elevator, rolling from heel to toe with each step, making no noise whatsoever as he walked smoothly down the hall.

Alex heard once that SEALs had a saying. Slow is Smooth, and Smooth is Fast. They were not wrong.

A door squeaked in Alex's earbud and he tensed.

"In the stairwell. Moving up to four," Nick murmured.

He was only silent for perhaps ten seconds before he whispered in Alex's ear, "Tallyho."

"Scorpion on your neck?"

"Roger that," Nick breathed.

"Any visual on Gray or his guys?"

"No. But they're in one of two apartments. I'm knocking on the first door now."

Alex's whole body vibrated with tension as he heard

Nick's knuckles rap quietly, not so loud as to carry across the hallway into the other apartment.

Silence.

Nick knocked again.

Still nothing.

"Trying the other unit," Nick breathed.

Again, there was no response to his knocks.

Alex knew better than to bug Nick while he was operating in a high-threat environment. The man needed to focus all his awareness on his immediate surroundings and be ready to react instantaneously.

Two minutes or so passed in tense silence. *What was Nick doing down there?*

"Sonofabitch," Nick said in disgust.

"What?" Alex blurted, his nerves near the breaking point.

"So, I let myself into the apartment that felt the most scorpion-like."

"You broke in?" Alex squawked. "What if they were there, waiting for you?"

"They weren't. I cleared the place, and it's empty."

"Then, how do you know you have the right one?"

"My tracker is lying on the kitchen table beside a note that says 'You forgot something.'"

Alex's jaw dropped. "Does he know who you are?"

"No idea. But it's vintage Gray. He wants whoever is following him to know that he knows."

"So, he was in the car you saw take off, then?"

"That would be my guess," Nick replied heavily.

"We've lost him."

"Looks that way."

Alex was tempted to punch the brick wall beside his head. "What do you want to do next?"

"I'm gonna search the apartment across the hall to be safe."

"But—"

"I'm going now," Nick interrupted. He might as well have told Alex to shut up. Both of them knew he needed silence in his earbuds while he broke into and cleared the second unit.

Alex pictured Nick checking for alarms, picking the door lock and easing into the apartment. He would clear the space in a pattern—front to back, clockwise—it would depend on the layout. When he'd opened all the doors, looked in every closet, under every bed and anywhere else a human could conceivably hide, only then would he break radio silence.

"Clear. But his team stayed in this place last night," Nick announced.

"How do you know?"

"It's too neat for any normal person to leave it like this. There's not a fingerprint *anywhere*. Every glass in the cupboard is wiped clean. No normal person wipes down the glassware, and certainly not that thoroughly, when they unload the dishwasher."

"Good point."

Alex noted Gray's man at the north end of the street turning to walk back toward the building. He checked the south-end man, and he, too, was on the move. "Nick, you've got two tangos incoming. The guys on the street are coming toward the building."

"I'll bet they just get in a car and drive away. This place is already sanitized and buttoned-up. They won't come back here. I'm going to head down to the basement and see if I can get a license plate and description of their vehicle."

Alex squeezed his eyes shut. It was exactly what he

would do, so he couldn't fault Nick for doing the same thing. But he didn't like it. The risk of being seen was considerable, and a two-on-one fight of any kind rarely went well for the solo guy. It took a ridiculously skilled fighter to hold off a pair of attackers.

He heard Nick breathing hard, which meant he must be charging down the stairwell at top speed. Abruptly, Nick stopped huffing, took two long, deep breaths, and then a door latch clicked. He was heading back into the parking garage.

Alex heard an engine rev briefly.

"Got 'em," Nick said in satisfaction when the car noise had died away. "Pack up, and I'll meet you at the north end of the street."

Alex folded the Mylar tarps and stuffed them in his rucksack. He policed the roof for any wrappers or water bottles, then walked around, scuffing his feet until he had obscured any tracks that might have identified him or Nick in any way. Then he headed for the fire escape.

He spotted Nick standing at a bus stop in front of him, looking bored and annoyed…which meant he blended in perfectly with the other people waiting for the bus.

Alex walked up beside Nick and murmured, "Subway will be faster to get back to my place. We'll have to make two transfers if we take the bus. But there's a direct train to my neighborhood."

"Subway it is," Nick replied low.

They had to walk a block or so to the nearest entrance. But a train was pulling into the station as they reached the platform, and it was only a half dozen stops on this line to the subway station just down the street from his crash pad.

A busker played acoustic guitar and sang holiday songs in their car. As the stations flashed by, advertisements for live Christmas trees, department store holiday sales, and seasonal pop-up stores came into view and disappeared again. It was oddly cheerful, given the grim nature of the job they were in the midst of.

The morning rush hour was mostly past, and the subway riders skewed mostly to retirees and moms with small children. Both groups appeared to be interested mainly in their holiday shopping needs.

Nick and Alex walked to their building in the light layer of new snow, rode the rickety elevator up to the apartment, and while Nick took a shower, claiming a need to wake up, Alex scrambled a pile of eggs for them and made toast in the oven. It felt good, right, to cook breakfast for the two of them like this.

Since when did he like playing house, solo or otherwise? Sure, he fed himself and cleaned the spaces he lived in. But he'd never registered enjoyment of simple tasks like this, let alone enjoyment of doing them for someone else.

With a jolt, he smelled something burning. He lunged for the oven and pulled out the rapidly blackening toast.

He scraped off the blackened part with a knife over the sink, shaking his head at how much Nick distracted him. He popped a pod into a single-serving coffee maker and inhaled gratefully as the scent of the steaming brew rose from the machine.

"Oh man. That smells good," Nick said from behind him.

Alex tensed reflexively. He wasn't used to being around anyone who could sneak up on him like that. It took a very, very quiet human being to get close to him without him hearing or at least sensing them.

He turned to face Nick. *Hoo, baby.* With his hair towel dried and brushed back from his freshly shaven face, the full impact of Nick's good looks was on display. His tanned skin and manly features stole Alex's breath away. He wasn't a pretty man, per se. But he was hard to look away from.

Alex's gaze dropped, taking in the fact that Nick's shirt wasn't buttoned. He'd donned the starched white tuxedo shirt from before, and he'd rolled up the sleeves—he probably didn't want to fuss with cuff links—and he hadn't bothered with the studs that would close the garment, either.

His chest was covered in dark hair that looked fantastic against his darkly tanned skin and bulging pectorals. An urge to crawl inside that shirt and lick the man's chest startled Alex badly. "Where'd you get a tan like that at this time of year?" he blurted.

Nick arched one dark, sexy eyebrow at him and said dryly, "You know better than to ask a guy like me stuff like that."

"Yeah. Right. Sorry," he mumbled, picking up a plate of eggs and toast and shoving it practically into Nick's belly button.

He fetched his own plate and followed Nick to the table with it. "I would've made you coffee, but I thought you might want to sleep some more. You've got some catching up to do after the past week. After that, we can figure out how we want to proceed with picking up Gray's trail."

Nick looked longingly at Alex's mug of black coffee but nodded in acquiescence. "What are you going to do while I snooze?"

"I thought I'd go out and do a little sightseeing. Maybe do a little Christmas shopping."

Nick looked startled. As if he hadn't had anyone to shop for at this time of year for a very long time.

His own family wasn't great—he could do without their hypocrisy—but at least they didn't reject him outright.

To be honest, he was probably as hypocritical as they were, buying Christmas presents and sending birthday cards with cheerful messages as if nothing was wrong between them. As if it didn't feel like a hot knife in his belly every time he thought about the things his family said about him behind his back that they thought he wouldn't find out about.

Maybe Nick had the right of it. Maybe he should just make a break and tell them they could come back into his life when they could fully embrace him as he was, or at least be honest with him about how they felt about him being gay. But it was a big step. And he was already completely alone in the world. Did he have the courage to cut off his only lifeline to family?

Alex asked, "When's the last time you celebrated Christmas with your family?"

Nick very obviously deflected the topic, snapping, "I hate Christmas."

"With a name like Nicholas Kane? As in Saint Nick and candy canes? And you hate Christmas? Say it isn't so!"

"Sorry. I'm a born-again holiday hater."

"Okay. Then, when is the last time you celebrated a holiday with anyone? A birthday, New Year's, Independence Day. Any holiday," Alex asked in surprise.

Nick frowned for a moment and then shrugged. "Can't remember."

"Aww, c'mon. A guy like you has to have a pretty decent memory."

"I have a great memory but a lousy family. I guess my last Christmas at home would've been before I joined the navy, so maybe…eighteen years ago?" he guessed.

"Dang, you're old," Alex teased.

"How old are you?" Nick demanded.

"Thirty-four. You?"

Nick snorted. "You're a babe in arms. I'll be thirty-eight in January."

"Man, you really are ancient. You're just about ready for the retirement farm."

Nick scowled and made a rude hand gesture to him.

Alex grinned even more broadly. His smile still fading, he said to Nick, "Tell me something your family did together to celebrate the holidays when you were a kid."

"We never did much together. But let's see. Holidays at my house. On Christmas Eve, my dad usually went to a bar to drink. My mom went to her bedroom to drink. My older sister went to parties with her friends to drink, and my younger brother snuck booze out of my mom's hidden stash and drank it."

"I'm sensing a theme with your family," Alex responded.

Nick shrugged. "I remember making Christmas cookies once with my granny. She let me decorate them however I wanted. That was fun. She made popcorn for me and her, and we watched a Christmas movie while we worked on those stupid cookies."

"Do you remember what the movie was?"

Nick shook his head. "No clue. She was babysitting me that night. And she brought over Christmas lights and ornaments for our tree. My dad refused to spend money on frivolous crap like decorations, and my mom was too depressed to fight him on it. In his defense, do you know how many fifths of vodka you can get for the same money it takes to buy a tree?"

The pain in Nick's voice was hard to hear. He couldn't

think of anything to say in response, so he put his head down and ate in silence.

"Do you actually like Christmas?" Nick blurted without warning.

He looked up, startled. "Yes. Actually, I do."

"Why?"

"Hope. It's a season of love and peace, family and new beginnings. It gives me hope."

"Hope for what?"

"For me finding a little of all those things one day, I guess."

"Whew. For a second there, I thought you were going to say you wish for world peace."

"Umm, I do. Of all people, you and I know the cost of there not being peace on earth."

Nick exhaled heavily. "Yeah. I guess we do. Maybe that's why I hate the holidays."

Alex blinked, shocked. "Are you saying you're a pessimist at heart? I don't believe it. I may not have known you all that long, but you strike me as the kind of man who always believes things will turn out okay for you."

"Maybe professionally." Nick shrugged. "Can't say the same for my personal life."

"Maybe the right person just hasn't come along for you. Maybe happiness is waiting for you right around the corner."

"Dang. You really are a Pollyanna."

Alex merely shrugged in response. He stood by his declaration of affection for the holidays. It was the one time of year when he felt a tiny bit optimistic about the future.

As they finished eating and Nick pushed his plate back in satisfaction, Alex said quietly, "Regarding your death wish. We need to have a conversation about that."

"What about it?"

Interesting. He didn't deny having one. "It's not a good trait for an active covert operative."

Nick sighed. "I've always expected to die in the line of duty. Don't you?"

"No!" Alex exclaimed. "I don't. I fully expect to retire safely from my job and settle down to a nice, quiet life. And you should, too."

Urgency to get Nick to give up his crazy notion of dying in the line of duty pulsed through him and through his words. Nick had to live if he was going to get his shot at a family of his own.

Nick shrugged. "I guess I've never pictured myself getting a happily-ever-after."

"Why ever not?"

Nick frowned at him. "You know why not."

"Because you're gay?" Alex asked, startled.

"Well. Yeah."

"It's not a crime to be gay. And it certainly doesn't mean you're not allowed to find happiness in your old age."

"I'm not forty yet. I'm not exactly in my dotage, here."

Alex rolled his eyes. "You know what I mean. You're allowed to find a nice guy, settle down, have some kids if you want. Be happy."

"Happy," Nick murmured reflectively. "Not a word I've ever used to describe myself."

"Well, that's grim."

Nick shrugged.

Alex had no idea why it was suddenly so important to him that Nick get a happily-ever-after in spite of all the bad family and bad luck life had thrown at him. But it was important to him. In fact, a desire to be the person to give love and laughter and family to this grim man surged through him.

Alex leaned forward. "I'm serious. You need to get over this eagerness to die. If nothing else, it makes you bad at your job. I'd hate to have to pull you out of the field because of it."

"You'd pull me out of the field?" Nick exclaimed. "Do you even have that power?"

Alex shot him a withering look. "I have the power to execute you, no questions asked. I most certainly have the power to tell my superiors you need to be brought in and taken out of field operations."

"You wouldn't!" Nick sounded aghast.

"I don't want to. Please don't make me do it."

"So…what? I'm supposed to act as if there's a permanent ray of sunshine up my ass?"

"No. And don't be crude." He drank the last of his coffee and set the mug down on the table. "But do think about pulling your head out of said ass long enough to find a compelling reason to stay alive."

"Has anyone ever told you that you're a bit of a jerk?" Nick grumbled.

Alex grinned. "All the time, my friend. All the time."

Nick just scowled, shoved back his chair and carried his plate over to the sink.

Alex insisted on doing the dishes. He waved Nick over toward the mattress in the corner, and thankfully, Nick didn't fight him on it. Which was an indication of just how beat the guy was.

By the time Alex washed the two plates, skillet and coffee mug, Nick was passed out cold, still fully dressed except for his shoes, which he'd kicked off. Shaking his head, Alex fetched a blanket and pillow out of the front closet. He considered waking Nick to hand him the pillow but settled for laying it gently beside the guy's head. He unfolded the blanket and draped it lightly over Nick from neck to toes. Nick didn't even stir as the blanket settled over him, which was indicative of just how deeply the guy was already asleep.

Alex set the alarms for the apartment and headed out. He had an idea. He didn't know if he could pull it off, but he would give it his best shot.

Chapter 7

Nick woke slowly, groggily. What was the sun doing coming in the window from that angle? When he'd closed his eyes for a quick nap, the sun had been behind the building in the east. Now it was flooding the tiny studio from the west.

Surely he hadn't slept all day—

As the thought occurred to him, he lurched up to a seated position. Where had that pillow come from? And the blanket? And where was Alex?

He looked around and several other things registered in him all at once. In his absence from consciousness, someone—Alex, no doubt—had decorated the apartment for the holidays. A fake Christmas tree perhaps two feet tall stood on the table. Small, shiny objects hung all over it.

Nick climbed to his feet and noticed the window behind him was surrounded by a string of orange-and-green–chili pepper lights held up with black duct tape. The dude version of Christmas lights amused him. He wandered over to the table and grinned at the tree's decorations. Ammunition in various calibers hung all over it from black thread that look suspiciously like trip wire.

He turned on the television to catch the news, pondering how many times he'd found out where he was about to be deployed over the years by watching twenty-four-hour news channels like this one.

The hallway doorknob rattled, and Nick reacted fast, jumping up and moving swiftly to the corner of the kitchen, out of sight of the short hallway. He waited, poised for violence.

"Hi, Lucy. I'm home," Alex called out.

Nick exhaled and lowered his hands as he stepped out into the middle of the living area. "Hey. I love what you've done with the place, Ricky."

Alex set down a pair of flat cardboard boxes on the table beside the tiny, homicidal tree. "I brought us a holiday-themed meal."

"Pizza?" Nick blurted. "How is that Christmas themed?"

Alex grinned and opened the lid of the top box. "Easy. One is topped with tomatoes and basil, the other has pepperoni and green peppers. Get it? Red and green?"

Nick just shook his head. "Pathetic, man."

"Admit it. This is more Christmas-y than anything you've seen in years." Alex waved a hand to encompass the pizza, tree and window dressing.

"How are chili peppers Christmas-y?" Nick asked, reaching for a slice of pizza.

Alex shrugged. "The store I went to was out of lights, and those were the only ones they had left."

"The duct tape really makes the pepper lights special," Nick commented dryly.

Alex grinned and handed Nick one of the pizza boxes, then picked up the other. "I thought you of all people would appreciate my ingenuity in figuring out how to hang them."

Nick sat down on the sofa and commenced eating pizza straight from the box.

"Speaking of holiday moods," Alex said cheerfully, "I got us a couple Christmas movies to watch, too."

"You really went all out. Beneath all that cool, calm killer, are you really a secret Christmas junkie?"

"Guilty as charged," Alex replied, crouching in front of a DVR player sitting on the floor below the flat-screen TV. The screen went dark for a moment, and then a movie started to play.

Nick watched about ten seconds of it and started to laugh. "Really? *Die Hard* is your idea of a Christmas movie?"

Alex grinned at him. "Hey. I'm totally down for watching *White Christmas* or *It's a Wonderful Life*. But I thought you'd prefer a little shoot-'em-up with your holiday cheer."

"You would not be wrong. Nothing says Peace on Earth and Goodwill to Men like a hostage crisis and a little gratuitous violence."

Alex laughed. "Great. Because I've got *Home Alone* for us to watch, too."

Nick had to shake his head. Truth be told, all of this was really thoughtful. He really hadn't celebrated the season, not once, since he'd left home at eighteen years of age. During his military career, he had always volunteered for Christmas duty so the guys with families could stay home with their loved ones. More times than he could count, he'd ended up deployed in some remote corner of the world anyway, chasing bad guys who didn't care if it was December 25 or not.

"Shouldn't we be trying to track down Gray's guys and the car I saw them leave the garage in?"

Alex scowled. "I already had the plates run. It was a rental car. Got turned in around noon. We lost Gray and his men."

"Well, hell."

"I don't know about you," Alex commented, "but if I do something innocuous to keep my conscious mind occupied, my subconscious usually figures out what I should do next. Right now, I've got it working on how to pick up Gray's trail again. In the meantime, I'm going to pop some popcorn and watch a movie."

Nick shrugged. The plan worked for him.

As Bruce Willis entered the high-rise tower where his ex-wife worked, Alex surprised him by asking randomly, "If you were actually going to celebrate the holidays, what would you want to do?"

"I have no idea. Maybe go sit on a beach somewhere and listen to country music."

Alex laughed. "My sister calls country music the music of pain."

Nick grinned. "She's not wrong. Maybe that's why I like it."

"Party pooper," Alex retorted.

"Why? What would you do for the holidays if you didn't spend it with your perfect family?"

"My family isn't perfect. Far from it." He paused, letting the wave of sadness that washed over him pass. "In answer to your question, though, I would head somewhere snowy. A small town that goes all out for Christmas. Every house would have lights on it and a tree in the front window. There would be snowmen in the yards and kids sledding. I would bake cookies and wrap presents and wrap presents and spend the holidays with my family, hanging out, catching up on one another's lives and laughing."

Nick tilted his head. "What does your family think you do for a living?"

"They think I do financial audits of government agencies and fix any discrepancies I find."

Nick's mouth twitched with humor. "When I was still speaking with my sister, I told her I was a tropical fish importer. Every time I visited her and her kids, I had to stop at a store and buy them a plastic bag full of fish. Lousy legend. Pain in the ass, having to keep getting all those stupid fish."

"Why don't you speak to your sister anymore?"

"Her husband won't let her contact me. He says that, as a former SEAL, I pose a danger to her and the kids."

"Do you?"

Nick rolled his eyes. "They're family. I'd die to protect them, and I would never, ever harm them. Not that they understand for a second what loyalty to family actually means."

Alex put down a strip of uneaten crust and picked up another piece of pizza. "Mine understands loyalty. But they have a real problem with telling the truth. Not to mention they have no idea what it takes to keep a government the size of ours from going off the rails."

"Is that how you see yourself?" Nick asked. "A guy who keeps Uncle Sam honest?"

"Something like that. I'm not so naive as to think we don't need bad people to do bad things from time to time. But those people can't be allowed to slip off their leashes. That's my job. To keep them from losing control and using the government's resources to do terrible things they weren't ordered to do."

"I've never met a fixer before," Nick reflected. "I mean, I always knew at some peripheral level that guys like you must exist, but nobody ever talks about it."

Alex shrugged. "It's interesting work."

"Don't you get cynical after a while?" Nick asked.

"How so?"

"Don't you get jaded, seeing good guy after good guy making a bad decision or losing control and doing something they shouldn't?"

Alex frowned at him, and Nick gazed back, interested in Alex's answer.

"Honestly, I try not to think about it. It's too depressing. I remind myself that, for every person I have to take out of the field, there are dozens or hundreds of operators who don't step over the line."

"How many people have you actually executed in your career?"

Alex grimaced. "You know the deal. I try not to keep count."

"You try. But you remember every face and every name," Nick said quietly.

Alex met his gaze, and for a second, naked pain and grief shone in his eyes.

Of course, Alex remembered every kill. Most of the SEALs Nick had worked with were the same way. In fact, the guys who didn't remember them, who didn't have nightmares about them, were the ones who worried Nick.

Alex said vaguely, "I'm up around fifty sanctions. Of course, those aren't all American operators, and they didn't all end up in a morgue. When there aren't any domestic bad guys to stop, I occasionally pick up a regular assignment."

Alex might have said the word *assignment*, but Nick

heard the unspoken word—*assassination*. "How many of your targets were foreign?"

"A dozen, maybe. And only about half of my American caseload ends up in a kill."

"But still, half are guys like me."

"Not guys like you. Guys who've gone rogue."

Nick shook his head. "Still. You're talking about multiple guys of our own who've crossed over to the dark side. That is depressing. I hoped there might be one guy go bad every decade or so."

"If only," Alex said soberly.

Nick turned back to the movie to watch Alan Rickman's villain character burst into a boardroom and shoot it up.

"Promise me something," Alex blurted suddenly.

Nick looked over at him. "What's that?"

"Swear to me you're one of the good guys. That you're not a plant by Gray to track me and stop me from getting to him."

Nick lurched. "I swear. I want to take down Gray as much as you do. The bastard corrupted my entire team and dragged them into whatever criminal enterprise he's got going."

"Where are your former teammates, anyway?" Alex asked. "You said something about them being apprehended. But, they're not listed in any prisoner database I have access to."

"Black site. In the custody of a group I trust absolutely. Not CIA, though. Military."

"Are they giving up any information?"

Nick rolled his eyes. "What do you think?"

"I think people like us are trained to die before we give our interrogators the time of day."

"You would not be wrong," Nick responded.

Alex shrugged. "In my experience, everyone has a breaking point. With people like us, it just takes a lot longer to reach it. Give your teammates a few years sitting in a hole. They'll talk, eventually."

"And what will that accomplish?" Nick asked bitterly.

"Well, if we manage to take Gray alive, he'll also be sitting in a hole somewhere. And when your guys finally talk, we can prosecute him and put him away—or put him down—for good."

"We won't take Gray alive. That I know for sure. The man always has a cyanide pill or something similar on his person. He'll kill himself long before he lets himself be arrested."

"Oh, I don't arrest my targets. Capture them, yes. But I don't do anything so mundane or formal as arresting anyone. That would leave a paperwork trail."

Nick studied Alex intently. "Who fixes the fixers? What if one of you goes off the rails?"

Alex let out a whoosh of air as if Nick has punched him in the gut. "That would be bad. Real bad. I imagine we would join together to go after the rogue fixer."

"Do you know how many of you there are?" Nick asked.

"I have no idea. And if I did, I surely couldn't tell you."

"Aww, c'mon. I've got *all* the security clearances," Nick protested.

Alex shrugged. "I'm afraid there are a few clearances you don't have. There are some whose names are even classified."

Nick never had felt a need to one-up other operators. He was comfortable in his own skin and at peace with the idea that there would always be others who knew a little bit more than him. It was the nature of working in the intelligence community. All information was tightly compartmentalized. He knew everything he needed to know to operate in his own little sandbox. He didn't need to know what was going on in the next-guy-over's sandbox.

Alex said, "Here's where the movie gets funny."

Nick watched, and guffawed, as Bruce Willis ran around barefoot on floors strewn with shattered glass. "What technical advisor let them film anyone barefoot running around on shards like that?"

Alex grinned over at him. "It's the magic of Hollywood."

Nick shrugged. "I mean, sure, he's playing up wincing and limping a little. But he would be debilitated by the pain of running on that much glass. And he would be bleeding everywhere by now."

Willis climbed up into a ventilation duct and commenced crawling through it while Nick shook his head and commented, "How many buildings have you ever been in that had ductwork that easy to access or that went exactly where you needed it to go?"

Alex rolled his eyes. "Or buildings with banks in them that don't have alarms wired directly to police stations?"

Nick grinned, and the nitpicking was on. They surgically dismembered the movie, discussing in detail how they would have gone about freeing the hostages, stopping the bad guys and liberating the building. Alex was a creative and out-of-the-box thinker who challenged even Nick's problem-solving prowess.

They laughed and compared notes—in general terms that didn't violate security protocols, of course—on various missions they'd run, and they discovered their backgrounds were more similar than they expected. They'd found kindred souls in each other.

Except for country music. Alex hated country music. While Nick had been running around with his SEAL team, Alex had gone the civilian route, working his way up through the ranks of the CIA, picking up training all around the world with various intelligence agencies, like MI6 and the Mossad. He'd run undercover with mobsters and terrorists, and had even embedded with a few private security firms to do mercenary work. The end result was that he was trained much like Nick had been, first in the military and then in the CIA's Special Operations Group.

They both had been all over the world and, sitting here now, expressed fatigue at all the travel. When Alex challenged him to imagine surviving his career, his mind turned to a quiet retirement where he settled down someplace exceedingly dull. To that image, Alex added putting their feet up on the porch railing and watching the world go by for a good, long time.

Yep. That sounded almost good enough to stay alive for.

As the big shootout and explosions at the end of *Die Hard* commenced, Nick asked, "Have you ever thought about having a family of your own?"

Alex winced. "Of course I've thought about it. But it's hard enough to find a partner who won't drive me crazy, let alone one who can put up with a guy like me. I surely don't expect to find someone who can tolerate me *and* who wants a picket fence and kids."

"Why? What's wrong with you? I mean, if you have no hope, surely I have even less chance," Nick said.

Alex shrugged. "It's not as if I can talk like this about my career with anyone else. The first time I casually dissect the best way to kill someone in a movie, any reasonably nice civilian guy will run screaming from me."

"Damn. I hadn't ever thought of it like that," Nick said low. "I mean, I haven't really given serious thought to what comes after my career, because you know, death wish and all."

"You should really give some thought to the idea of building your own family after the one that raised you turned out…badly."

He snorted. "*Badly* is hardly the word I would use. They're a freaking shit show— Sorry. A freaking disaster."

"I'm sorry about that, too. You're a decent guy and deserve better."

"Yeah, well, we don't get to choose our parents."

Alex rolled his eyes knowingly.

"What's that all about?" Nick asked. "Why did you roll your eyes when I mentioned your family?"

Alex stared at a spot over Nick's shoulder and didn't look him in the eye. "Let's just say I have a very black-and-white sense of honesty, and they do not."

"Ouch." Nick nodded in understanding. "It sucks being in a business where absolute honesty is required or else people will die. The rest of the world doesn't tend to live that way, do they?"

Alex sighed. "No. They don't. And it worries me for down the road when I rejoin the civilian world. How am I going to compromise my standards and live with someone who can't or won't be totally honest with me at all times?"

It dawned on Nick that he was going to have the exact same problem. Particularly after his team had lied to him and betrayed him the way they had. It had been more devastating to him than he would've anticipated. "Who the hell knew that finding one truthful man to love would turn out to be such a hard thing? If you'd told me back when I was seventeen that honesty would be the one issue that was my deal breaker for relationships, I'd have laughed my head off."

"Why's that?"

"Because being gay and not out of the closet is a completely dishonest way to live. Granted, I needed to stay closeted for my own safety. But I became a fantastic liar out of sheer survival necessity."

"At least you'll be a much better dad to your own kids because of what you went through. I'll bet you create a safe space for your children to be totally candid with you and not face repercussions for it."

Nick's gut tightened at the thought of having children of his own one day. It was his fondest wish to have kids, but he knew full well how unlikely he was to attain it. He barely admitted to himself that he would love to have a family of his own, let alone to anyone else.

"...you'll know what not to do as a parent," Alex was saying.

"That's something, I guess." Nick looked over at Alex. "Are you always Mr. Optimism-and-Find-the-Silver-Lining?"

"Me? My family insists I'm the doom-and-gloom guy of our clan. Apparently, I always have a contingency plan for the worst-case scenario."

"Well...yeah. That's how you've stayed alive this long. People like us always have to be prepared for the worst, the unexpected, the shot out of left field."

"I know, right?" Alex exclaimed. "That's what I keep telling them. But then they remind me that financial audits are not the stuff of life and death."

Nick grinned. "Neither is selling tropical fish."

They traded smiles of commiseration. Their families never would understand them. Not as long as they had no idea what kind of work they'd really done in their careers.

Nick asked thoughtfully, "Do you suppose the day

will ever come when you can tell them what you actually did?"

Alex answered quietly, "Would you tell the people you love how many human beings you've killed in your work?"

Nick jolted. "Good grief. I haven't had any contact with anyone I love for so long that I haven't had to consider how they would react to knowing what I do."

"Hah. And you thought I was the Sunshine Guy," Alex said a shade bitterly.

"Point taken."

The movie ended, and Alex fast-forwarded to the end of the credits and started playing *Home Alone*. The ridiculous humor of a boy getting left behind by accident when his family went on Christmas vacation was just what they needed after the heavy conversation about their careers and families.

One thing Nick knew for sure. If he had a kid, he would never leave him or her behind, by accident or otherwise. Ever. He knew all too well the pain of being abandoned and rejected by the people he loved.

Thankfully, the antics of the dumber-than-dirt robbers trying to break into a family's home, foiled at every step by the boy who'd been left behind, were so silly that Nick felt no need to dissect the tactics or strategies employed by the bad guys or the kid.

He and Alex laughed through the film and munched on the popcorn Alex popped on the stove. They sat side by side, their elbows brushing against each other, balancing the big bowl of popcorn between them. They grabbed handfuls of the buttery, crunchy goodness, and for a little while, life was simple. They ate, they laughed, they relaxed. And it was nice. Really nice.

After the movie finished and twilight was falling

across the city outside, Alex sighed. "We probably ought to have another serious conversation."

"About?" Quick alarm buzzed in Nick's gut.

"Gray. We've got to acquire him again, and this time, we've got to figure out what he's up to before he loses us."

Whew. For a second there, he thought Alex was going to tell him he was in trouble, if not for the death wish thing, then for something else. That for some reason, he'd popped up on the fixer network's radar as a criminal. He would've argued stridently against the accusation if that were the case. He really was a Boy Scout at heart.

Relieved, Nick said, "I have a few thoughts about finding Gray. But before I share those, what exactly are you planning to do to him when you discover what he's involved in?"

"If he's doing something criminal, which I have reason to believe is the case, given his paranoid behavior, I have the authority to decide whether what he's done warrants capture or if it warrants more extreme measures."

"So, you really do have the authority to kill anyone who you decide is in need of killing?" Nick blurted. "Isn't Gray a stupidly high-level asset for the US? I mean, surely you need someone's permission to take out someone like him."

"Nobody's above the law, Nick."

He rolled his eyes. "I know that. But...you can kill him if you want to?"

"I never want to kill anyone. But it is my job. If he's done something bad enough, yes, I'll put him down."

As if calling it "putting someone down" made it anything less than what it really was. Cold-blooded murder.

Not that he had any right to cast stones over eliminating people. It was part of his job, too. Except he killed enemy combatants. Not members of his own government and fellow countrymen.

"You are aware that Gray's team murdered three American marines on their way out of the compound where they stole the crate, aren't you?" Nick asked.

"I am."

"Not that I'm trying to tell you how to do your job, but isn't that…well…put-down worthy all by itself?"

"Indeed, it is," Alex answered soberly. "Which is why I'm delighted to hear that team—Gray's team—is off the street and in custody. But I have yet to determine if Gray ordered them to kill those marines. I won't sanction him over the deaths of those marines if he had nothing to do with the decision to take them out."

"Oh, he totally had something to do with the decision," Nick declared.

"How do you know that?" Alex asked quickly.

"I worked for the man for four years. We didn't sneeze without his permission. I'd lay odds he had his own surveillance drone hovering over that compound, and he was directing every bit of the operation to infiltrate the place, steal the crate and get out."

"But you don't know that for certain," Alex said gently. "Would you want me to kill you because someone had a strong gut feeling that you'd done something wrong? Or would you want me to do my due diligence and find actual proof of your wrongdoing before I put a bullet in your brain?"

Nick huffed. "I get your point. Your job is to be impartial and have proof before you act. But I'm still dead sure Gray told them to hijack the Hummer those marines were in by whatever means necessary. Including killing the marines inside it."

"Time will tell. And once I know for sure, only then will I take action."

"And in the meantime, Gray knows someone is following him. He will be insanely dangerous to tail from now on. He even left the tracker from the limo and that note to warn us off."

Alex retorted, "I'm not intimidated because one of his guys spotted a tracker planted in plain sight. Even a routine inspection of the vehicle by a total amateur would've gotten that tracker found."

Nick frowned and said urgently, "Listen to me, Alex. Gray isn't like anybody you've gone after before. There are dangerous people out there, and then there's Gray. He's in a whole other class of nasty."

"I'm not worried—"

Nick cut him off. "Then, you're a damned fool. You should be scared silly of going up against him. He has his own private army, for crying out loud. It may not be that big, but it's *all* men and women like me. Like *you.*"

Alex studied him intently for a long time and finally said quietly, "Okay. I hear you, and I believe you. I'll take this guy and his people very seriously."

"You have to do more than that. You have to be careful like you've never been careful before. And you should probably get help. You said there are other fixers. This is the guy you should call in the *whole* cavalry for."

Alex opened his mouth to say something. Given the stubborn set of his jaw, Nick guessed he was about to declare that he didn't need that much help, and he cut off Alex again. "I know you're very, very good at your job. I don't doubt that for a second. In fact, I've heard about you before. You're a bit of a legend in the business."

Alex looked surprised and not superpleased.

Nick continued, "It's probably why you were assigned

to deal with Gray in the first place. But please, for the love of God, don't take him on by yourself."

Alex was silent for a long time. Thoughtful. And then his gaze hardened. "Will you help me?"

"Me?" Nick exclaimed. "I'm not a fixer."

"But you know him better than anyone. You worked inside his organization. You know his habits, how he thinks, what he's likely to do in any given situation. Help me investigate him…and, if necessary, take him down."

Nick said grimly. "It'll be necessary to take him down. I feel it in my bones. He's done something very bad. His grand finale on the way out the door, as it were."

"So, you do think he's gone fully rogue?" Alex asked.

"I know it."

Chapter 8

Alex wasn't sure if he fell for Nick while listening to the outrageous ideas Nick had for how to take over the Naka-tomi Tower in *Die Hard*, or if it was when they laughed together at *Home Alone*. Or maybe it was when Nick's whole face softened as he talked about having a family of his own someday. But regardless, Alex had a problem.

He liked Nick. Really liked him.

Now he just had to pray Nick wasn't lying to him. He wanted to believe Nick was telling the truth and not still working for Gray. In fact, he was probably staking his own life on that being true. Nick was not wrong about Gray. The man was exceedingly dangerous. No way would Alex survive both Nick and Gray if they teamed up together to kill him.

Alex looked over at Nick. "Talk to me about how we reacquire Gray."

"The art gallery. Gray was definitely interested in the

gold statue there. I think we should go back and stake the place out. See if we can find out why he's so interested in the statue and then wait for him to show up there to buy it. My impression was that the horse-and-rider piece is part of an auction at the gallery in a few days. At least, everything else on display was going up for sale. It makes sense the statue would be auctioned off, too."

"That's a good plan. Is your tuxedo clean enough to wear again after our scuffle, or do we need to get you a decent suit?" Alex asked.

"The tuxedo is destroyed. I ripped out a sleeve in that move to keep you from breaking my neck and killing me."

He couldn't help but smile a little at the memory of being pressed up against Nick's entire backside and having his arm around all that vital energy. "I wasn't planning to kill you, Nick. I just needed you to quit trying to kill me for long enough so I could talk with you."

"Hah! I wasn't trying to kill you, either!" Nick exclaimed. "If I'd been trying to kill you, you'd be dead now." He shot Alex an impudent grin, but there was a hint of seriousness in his dark eyes.

He answered with a hint of his own seriousness, "No, you'd be dead."

They exchanged frank stares, acknowledging their mutual lethality. Alex dipped his chin in a slight nod of respect.

Nick scowled but followed suit, nodding as well. But then he went and ruined it by muttering, "You didn't win. It was a stalemate."

As Alex smirked skeptically enough to visibly irritate him, Nick snapped, "I was not planning to enter high society when I came to New York. I'm equipped to hide in the underbelly of the city. Which means I didn't pack a spare tuxedo."

Personally, he rather liked Nick lounging around like he was right now in a T-shirt and jeans that were both just a smidge too tight on his muscular physique.

Realizing he was staring at said physique in fascination, he jerked his attention off Nick's bulging biceps and nodded briskly. "A new suit it is. I know just the place. Are you feeling up to a shopping trip?"

"Yeah, sure. I feel great after getting eight hours of solid sleep. Thanks for that, by the way."

The rough gratitude in Nick's voice sent a little shiver of delight down his spine. He shrugged and had to clear his throat before he choked out, "Gotta keep my assets sharp."

"Oh, I'm an asset now, am I?" Nick teased.

"You are if that means you understand I'm in charge of this operation."

A snort from Nick. "No way. I'll work *with* you, but I don't take orders from anyone."

Alex couldn't resist poking. "That sounded like a challenge, Mr. Kane. Do you want to place a small wager on who'll take orders from who when things heat up?"

Nick's gaze snapped sharply to his. He'd been talking about things heating up as in the heat of combat. Danger. Like a gunfight. But it was clear Nick thought he'd meant when things heated up in the bedroom.

He reluctantly met Nick's gaze and was startled to see the guy's dark eyes blazing with something that looked a whole lot like interest. Romantic interest…not gunfight interest.

Well, okay, then.

Nick unfolded his tall body off the couch and strolled toward where he leaned a hip against the kitchen counter. It was all Alex could do to hold his position and not flinch away—or fling himself at Nick—as the man sauntered toward him.

At the very last second before Nick would have run right into him, he veered away and moved around Alex to head for the closet.

Alex let out a shockingly wobbly breath.

Jerk. Hot, *hot* jerk.

He took Nick to a menswear store that specialized in odd sizes off-the-rack. It was less of a big-and-tall-men's store and more of a bodybuilder's-physique or bulge-under-the-left-armpit kind of place.

The owner knew Alex and greeted him warmly when they came in. It was supper time, and the place was deserted, which suited Alex's purposes just fine.

"Hi, Tony. This is my colleague, Bob, and he needs a suit."

The tailor eyed Nick critically and then asked Nick, "Are you right-handed or left-handed?"

Nick frowned. "Right-handed. Why?"

"Then, you'll need the extra allowance for a holster under your left arm."

Nick glanced over at Alex, his eyebrows up around his hairline.

Alex said dryly, "I've done business here for a long time. Tony used to work for the Mafia but went straight some years back when I took down the family he was having to pay protection money to. One of my first jobs."

"Saved me a fortune, young Alex did," Tony said warmly. "I put both my kids through college on the money he saved me. I've got a nice retirement nest egg now, too. You're a good boy, Alex."

He smiled at the elderly man. "Any chance we could

have something off-the-rack for my friend this evening? We're pressed for time and need to go someplace nice."

"No problem. I've got a charcoal gray suit that I think will work well for him. The trousers will need hemming, but if you can wait fifteen minutes or so, I'll do that myself. These old hands still remember how to sew."

"That would be great."

"You'll be needing a dress shirt, too?" Tony asked,

"From the skin out, I'm afraid. Socks and shoes if you have them, as well."

"I'll keep my own shoes," Nick said quickly. "I like the custom soles."

Alex glanced down, startled. "Are those crepe? They look like leather."

"Yep. They're soft rubber, but the edges are finished to look like shoe leather."

"Nice. Where'd you get them? I could use a pair like that."

"I've got a guy in Istanbul. Hand makes every pair of shoes he sells. Doesn't take many new clients, but he'll make an exception for me because I always bring him good tobacco. I'll hook you up next time you're in Turkey."

Alex nodded his thanks to Nick. They made a weird pair of ducks, all right. He knew where to get suits cut for concealed weapons, and Nick knew where to get silent shoes for stalking targets.

Tony dressed Nick and marked the hemline of the pants, then shooed them out of the shop. He said he worked better without customers hovering over his shoulder, watching him sew.

As they sat in a coffee shop down the block, Nick commented, "Man, I'd love to see that guy's client list. Can you imagine the people he's dressed?"

Alex smiled. "Tony is the soul of discretion. Never names names. It's how he stays in business and alive."

He noted that they both watched everyone who walked past the coffee shop, assessing body language, looking at how people's gazes moved around, how they held themselves. He spotted a few people who looked like martial artists, but nobody that made alarm bells go off in his head.

Still, he did the courtesy of asking Nick, "See anyone of interest out there?"

"Nope. Coast is clear."

They headed back to the clothing store, and Nick dressed in the suit. Tony said he would have a second suit ready for Nick tomorrow by noon and promised to hang on to Nick's other clothes until they could come back to pick them up.

As they stepped out onto the street, Nick—looking darned sharp—said briskly, "To the gallery?"

"Let's do it."

When they arrived at the warehouse turned art gallery, it was lit up and crowded with customers. Apparently, the upcoming auction was a big one, and the establishment was stuffed with potential bidders interested in previewing the items that would be coming up for sale.

Alex murmured as they stepped inside, "Do you know anyone we can talk to about the statue?"

"I met one of the owners the other day. Nice guy. Flag-carrying Rainbow Mafia member. So, lean into being gay when we talk to him and be your most charming self."

"You think I'm charming? Aww."

Nick rolled his eyes. "By charming, I mean that you lie better than me."

"Now who's lying? You *do* think I'm charming. You have a crush on me, don't you?"

Nick's scowl was entirely too ferocious for the topic under discussion. Yep. The guy had a crush on him. But Alex also knew the harder he pushed Nick to admit it, the more stubborn Nick would become about not admitting it.

Still scowling, Nick reached out to straighten Alex's tie. It was a small, intimate gesture, the kind of thing one lover might do for another. Alex's heart pitter-pattered frantically under Nick's knuckles.

"There. Perfect," Nick murmured.

Alex got the impression Nick wasn't talking about the tie, but rather about the man wearing it. *Aww.* And there went his heart again.

Alex mumbled, "Um, okay. Are we on a date, then?"

"Sure." Nick grinned at him. "Just don't call me sweetheart."

Alex rolled his eyes. "There's nothing sweet about you, Mr. Grinch."

"There he is," Nick murmured. "C'mon. Oh, and he thinks my name is Stephan Clark. New Yorker. Real estate guy."

Alex always had an emergency legend metaphorically and literally in his hip pocket, and he employed it, now. "Call me Luca. Luca Serrano. Born in Spain, raised in New Jersey. Banker."

"Got it."

The beauty of working with a man of Nick's skill was that Nick really did get it. Both of them were completely adept at assuming cover stories on short notice and rolling with them smoothly. Not many people could do what they were both doing right now, and even fewer people could flow into a new identity quickly and seamlessly with another person.

Alex took his lead from Nick, who made no effort to hurry toward the gallery co-owner. He took the flute of champagne that Nick handed to him, and they clinked glasses, smiling intimately at each other over the crystal rims before sipping the bubbly. *Hubba hubba.* If Nick kept looking at him like that, this was going to turn into a real date, job to do or not.

He and Nick must have both calculated the path of the gallery owner identically, for they moved as one into the way of the man. It took a couple of minutes, as other patrons stopped their target to chat with him and the man said hello to various guests. But eventually, the middle-aged proprietor walked up to them and said pleasantly, "It's Stephan, right? Stephan Clark?"

Nick said warmly, "That's correct. I'm flattered that you remember me. Otto Katzinger, this is my good friend, Luca. Luca, Otto."

Alex's gut tightened a little at the possessive way Nick leaned into saying the word *friend*. He smiled at Otto, turning on the charm Nick had requested. "Stephan tells me you own this place. I'm so impressed."

Otto waved a heavily ring-clad hand. "Oh, I only own half of it. My husband, Yuri, owns the other half. We decided to go in on it together so we can never divorce each other. No matter how much we drive each other crazy, neither one of us could bear to part with this place."

Alex laughed. "An interesting technique for ensuring longevity in a marriage. And clearly successful." He looked over at Nick. "How do you feel about going halfsies on an art gallery with me?"

Nick grinned. "Maybe halfsies on a martial arts studio or firing range would be more my style, but sure."

"Oooh, dangerous," Otto purred, stroking Nick's bulging biceps through the fine wool of his new suit.

Alex was shocked when an urge to swat away Otto's hand passed through him. Since when was he possessive of anyone, let alone Nick? In the spirit of their cover story of dating, he let a hint of his actual jealousy show on his face. Nick must've caught it, for he grinned widely behind Otto's back. Alex rolled his eyes at Nick, and the infuriating man's smile only widened. If only those dimples of Nick's weren't so killer cute.

"By the way, Otto," Alex said lightly. "Nick was telling me that the last time he was here, he saw a fantastic statue. A man on a horse, done in gold. Can you tell me a little more about it?"

Otto's eyes lit with unholy avarice. "Ah, the crown jewel of our collection. It's going to take the art world by storm when they find out what Yuri and I have got our hot little hands on."

Alex said with real interest, "What's so special about it? Can I see it? Steph said it was stunningly beautiful."

"He doesn't know the half of it. Shall we wait for the elevator, or are you magnificently brawny beasts up for taking the stairs? It's on the third floor."

Alex gestured at Nick and Otto to go first up the hypermodern steel staircase. While Otto continued to pet Nick's arm all the way to the third floor, Alex consoled himself with an outstanding view of Nick's muscular rear end flexing in front of him as Nick climbed each step. Tony really did know how to fit a suit to a man's body. The gray wool clung to Nick's rear end to perfection— tight enough to catch every flex of powerful glut muscles but loose enough to leave just enough to the imagination.

Hubba hubba, indeed.

They reached the third floor, and Alex looked around casually, taking note of the intense security. Not only were armed guards stationed every fifty feet or so around the perimeter, but he spotted pressure plates in the floor, a steel drop-down portcullis overhead that would block off the stairs, motion detectors, cameras and what looked like some sort of infrared-beam system.

Otto led them forward to a white columnar display stand. The gold statue Nick had described stood upon the waist-high column, and the whole thing was covered by a glass tube that extended from the floor to the ceiling. Undoubtedly, that tube and the display stand itself had pressure and motion sensors built into it. If he were in charge of security around here, he might even fill the tube with some sort of knock-out gas. Break the glass and get a lungful of it.

Alex finally took a good look at the statue itself. Nick wasn't kidding. It *was* stunningly beautiful. If he didn't know better, he would say it was a real horse, miniaturized and dipped in gold, so perfectly was it rendered.

"Whoa," he breathed.

Otto said proudly, "Remarkable, no?"

"Yes," Alex said reverently. "It's incredible."

Nick, however, was more prosaic and asked, "Why the steep price tag? I get that the value of the gold alone is in the neighborhood of four million, but ten million? What gives, Otto?"

Otto leaned in close and said under his breath, "We've already got interested parties hinting they'll bid as high as fifty million for it."

Alex's jaw dropped. "Fifty? Million?" He turned to stare at the gallery owner.

"What the hell?" Nick muttered. "Why? What's so special about it?"

Otto said conspiratorially, "You didn't hear this from me. But we believe it to be a piece from the Magi Crèche. We've sent inquiries out to the right people, and we're hoping to confirm that any minute. If we do get confirmation, the price will rise into the stratosphere. Astronomical."

Alex frowned and said politely, "Forgive me for my ignorance, but what's the significance of this Magi Crèche?"

"My dear boy," Otto said, assuming a lecturer's tone, "the Magi Crèche is legendary. Historians say that the Three Wise Men—the Magi—who visited Jesus in the manger were Persian mystics. Astrologers and soothsayers, if you will."

Nick interrupted, "Are you talking about the frankincense, myrrh and gold guys?"

Otto pursed his lips disapprovingly. "Yes. The frankincense, myrrh and gold guys."

Alex jumped in to soothe Otto's ruffled feathers. "Please forgive him. He's so pretty to look at and so… athletic in certain departments…that he must be forgiven for his blunt way of speaking. Am I right?"

"Indeed," Otto murmured, ogling Nick appreciatively. Alex joined him in ogling Nick, who squirmed a little under their scrutiny. If Alex wasn't mistaken, Nick's cheeks were turning a little ruddy, in fact. He wore the color well.

Otto resumed his narrative. "Anyway, legend has it that when the magi returned to Persia, one of them carved a set of statues that depicted the birth scene of Christ."

Alex immediately grasped the significance of that and gasped.

Nick glanced over at him questioningly, and Alex explained, "A nativity scene created by someone who was really there would likely be the closest to an accurate depiction of what the actual stable, the actual manger— heck, even the Baby Jesus and Mother Mary—looked like. It would be the only existing firsthand representation of the nativity anywhere."

Comprehension lit Nick's gaze. "Something like that would be *priceless*."

Alex nodded. "Every major religious group would want to have it for their own, not to mention wealthy art collectors and museums the world over would lust after it."

"Exactly," Otto piped up. "We've already got interest from the Vatican, from a coalition of Jewish bidders, from various major Protestant churches—even the Louvre is setting up a bidding line with us. If the provenance comes through, most of the wealthiest art collectors in the world are expected to bid on this piece, as well."

"When does it go on sale?" Alex asked.

"We're planning to offer it tomorrow evening, but we'll delay the sale if we don't have the provenance on it by then."

"Where do you get provenance papers on a thing like that?" Alex asked.

Otto shrugged. "It's difficult, of course. Legend has it the Magi Crèche stayed in the possession of an order of Persian mystics for centuries. It's said that sometime around the end of the Seljuk Dynasty of Persia—that would have been in the 1190s—the ruling family took it for themselves. The various rulers of Persia passed it down from generation to generation, from dynasty to dynasty, all the way to the Pahlavi Dynasty that fell in 1979. They kept it a closely guarded secret in their personal collections."

"Fascinating," Alex murmured. "They must have known how great a prize it would have been to Christians the world over."

Otto smiled mischievously. "They were very naughty

to keep it for themselves, no? It is said that various sultans and emirs added pieces to the original nativity scene. We believe this is one of those pieces. Supposedly, the pieces got more elaborate and exquisite as the centuries passed, each dynasty adding ever more spectacular pieces to the crèche. Rumor has it the entire crèche consists of fifty or sixty pieces, by now."

When Otto fell silent, Alex prodded gently, "What happened to it after the fall of the last shah of Iran?"

"When Mohammed Reza Pahlavi was deposed, nobody knows what happened to it. There was chaos in Iran and the Revolutionary Guard was allowed to loot national treasures at will. Many of those treasures have turned up on the black market. But this is the first sign of the Magi Crèche having found its way out of Persia at last."

Nick asked, "Where did this piece come from? Who's selling it?"

"Ahh, ahh, ahh," Otto said reprovingly, wagging a finger at Nick. "Our consignors are guaranteed anonymity, if they so choose."

Nick shrugged. "I'm sorry, Otto. I must confess, that was a test. I thought you knew Luca and I work for Harlan Gray. I was part of the team that brought the whole crèche out of Zagastan last spring. Heavy sucker. Big crate. We kept everything wrapped up for safety, of course. I never got to look at it. I'm delighted to get to see at least one of the pieces we rescued. Luca handled details at this end, arranging for us to transport the whole thing in the United States."

Alex was startled that Nick had chosen to play such a dangerous gambit. If he was wrong, and Gray hadn't consigned the statue, they would be thrown out of here on their ears and not allowed back inside. Not to mention, Otto would warn Gray that he and Nick were investigating him.

Hah. And Nick called him the better liar. Nick had just rattled off all that information with such casual ease that he almost believed the story—and he knew it to be false.

"I had no idea," Otto said in a tone of distinctly more respect. "Mr. Gray told me he would have his own security keeping an eye on the statue at all times, of course. But I didn't realize you were his men."

Nick smiled warmly at Otto. "No worries. You passed our little quiz with flying colors. And we're not nearly as…tense…as Mr. Gray can be." Alex smirked as Nick rolled his eyes for good measure. Otto visibly relaxed.

Alex said lightly, "Mr. Gray spoke initially of planning to liquidate the entire crèche in a single sale. Now that I've seen this piece, and assuming the others are as exquisite, I can see why he changed his mind and decided to offer them one at a time. Has he made any mention to you of being willing to sell the whole crèche off market if someone were to bid high enough?"

"I do not know. You would have to ask your employer that. I sincerely hope not, however. Yuri and I have our eyes on a charming little Greek island we plan to buy with our portion of the proceeds of fifty more pieces like this one. Can you even imagine what people will pay when the figures of the Christ Child and Virgin Mary come up for sale? What is the worth of knowing what they looked like? What they were wearing? If the baby really slept in a manger or if that's a myth?"

Alex just shook his head. The mind boggled at the idea of glimpsing a firsthand snapshot of the event. "If there's anything we can do to help you with obtaining the provenance papers, do let us know. Here's my card."

He pulled out his wallet and fished around through

various fake IDs and matching business cards until he found the one with the name Luca Serrano on it. God bless the legend-building crew at the CIA for their thorough work.

"...historical source in Iran has been most helpful," Otto was saying. "Apparently, no photograph was ever allowed to be taken of the crèche. But there's an eighteenth century sketch of the piece, and various inventories of the Persian rulers that mention it. The only tricky bit is accounting for the crèche between when it left Iran and when it came into Mr. Gray's possession."

Nick rolled his eyes. "It's not as if my teammates and I can offer affidavits of where we got it. At least we got it out of the hands of warlords and back into the legitimate, elite art world."

"Why, thank you," Otto gushed. "We like to think of ourselves as one of the best houses in the business. Christie's and Sotheby's strut around selling fifty-million-dollar paintings, but we're going to put all the big galleries to shame when the identity of this little gem is revealed to the world."

Alex added warmly, "You and Yuri are going to be the most famous art dealers on the planet."

The man preened some more.

Nick said lightly, "I assume Mr. Gray is still planning to attend the auction in person? He mentioned wanting to be there for the big event."

"Most definitely. Of course we've got a discreet viewing area for consignors such as him who would like to attend the sale without being seen."

"Of course," Nick said quickly. "I believe Luca and I will be assigned to the security detail for this beauty, and other colleagues of ours will see to Mr. Gray."

"I'll look forward to seeing you then," Otto said.

"As will we."

"Mum's the word on what I told you. We wouldn't want rumors leaking out to the press, now, would we?"

Alex matched Nick's smile as he murmured to the art dealer, "We work for Harlan Gray. Discretion is our middle name."

Otto got called away by another guest to answer a question, and Alex looked over at Nick significantly. "Wanna scope out the private viewing area that Gray will be sequestered in the night of the auction?"

Nick nodded. "It's probably on the second floor. I'm told that's where auctions are held. I found a back staircase the last time I was here. I'll bet the private viewing room is near that."

Alex followed Nick downstairs and into the large, open second floor. As they strolled around the perimeter of the room, the hairs on the back of Alex's neck felt itchy. "Um, Nick?"

Nick glanced over at him, frowning.

"Do you feel it, too?"

"Yeah," Nick answered grimly. "We have company."

Alex muttered without moving his lips, "Gray's guys are here. And they've spotted us."

Chapter 9

Nick sincerely didn't want to fight men he'd personally trained to be lethal hand-to-hand combatants. "Let's take this away from all these civilians, shall we?" he muttered to Alex.

"Agreed. Front door or back?"

"There's a big warehouse and a fenced security yard out back. We'd be trapped."

"Front it is," Alex said calmly.

As they moved swiftly through the crowd toward the exit, surreptitiously slipping in their earbuds, Nick talked low and fast. "They'll use team tactics. Don't underestimate their hand speed. They'll fight dirty. And they'll be carrying knives. If they plan to kill us, those will come out midfight after they've lured us into thinking we're just in a fistfight."

As they reached the front door, Alex turned briefly to

face Nick. "Thanks for your concern, but I can handle myself. I beat you, didn't I?"

"It was a stalemate," Nick snapped in irritation.

"Better," Alex murmured as they crossed the street in front of the gallery. "I need you pissed off, not panicked over my safety."

"If they outnumber us, we'll need to fight back-to-back. Have you ever trained like that?"

"Yes, dear. I've trained like that. I've even fought like that for real. Quit being such a worrywart. And stop fussing over me. We've got this."

He rolled his eyes at Alex. Oddly enough, Alex was right. He wasn't worried for himself at all, but he was completely freaked out at the idea of Alex getting hurt or killed. What did it mean?

He didn't have time to contemplate the implications of it because Alex said low, "Should we split up? Rendezvous a few blocks from here?"

It was a good idea. Gray's team wouldn't expect it. They never, ever split the team. It was a fundamental protocol Gray insisted upon. "Let's meet at the spot where you attacked me."

Alex flashed him a quick, sexy grin. "I like the symbolism of it. See you there in five."

While Alex turned left, he turned right, walking as fast as his long legs would go without breaking into a run. The moment he turned the corner, though, he took off running.

No surprise, he heard footsteps slapping the pavement behind him. Sloppy. The guys should be wearing quieter shoes. It was not a mistake he would've let the team make if he were still part of it.

Alex spoke in his ear between deep breaths, "I've got two…on me. Don't worry… I'm faster."

He replied, grunting on exhales, "I've got…two on me…also. Don't know…if I'm faster."

"Be faster, Nick…can't lose you…need you."

And it didn't sound as if Alex was talking about needing him for the mission. Warmth that had nothing to do with the exertion of sprinting spread through Nick's body. He dodged left, down a side street, and stretched out into a maximum sprint, arms pumping, legs churning. He focused, the way he'd been trained, on relaxing his entire body and letting his legs, arms, and lungs do all the work.

He swerved right at the next corner and put on another burst of full-out speed. His plan was to circle wide of the rendezvous spot and come in from the other direction—also a tactic Gray's men might not expect. They tended to be direct when entering combat, choosing to rely on their superior strength and training, rather than tricky tactics. But, with Alex's neck on the line, Nick was prepared to pull out every trick in the book.

"I'm one block out," Alex huffed.

It was good to know he wasn't the only one out of breath. Nick replied, "I'm two blocks out. Coming from… the other direction."

Alex must've stopped abruptly, for Nick heard shoes skidding on concrete. Then a grunt as if someone had just slammed into Alex.

Nonononono…

Nick found another gear he didn't know he had. The one where a man he cared about was under attack alone and going to die if Nick didn't get there ASAP.

He spared just enough oxygen to gasp, "Coming in hot."

He rounded the corner and raced the final twenty yards or so to the fight in front of him. Thankfully, his eyes adjusted fast to darkness. He made out Alex's lean form twisting and spinning as he attempted to fight and dodge two men at the same time.

Nick barreled into the back of the attacker directly in front of him, the one who kept trying to get behind Alex, and he and his target hit the ground. Nick had the advantage of landing on top, which meant the other guy acted as a crash cushion for him. Also, he expected the fall and was able to roll and leap back to his feet in a single motion. The other guy lay flattened on the pavement, his breath knocked out of him by the impact with the sidewalk and a two-hundred-pound-plus man crushing him.

Nick spun to put his back to Alex, backing up until their rear ends touched as they crouched in fighting stances. The two men chasing him caught up, and suddenly, Nick was fighting two on one.

Arms bumped into his back. It felt as if Alex's second attacker had closed to grappling distance and had Alex wrapped in his arms. Nick started to turn, to reach for the attacker, but one of his assailants slid around to the side to help the guy on Alex while the other one threw a flurry of punches at Nick.

Nick warded off the flying fists and jumped to his right to block the other guy from grabbing Alex.

All four of Gray's men backed up momentarily to regroup. For the time being, they were all in front of Nick and Alex. Standing shoulder to shoulder for now, they braced for the rush of the four attackers.

Nick muttered, "The end guys will try to flank us. You hold your position and I'll spin to put my back against yours."

"Got it."

Here they came, prowling in slow and dangerous, like circling wolves.

"Knives," Alex muttered.

Nick hadn't seen any blades—Gray's men probably had them tucked against the sleeves of their coats, hiding them until the last possible second. Good thing Alex had spotted them. He dropped his own down into his right hand out of its wrist sheath, and reached down to his left ankle to pull out the field knife strapped there. With renewed caution, he waited for Gray's men to charge.

Sure enough, the two guys on the end did a wrap-around maneuver, both of them ending up in front of him. Holding his knives low, in front of his body, he waited for them to attack.

The fight was fast and vicious. If any single stab from any one knife plunged into someone, the odds were good the target would be seriously injured and definitely knocked out of the fight. Better to take a few slices across the forearms or face than let the enemy gut him. Hence, it became vital to parry incoming swings of the knives with his own blade or his arm, and to jump back from direct thrusts.

Nick was pushed to the limit of his speed and skill, keeping two flashing knives in sight and staying out of the way of them as Gray's men slashed and stabbed at him.

In a fight like this, Alex truly did have the advantage on everyone, given how unbelievably fast he was. Nick had great reflexes but nothing like Alex's.

Nick took a glancing cut to the jaw that hurt like hell and left him more distracted than he liked. He resorted to lashing out with a hard kick to the guy's belly, driving the heel of his shoe hard into the man's stomach. The attacker staggered back, gasping for air.

Nick wanted to pressed his advantage, to follow the guy as he fell back and deliver a debilitating stab of his own, but that would mean leaving Alex's flank unprotected. He held his ground and let the moment of advantage pass.

When Nick didn't follow him, the guy he'd kicked straightened suddenly, less injured than he'd been feigning. It had been a trick to try to draw Nick away from Alex.

Bastard.

Alex pivoted, putting them shoulder to shoulder again as the guy he was fighting slid around to stand next to the man directly in front of Nick. Alex lunged forward, and Nick went with him, protecting his flank, also concentrating on taking down the assailant in front of him as fast as possible. He lashed out with his foot and the guy's knife went sailing in a high arc, away into the darkness. It skittered metallically on the sidewalk.

Without warning, something clamped around his ankle and gave a hard yank.

Sonofabitch. The guy he'd knocked down initially was coming around and had grabbed his leg. Nick staggered, nearly going down before he caught himself. But, in that moment of unbalance, the guy in front of him punched hard, a big roundhouse blow. Nick ducked and the man's fist impacted just above Nick's ear.

He saw stars, and the world started to spin around him. Not good. If he went down, Alex was screwed.

With that thought foremost in his mind, he fought on grimly, swinging his knives wildly in arcs in front of his body and throwing a flurry of kicks to hold off his attacker until his head cleared.

The guy on the ground must've grabbed Alex's ankle, too, for without warning, Alex fell down, pitching forward. The attacker who'd faked being hurt immediately leaped forward to stab Alex, but apparently forgot Nick was still there or chose to ignore him. A mistake, that.

It exposed Nick to the unarmed attacker, but he turned and chopped down as hard as he could with the butt of his knife on the back of the neck of the guy who'd jumped Alex. That attacker went limp, and Nick half turned, throwing his forearm up at the last instant to prevent a similar blow from landing on his own neck.

Well and truly pissed off that these jerks had nearly taken down Alex, Nick surged upward, driving his head into the gut of the guy who'd just tried to karate chop him. He wrapped his arms around the dude and drove him backward.

He got lucky and stepped on the guy's foot, which caused the attacker to topple over backward. The two of them hit the ground, and the other man's head made a sickening, cracking sound as it hit the concrete sidewalk. He went limp beneath Nick.

No time to gloat. Nick shoved upright and turned in a crouch, all in one frantic movement. The lone remaining attacker was squaring off with Alex.

As Nick straightened and prepared to charge in like a bull to defend his man, Alex parried a slicing knife attack and stepped toward his attacker fast, punching him right on the bridge of the nose. As the attacker doubled over in pain, Alex drew his knee up fast and clocked the guy in the jaw. Hard.

Down he went.

Three of the four attackers were on the ground. Two were groaning in pain. The one who had hit his head was still, and a pool of black liquid was growing under his upper torso in the dark.

The fourth man, ankle grabber, had climbed to his feet, assessed his downed teammates, noted Nick brandishing his knives and advancing to stand beside Alex, and thought better of continuing the fight. He turned and ran.

"Chase him?" Alex panted.

"Nah," Nick panted back. "He's got too much of a head start. Besides, Gray will be plenty pissed off that we whupped his guys. It might just bring him after us."

"Cool. So instead of chasing the killer, now he'll be chasing us," Alex said dryly.

"Something like that."

"Shall we disarm these yahoos?" Nick suggested.

"Grab their cell phones, too," Alex said as he punched the guy groaning at his feet in the temple. The man went still, and Alex commenced searching him.

Nick did the same to the other moving guy, knocking him unconscious, ideally for another minute or two, then reaching into the man's coat for his cell phone. Nick yanked the man's pistol out of its shoulder holster and picked up the knife lying on the ground beside him. The dude probably had at least one more blade, somewhere. Nick patted him down and found it in a sheath tucked inside the back of his pants' waistband.

Nick spotted something rectangular lying on the ground where the ankle grabber had originally gone down. "Oh, look. Runner guy dropped his phone." He bent down and scooped up the device, pocketing it with the other cell phone he'd retrieved.

"Sloppy of them to lose all their phones," Alex commented dryly as he moved over to the man lying motionless in a pool of blood. "This one's not breathing. Want to try resuscitating him?"

Nick sighed. "We're gonna get blood all over ourselves, but yeah. You do the chest compressions. I'll breathe into his mouth."

As he knelt down to administer CPR, Nick got his

first good look at the man. "Hey! I trained this guy a while back! Name's Jed. He's not a bad guy. Decent knife fighter."

"But not as good as you," Alex commented.

"Nor you," he murmured back as he pinched Jed's nostrils shut and tilted his head back to begin breathing into his mouth.

It took them nearly two minutes, and administering CPR was more strenuous than it looked. But they got the guy breathing again. True to his forecast, though, both he and Alex got covered in Jed's blood.

"Shall we call an ambulance for him?" Alex asked as they stood up.

"The other two are coming around. They can take it from here."

Alex nodded. "Then, let's get the hell out of here before the runner arrives with reinforcements."

In the concentration of getting the fourth man breathing again, Nick had forgotten about the one who got away. "Yeah. Let's split."

"Do we need to police the area for fingerprints?" Alex asked doubtfully.

"With all the blood you and I went swimming in, there's no way we'd erase every print. We would need a power washer to spray down the whole vicinity. Besides, Gray's guys won't call the police. There would be too many questions about who they are."

Alex nodded and murmured, "Feel up to running? Your face is bleeding, and you took a couple of nasty hits there at the end."

"I was defending you, thank you very much," he snapped as he took off jogging down the street. He certainly didn't feel like doing any more full-out sprints, but he did set a steady, ground-eating pace away from the scene of the fight. His head throbbed, harbinger of a splitting headache to come. He supposed it was better than being dead.

Alex let him set the pace. They ran all the way to the apartment building, keeping an eye out for any kind of pursuit. He hoped that the immediate need to get their fallen comrade to a hospital had distracted Gray's security team from pursuing them.

The elevator door opened, and they made their way quickly to the tiny apartment.

The door had barely closed behind them before Nick turned and grabbed Alex, wrapping his arms around him in a tight bear hug. "I don't ever want to be in a fight like that with you again," he muttered.

He was shocked to register that his knees felt weak, so profound was his relief at having made it back here in one piece with Alex. So much for his death wish, apparently. This was the first time in years that he was actually freaking out a little at the idea of himself or his teammate getting killed.

And there went his pulse, galloping off toward panic-land again.

It dawned on Nick that Alex was hugging him back fully as tightly.

"All I could think about was what would I do if something happened to you," Nick admitted raggedly.

"Funny. I was thinking the exact same thing. That, and planning how to kill each one of them slowly and painfully if they did anything bad to you."

Nick smiled a little over Alex's shoulder. He'd brought out the guy's protectively vicious streak, had he? That was so sweet. He felt a shudder pass through Alex. He knew the feeling. They might've won that fight, but things could always go wrong in a violent situation. A slip of the foot, a blink at just the wrong moment, a tiny distraction…and the outcome could've been very different. Nick's arms tightened even more around Alex.

"A little air here," Alex wheezed.

"Sorry." Nick turned him loose and stepped back, chagrined. So much for keeping a professional distance from his partner.

Alex looked a little annoyed with him, so Nick expanded upon his apology. "I shouldn't have up and grabbed you like that. Not with us having to work together and all—"

Alex reached up with those lightning-fast reflexes of his and pressed his hand against Nick's mouth, stopping any more words from coming out. "I was frustrated that you let me go, not that you hugged me in the first place."

Nick stared. In the darkness, Alex's eyes were black. But he could swear he saw a glow in them anyway.

"Oh." It was all Nick could think of to say as his mind went blank.

Alex stepped forward and planted his hand on the back of Nick's neck. As he tugged Nick forward, he muttered, "You're such a jerk."

As their faces drew together, he murmured back, "Yeah, but you like me anyway."

"Shut up." Those were the last words Alex breathed before their lips touched.

An urge to grab Alex and devour him alive nearly overcame Nick, but he held himself completely still and let Alex set the pace. He had no idea how much experience Alex had with love, and at a minimum, he gathered it had been a long time since Alex had let down his guard with anyone, let alone kissed someone.

Alex's mouth was warm and smooth against his, and surprisingly confident. But then, Alex was a direct man.

He spoke the truth and apparently acted with truth, as well. He wanted to kiss Nick, so kiss him he did.

It was sexy as hell.

Nick kissed him back, enjoying the slide of their mouths, the way their breath mingled, the way Alex took his time. They traded several light kisses, adjusting angles of chin, tilts of the head and body posture until they fit together perfectly. Then Alex leaned in and really kissed him.

Hello, sailor. Nick was startled by the frank intensity in Alex's kiss. This was not a man who played games. There was no coy flirtation, no advance and retreat, no head games whatsoever. And he kind of lived for it. He slipped his fingers into the short, soft hair at the back of Alex's head and opened his mouth, deepening the kiss.

Alex met him halfway, and as their tongues swirled together in a sexy slide of hot, wet flesh, Nick groaned at the exact same moment Alex did.

Simultaneously startled, apparently, they both pulled back from the kiss at the same instant, their fast, shallow breaths panting in exact rhythm.

"Well, then," Alex said breathlessly, "I think we've established that both of us are alive and well after the fight."

More like alive and horny. Nick's body was reacting in all kinds of ways it shouldn't be. He tried to speak, but his throat was too tight for words, and he ended up making a pained sound as lust pounded relentlessly through his body.

Alex took another step back. Nick was relieved the man was no longer in range to grab and throw down to the floor, but it was also all he could do not to stalk after Alex and kiss his lights out again.

"Go take a shower," Alex said lightly. "You smell like

blood. We can pick this up later, when we're both cleaned up and patched up."

"Uh, right," Nick mumbled, feeling about as smart as a fencepost at the moment. Alex had wanted to kiss some more? Well, color him totally on board for that plan. But where had that kiss come from? Alex had given no hint, prior to grabbing him and laying a big wet one on him, that he was interested in jumping anyone's bones. So closed off that man was.

Usually, he was so much better at reading people—

"Go on." Alex waved him toward the bathroom. "You wash up first. And pass out all your clothes to me when you've stripped down."

"Why?" Nick asked.

"I'm going to scan them for tracking burrs."

"You think Gray's guys managed to plant one on me in the middle of a fight like that?" he blurted.

Alex shrugged. "I think we can't be too careful, given who we're up against."

"Sheesh. And I thought I was paranoid," he muttered under his breath.

"How do you think I stay alive, chasing the kind of people I do?" Alex bit out.

Nick threw up his hands. "I bow to your superior caution. I'll pass my clothes out when I'm naked. But first, are there any painkillers to be had around here?"

"Prescription or nonprescription?" Alex asked dryly, heading for the closet that Nick was beginning to think was magically stocked with everything the spy-on-the-go could need, and more.

"Nonprescription, for now," he answered.

Alex emerged a moment later, carrying four white tablets. "This should knock out what ails you. Or at least knock it back significantly."

"Bless you," Nick murmured, swallowing the pills dry.

Alex groused over his shoulder, from the kitchenette, "Hasn't anyone ever warned you that pills can get stuck in your throat if you take them dry like that?" He filled a glass of water and thrust it at Nick.

"Really? We're attacked by four commandos with knives and you don't bat an eyelash, but you're worried I'm going to choke on an aspirin and die?"

Alex scowled. "Drink the water."

"Fine." Nick tossed down the contents of the glass, amused at how Alex was fussing over him. He handed the glass back to Alex, saying, "I didn't peg you as the Nervous Nellie type."

"Me? Nervous?" Alex exclaimed. "I have nerves of frozen stainless steel."

Nick merely arched an eyebrow at him.

"I do!" Alex exclaimed.

Then, how did Alex explain his sudden and excessive worry about their safety? Bemused, Nick headed for the bathroom. He turned the hot water on full blast and stripped down to his skin. He wadded up his underwear and shirt, socks, shoes, tie, and the remnants of the ruined suit and cracked open the bathroom door. Alex's eyes went a smoky shade of blue green, and his gaze dipped downward as Nick leaned around the door frame, flashing a lot of brawny chest and a muscular, dark-haired leg.

The heat in Alex's gaze scorched him, and Nick jerked back, startled. He closed the door, breathing hard. He was just winded from all the exertion before. Yeah. That was it. He was out of air from running all the way back here.

Except he'd fully caught his breath in the elevator. Nope, this puffing like a broken-down racehorse was all about that smoking-hot look Alex had thrown him. And that kiss. Good grief, that kiss. He couldn't wait to do that again. And to take his sweet time about it next time—

Whoa, whoa, whoa. What was happening here? He was a bundle of...*emotions*. He wasn't an emotional guy. And he certainly didn't come off dangerous missions all rattled and discombobulated like this.

Except Alex could have died.

And that scared the hell out of him. Now what was he supposed to do about that?

Kiss him again, apparently.

Parts of his body that he really wished would behave themselves suddenly were totally ignoring him and developing a mind of their own.

Just as suddenly, he was thinking about taking a cold shower instead of a hot one to ease his body's aches.

Well, hell.

Chapter 10

Alex looked up as Nick emerged from the bathroom with a towel slung low around his hips. It took him a moment to realize he was staring, literally transfixed, at all those acres of muscle. He cleared his throat as he dragged his gaze away. "Uh…nice tan lines," he managed to mumble. Which was to say, *no* tan lines.

"My clothes have any trackers?" Nick asked rather more gruffly than usual.

"Nope. Clean. I'll just, um, jump in the shower, too. I've checked my clothes already, and they're clean. Well, not clean. I mean, they're ruined from that guy's blood. But there aren't any tracking devices on them," he babbled.

Cripes. He never babbled. But Nick's chest was so…bulgy…and in need of crawling all over…and…

"You okay, there, Al?" Nick murmured, smirking faintly.

Do not jump on your partner. Do not yank off that towel.

Do not even think about touching Nick. No way could you stop once you started with him—

Alex gave his head a hard shake and stood up. He'd stripped to his underwear to check his clothes for trackers and to get out of the blood-soaked garments. All he wore now were stretchy, athletic trunks that extended several inches down his thighs. They did little to hide the interested bulge in his crotch that was rapidly growing in response to Nick's décolletage.

Vividly aware of Nick checking him out—checking *all* of him out—and of the revealing nature of what little clothing he wore, Alex strode across the tiny living space fast and all but dove into the bathroom. He closed the door quickly and leaned against it, breathing hard.

Work. This was work. Yes, Nick was too sexy for anyone's own good. Hard-to-look-away-from sexy. Hard-to-keep-his-hands-off sexy, apparently.

What the heck had he been thinking to kiss Nick like that? Nick had let him go from that hug. Had stepped back. And then he had to go and grab the guy and try to give him a tonsillectomy with his tongue.

But, it had felt right. They…fit.

And it felt so very, very good to touch another human being intimately. To have another human being touch him back. He'd had no idea how much he was missing and craving human contact until he kissed Nick.

But what to do about that, now? He couldn't un-know how much he wanted to kiss Nick again and have Nick kiss him back. He wanted to crawl into bed and just cuddle with the man for about a week.

Okay, he wanted to do more than just cuddle.

But they didn't have a week to disengage from hunting Gray. For that matter, Gray might very well be hunting them now. And that changed everything. Their lives were on the line. And both of them needed to be as sharp and alert as they were both capable of being. There was no telling when or how Gray's men might come after them.

With a sigh, he turned on the water and stepped into the shower.

As the hot spray pounded his muscles into delicious mush, he thought about their embrace again. It had felt so good to have Nick's arms wrapped around him, as if he wanted to use his entire body to shield Alex and keep him safe forever. He felt the exact same way. If he were to be in another fight and able to choose only one man to have at his back, it would be Nick.

Out of the corner of his eye, he'd seen the moment in the fight when Nick's assailant had tried to fake an injury to get Nick to move away from Alex's flank. And Nick hadn't gone. They guy had given Nick a wide-open shot at him, and Nick hadn't taken it. Instead, he'd chosen to ignore the chance to win against his opponent and protected Alex.

It gave him warm fuzzies all over again, just thinking about it. Nick was an aggressive fighter, offense-minded all the way. It had to have killed him not to jump on the opening the other guy had given him. But Alex's safety had been more important to Nick than every instinct in his body to attack.

An urge to barge right back out into the living room and kiss Nick—and more—nearly overcame him. But, he couldn't go there with Nick. Not yet. Not until Harlan Gray was caught and this mission was over. They had to be safe before they could explore whatever was happening between them. It was the right decision, even if it was the incredibly hard and grumpy-making decision.

But *day-umm*, that man could kiss.

Soon. They would take down Gray, and then he would lay that kiss on Nick. And more. Much, much more.

He scrubbed himself from head to toe with soap and a loofah. When he was covered in suds, he stepped under the hot spray, rinsing off the dried blood and watching it swirl down the drain in a wash of rusty brown. He noticed a faint swirl of bright red in the water running past his feet. He must have a cut somewhere that was still bleeding. No surprise. Nicks and cuts were inevitable in knife fights.

Thank goodness Nick had been there beside him. He hadn't had to worry at all about protecting his back in the fight, which was the only reason he'd successfully been able to hold off two attackers in front of him at once.

As the hot water pounded his muscles into relaxation, fatigue set in, making his body feel heavy and lethargic. That fight had demanded every bit of his skill and speed. But no way had he been willing to lose and put Nick in even more danger than he was already in. Funny how having Nick there to fight for had sharpened his focus and intensified his will to win.

Reluctantly, he turned off the water and climbed out of the shower. As he'd expected, various aches and pains made themselves known quickly as his body cooled down to room temperature. He contemplated pulling on his underwear again, but then he got a better idea.

Why not wrap a towel around his hips and torture Nick the same way the guy had tortured him by strolling out of the bathroom more naked than not?

Smirking, he tucked the end of the terry cloth in securely and opened the bathroom door.

Sure enough, Nick looked up as he emerged from the steamy bathroom and did a hard double take.

His skin burning from the blistering heat of Nick's

stare taking in every inch of his exposed skin, Alex sauntered over to the closet and went inside to rummage around. The shelves were stocked with a small selection of men's and women's clothing, and he grabbed a pair of dark slacks and a dark mock turtleneck. His courage failing him, he dressed in the cramped confines of the closet.

When he stepped out, Nick said lightly, "Planning on breaking and entering later, are you?"

Alex glanced down at his black-on-black ensemble. "They were clean and my size. There's stuff in the closet that will fit you if you want to put on more than that towel."

Nick shrugged and made no move to stand up.

Alex frowned. It wasn't as if he could ask Nick to go get dressed. Then the guy would know how wildly distracting he found Nick's bare chest and muscular arms. And those powerful calves and deeply cut thighs—he wanted to crawl all over them, to feel them pressed against his body, to feel the weight of the man pressing down upon him, into him, around him—

Work, dammit.

Except telling himself that didn't curb the creeping sense of longing overtaking his gut. When would he have worked enough? Sacrificed enough for his country? When would there be more than his job in his life? A partner? Heck, he would settle for just a temporary man. Especially a man very much like this one.

He sighed and said, "I grabbed the first-aid kit while I was in the closet. You've got a cut on your chin, and I have at least one somewhere that was bleeding in the shower. I'll patch you up if you'll patch me up."

That did induce Nick to stand up. The towel slipped perilously low, and only a last-minute grab by Nick's fist stopped it from falling off completely. Too bad. His curiosity to see what the towel was hiding was almost more than he could stand.

For lack of anything else to do to cover his reaction to seeing Nick more naked than not, Alex made a production of unpacking medical supplies from the tightly packed first-aid kit.

Carefully, he laid them in a neat row in the order he was likely to use them. Gauze swabs, alcohol, antibiotic cream, medical tape and butterfly bandages. Most knife wounds required more than a simple bandage. They needed something to hold them closed for a day or two until the edges of the wound started to knit together. Of course, puncture wounds were a different story. They required deep cleaning, draining and potentially being held open to heal from the inside out—

"I don't think some little scratch on my jaw requires all of this fussing," Nick said from directly behind him. Alex jumped, startled. He didn't begrudge the man his silence. After all, it kept Nick safe. But it did freak him out a little to get snuck up on like that.

He looked over his shoulder. "Fine. I won't clean it. But when it gets infected and you have to go to a hospital to reopen it, clean it, stitch it closed and get a nasty scar, I get to say I told you so."

"It's not that bad," Nick protested, fingering the three-inch-long line of red just under his chin, following the curvature of his jawbone.

"Can you even see it?" Alex demanded.

"Well, no."

"Look at your fingers."

Nick looked down, and fresh blood stained his fingertips. "I just got out of the shower. Of course it's bleeding. I knocked the scab off of it."

"I took a shower, dried off and got dressed between

you getting out of the shower and now. It should've quit bleeding in that time," Alex pointed out. He picked up the bottle of alcohol and a gauze swab, waiting patiently for Nick to get his head out of his ass.

It took a minute, but finally, Nick shrugged. "Fine. Take a look at it and tell me what you see."

Alex pulled out a chair and Nick sat, leaning his head back to rest on the high back of the chair, exposing his chin. Alex stepped close and leaned down to take a look at the slice along his jawline. Nick smelled clean, like shampoo, and it was the sexiest thing he'd ever sniffed. Up close like this, Nick's eyelashes were long and dark resting against his cheeks.

With his hair wet and slicked back from his face, Alex was struck again by just how good-looking a man Nick was.

"Have you always hidden your face the way you do now?" Alex asked before he could bite back the words.

Nick's eyes opened and they stared at each other from a range of about twelve inches. Nick's eyes were a dark, rich brown, but from this close, Alex spied hints of cinnamon and gold in the depths of Nick's irises. He should've known the man's eyes wouldn't be any simpler than the rest of him.

"I may hide my face, but you hide your entire identity," Nick retorted.

"I beg your pardon?"

"You're so locked down—emotionally, psychologically, physically—that you don't let even the slightest hint of who you really are leak out."

Alex frowned. "I'm not locked down."

"Dude. You could hardly walk across this room in your underwear in front of me. I thought you were going to faint before you made it to the bathroom."

Alex felt the heat of a flush rise to his face. What could he say in response to Nick's accusation? The man was not wrong. "A little modesty does not constitute being emotionally locked down."

Nick just stared up at him steadily.

"Fine. I'm locked down. My job demands it of me."

"Agreed," Nick said evenly. "But what about when you're off duty? When do you let down? Relax?"

"When I go home to see my family."

"The family you don't trust and don't approve of? Do you actually relax when you're around them? But even if I'm wrong about that, when was the last time you did go home and take a break?" Nick asked quietly.

"Two…no, three…years ago."

"I rest my case."

Alex sighed. "Look. I'm not accustomed to having a partner when I'm working. I'm sorry if I'm not being sociable enough for you."

"It's not about me needing you to be sociable. It's about you letting go of the reins a little."

"What reins?" he blurted.

"I'm talking about all that control you exert over every aspect of your life. You've got to loosen up from time to time. Before you, I don't know, explode."

"I wouldn't explode. If anything, I would implode."

"Same diff. You'd end up wrecking yourself. If you don't learn to chill out a little more, you'll be broken-into-little-pieces Alex."

Was Nick right? Was he wired too tightly for his own good? Or was Nick not wired tight enough to be a fixer like him? Frustrated, Alex ripped open another paper package holding a sterile gauze pad.

Nick sucked in a sharp breath and flinched as the alcohol on Alex's pad hit the open wound.

"Seriously?" Alex murmured. "You get sliced by a knife in the first place and don't say a thing about it, then you come all the way back here and take a shower without even realizing you're cut open, and now you get all wimpy about a little alcohol in the wound?"

"I was distracted before. In the heat of the fight, I surely wasn't going to register it. And then, on the way back here, I was too worried about you to let the pain in."

"Aww," Alex murmured before he could bite off the sound.

Nick scowled up at him. "Now that my adrenaline has come back down to normal, of course I'm going to notice. We'll see how painful you think it is when I slap rubbing alcohol on your cuts."

"I make no claims of being a superhero about pain," Alex retorted, getting out a fresh gauze pad to replace the bloody one and then continuing to clean off Nick's jaw and neck.

As he leaned in close, all but sitting in Nick's lap, Nick put his hands on his waist. Maybe the intent was to steady him, maybe the intent was to rattle him. Either way, it worked.

He cleared his throat. "That's a nice little gash, you've got there. Hasn't anyone ever told you it's not a good idea to use your face to block sharp blades?"

"I got that memo, thanks," Nick retorted. "How does it look?"

"It's not quite deep enough for stitches. But that's only assuming you don't go running around getting into more knife fights in the next few days."

"I can't promise that won't happen," Nick responded.

Alex leaned in even closer to examine the angry line of red flesh. "Hence, I'm going to close your wound and hold it shut with a few butterflies after I put this antibiotic goop on it to keep it from getting infected."

He spread a thin layer of the gel on the wound, then carefully cut thin strips of surgical tape, pulling the wound closed and securing it with a half dozen tiny lines of white tape across the wound.

"How does it look now?" Nick asked as Alex stepped back to examine his work.

"The dressing makes you look like quite the pirate. But you'll live."

Nick rolled his eyes and stood up. "Your turn. Let's find out where you're bleeding from."

Alex stood still in front of Nick, startled to feel butterflies flitting around in his stomach. Surely, they had more to do with someone, anyone, staring intently at him than with how warmly Nick was looking at him.

Yeah, that was it. He just didn't like people in general to notice him. It had nothing to do with how Nick put a finger under his chin to lift his face slightly. Nick was only an inch or two taller, but significantly bulkier, and a thrill passed through Alex's still fluttering flock of stomach butterflies. He stared at Nick's intent features as the man leaned left and right, examining his face, neck and shoulders.

"The cut must be somewhere you can't see it," Nick murmured. "Behind an arm, or the middle of your back."

"I don't feel anything," Alex replied, frowning.

"Adrenaline. I've seen guys get shot and not know it. They can go an hour or more in the heat of combat without ever realizing they're bleeding from a giant hole."

Alex had seen the same thing a time or two, but he elected not to share that with Nick. The guy would no doubt point out that he should know better than to believe only his body's pain was an indicator of overall health and well-being.

"Your black clothes aren't showing me any bloodstains. Sorry, but you're going to have to strip down again."

Alex blinked up at him, startled for a moment. Right. Get naked in front of his hot partner. Okay, then. He could do this. He reached for the back neck of his shirt and pulled it over his head. As his face popped free, he thought he caught a glimpse of Nick ogling his torso hungrily. But then Nick's eyes went shuttered, their expression closed.

Feeling a little like a stripper, and kind of loving it more than he cared to admit, he unbuttoned his pants, pulled down the zipper, and pushed the black denim down his hips. He bent over to push the trousers down his legs, and when he straightened, he again caught a glimpse of raging interest in Nick's heavy-lidded gaze.

Must. Not. Pant.

But it was a struggle to keep his breathing light and even to pretend a calm he entirely didn't feel.

He chickened out at stripping off his cotton-spandex undershorts. Besides, they were white, and if he was bleeding beneath them, Nick would be able to see a red line of blood.

He'd never been a huge exhibitionist, but he also hadn't been bothered getting naked in front of his colleagues over the years. Of course, he'd been careful to make sure none of them knew he was gay. He didn't want his coworkers worrying about him eyeing them in *that* way nor did he want them eyeing him weirdly, either. But that particular cat was already out of the bag with Nick.

He'd been right for all those years not to let on about his orientation. This was awkward as hell.

Of course, it wouldn't be awkward at all if he weren't so freaking attracted to Nick.

But that cat, too, had long ago departed the bag for parts unknown.

Unsure of what to do with his hands, he let them hang loosely at his sides. He supposed that was better than grabbing Nick by the back of the neck and dragging him in for another hot wet kiss. Right?

As inappropriate thoughts roared through his brain, one after another, he managed to stand perfectly still. Which, frankly, was a minor miracle. Please God, let his trunks be tight enough to contain the growing arousal he felt starting to build in his crotch.

Nick walked around him slowly, checking for wounds. His belly tightened and got wildly jumpy as Nick moved out of sight behind him. Awareness rolled through him that a lethal predator was right there, right behind him, close enough for him to feel the heat of Nick's breath on the nape of his neck. A shiver chattered down his spine.

Nick knelt down, no doubt checking his legs, but the intimacy of it was almost too much to bear as Nick's warm breath drifted across his skin.

"Well, you've got several cuts that could be the bleeder," Nick announced. "There's this one on the back of your thigh—"

Alex about leaped out of his skin as a single warm, firm finger pressed against his right leg just where it turned into the first swell of his rear end.

"You've got another slice, long and thin, running across the middle of your back. Looks as if someone nicked you as you were turning during the fight. Blade got dragged across your skin. And then, as I suspected, there's a third cut up here, where your arm and back meet."

Another finger touched him lightly, just below his left armpit. He did jump that time. Not only did Nick startle him but he was ticklish, and that finger had come a bit too close to his ribs for comfort.

"Hand me a swab and the alcohol, will you?" Nick murmured.

Alex reached forward to the table for the supplies Nick needed. He was shocked to notice that his hands were trembling ever so slightly.

This was necessary wound care. Not two minutes ago, he'd harassed Nick about the stupidity of not cleaning and covering knife wounds. Metal blades could be dirty things that harbored all kinds of bacteria and dirt.

Nick's hands were gentle and efficient as he cleaned the wounds. When Nick ran a piece of breathable tape from his left shoulder all the way to his waist on his right side in a descending spiral, Alex was shocked. When Nick said the cut was long, he'd had no idea the thing ran all the way across his back. He was lucky he'd had on a lined suit coat, shirt and undershirt to take the brunt of the blade.

Alex said wryly, "Next time I have Tony make me a suit, I think I'll go ahead and take him up on his offer to put a Kevlar layer in between the lining and the outer shell."

"He can do that?" Nick exclaimed.

"Takes him a few days, but yes. He can put full body armor inside a suit coat if you want it."

"Wow. He really is a full-service tailor, isn't he?"

Alex shrugged. "In a town like this, plenty of people have dangerous enemies. Now that Tony has your measurements, you can call him anytime and ask for a suit, and he'll make it and ship it to you."

"Of course he will," Nick muttered, shaking his head.

"I think I've got you all patched up, my friend. You're good to fight another day."

Alex was too tense to sit still, so he packed up the first-aid supplies and burned the gauze pads in a bowl before rinsing the ashes down the sink.

Nick commented as the last of the ashes swirled away into the New York sewer system, "You take opsec to a whole new level."

Alex shrugged. "Operational security is a life-and-death matter to guys like me."

"You say that as if it isn't to someone like me."

Alex turned to face him. "Gray relies too heavily on the intimidation factor his bodyguards provide. That, and his high mobility. They've both become weaknesses for him."

"Weaknesses you think we can exploit?" Nick asked, sounding alert.

"Indeed. He also is too quick to go on the offensive."

Nick perched on the edge of the sofa. "Meaning what?"

"Meaning he's too fast to send his guys after a perceived threat with orders to eliminate it. He would be better off moving away from threats and hiding, rather than confronting them so aggressively."

Nick nodded slowly. "Now that you mention it, he has become more inclined to go on the offensive recently."

"How recently?"

"Say, the past year."

Alex frowned. "What has changed in the past year that has made him switch up his long-established, cautious behavior patterns?"

Nick frowned and was silent, appearing to think. "He did say something a while back about being forced to retire. Do you know anything about that?"

It was Alex's turn to frown. "Most field operatives

leave the business when they start to slow down. They have a close call with someone younger, faster, smarter, more up on the newest technology. They realize they're getting old and getting left behind. That's when they leave. I assume he has amassed a rather nice retirement nest egg for himself?"

"Ten-million-dollar gold statue notwithstanding?" Nick asked dryly.

"Do you think the theft was his retirement plan?"

Nick nodded. "I do. Of course, I think he and my teammates stole the entire Magi Crèche, not just that one statue."

"Why do you think that?"

"Because to get my guys to steal something, to risk their lives and throw away their careers and reputations—not to mention murdering American marines in cold blood—Gray had to have offered them each a crap-ton of cash."

"No amount of money could make me kill an innocent person—soldier or otherwise," Alex replied fervently.

Nick nodded. "Same. Whatever Gray offered to pay his guys, it was enough to convince them to give up everything they believe in for the payout."

Alex winced. "So, whatever he stole had to be worth enough to fund not only his stylish retirement but the comfortable retirements of at least four of his bodyguards."

Nick nodded. "A crap-ton times five. That's a lot of money. If Otto's right about how much the statue and other pieces will fetch at auction, we're talking several hundred million dollars at a minimum. Maybe closer to a billion before it's all said and done."

No wonder senior government officials had sent him after Gray to investigate and possibly kill. Alex asked,

"Didn't you say one of the four thieves died when you and that team of women operators ambushed them?"

"He did," Nick said heavily.

"So Gray is down to splitting the proceeds from selling the crèche with three other guys."

Nick shrugged. "You're assuming the other three will make it out of their—current incarceration—alive."

"You think he'd let his own guys die?" Alex blurted.

Nick stared at him a long time, the look in his eyes deeply troubled. At length, Nick answered heavily, "I think he would go one step further. I think he would kill his own guys if the payoff was high enough. Which it clearly is. At the end of the day, all that matters to Harlan Gray is Harlan Gray."

Alex stared back. "If you're right, then I'll have no choice. I'll have to put him down."

"And by putting him down, you mean you'll kill him?" Nick asked sharply.

"I do."

If the last pause had been long, this one was several times more drawn out. Then, slowly, painfully, Nick said, "I'll help you."

Chapter 11

Nick watched warily as Alex moved swiftly to the sofa and sat down beside him. Alex's body was visibly tense, and as he leaned in close to Nick and their knees brushed, Nick felt intensity vibrating through him.

"Are you absolutely sure you can kill your old boss?" Alex asked soberly. "Unlike Gray, loyalty means something to you. When the moment comes and you're looking at him through your gun sight, can you pull the trigger?"

Nick's emotions were turbulent as he considered the questions. It had been devastating to betray his teammates to the Medusas, who had only been planning to capture his brothers-in-arms. That was a far cry from planning to execute the man he'd worked for and been willing to die to protect.

Alex was speaking again. "...won't hold it against you if you can't do it, Nick. But I have to know now whether you can or can't kill him. My life is probably going to depend on you following through if you tell me that you can take the shot."

Nick nodded slowly, once. Twice. "You are correct. But here's the thing. It will take both of us working together to take down Gray. There's no telling which one of us will get the kill shot. But whichever one of us it is, neither of us dares hesitate to pull the trigger. With this man, we'll only get one try at him. After that, he'll kill us both and not think twice about it. To be blunt, you're going to need my help."

Alex laid a hand on Nick's forearm, which tensed beneath the light touch of Alex's palm. "No harm, no foul, Nick. If you don't want to be part of taking down Gray, I can do it alone."

He surged up off the couch, agitated. "No, you can't! That's what I keep trying to tell you! You still don't get how dangerous a man he is, do you?"

Alex gazed up at him steadily, waiting him out. Alex knew him too well. He sensed that Nick was spoiling for a fight and had no intention of giving one to him.

He shoved a hand through his damp hair. "Hell, Alex. *I'm* afraid of him. And you're a damned fool if you're not."

"Just because I'm afraid of someone, that doesn't mean I can't do my job and eliminate them."

He glared at Alex. "Maybe. But you and I both know that being scared of a target bloody well makes it harder to succeed in taking them out."

Alex shrugged. "I'll cross that bridge when I come to it."

"That's not how it works. You'd better get your head straight before you ever tangle directly with Harlan Gray or he'll use your mental weakness against you. He'll chew you up and spit you out."

"You think I'm not tough enough to do this job?" Alex challenged, rising to his feet and standing chest to chest with him.

Nick huffed. "That's not what I said."

"It's what you implied," Alex accused. "I took you in a fair fight, didn't I?"

"It was an *effing* stalemate," he ground out.

"Let's go again. Right now. I'll kick your ass again."

Exasperation exploded in Nick's gut. This wasn't about who was a better fighter. It was about Alex's mindset. If he didn't go into the fight with Gray utterly prepared for anything Harlan could throw at him, Alex would lose. And then he would die.

"Don't you get it?" he ground out. "You *have* to listen to me. You'll die if you don't!"

"I will not—"

Nick's exasperation overcame him, and in an excess of irritation at Alex and worry for him, he stepped forward fast, grabbed Alex by both shoulders and kissed him. Hard.

There was nothing soft or romantic about it. This was a kiss born of sheer frustration. Alex's mouth opened against his, whether in shock, delight or rage, Nick couldn't tell. Sensations slammed through him. The heat of Alex's lean, muscular torso against his. The resilient warmth of Alex's lips. The hunger vibrating through both of them as their lips and teeth and tongues clashed.

And then it hit him. He was *really kissing* Alex. And Alex was kissing him back. Neither one of them was holding back. At all.

And it was freaking wonderful.

Wonderful enough to give up everything and walk away from all of this. To run away with Alex and never look back. To find that quiet town and picket fence and settle down for good. Just the two of them. To start a family. A new life. A new love—

Nick stumbled backward, tearing his mouth away from Alex's and swiping the back of his hand across his mouth. Dammit, the swipe did nothing to erase the minty-toothpaste taste of the man. Nor did it eliminate the citrus and sandalwood smell of Alex's deodorant, or the clean, soapy scent of his skin.

Oh man. It didn't erase the feel of Alex's mouth against his, either. Not the warm, smooth texture of Alex's lips nor the heat of his surprised breath in Nick's mouth nor the way their mouths fit perfectly together, matched in hungry strength and in raging desire.

Nick swore under his breath, long and violently. Then he said raggedly, "I'm sorry. That was out of line."

Alex cleared his throat. "Uh, yeah," he mumbled. "It was. But given that I kissed you the first time, I can't very well hold this kiss against you. Care to tell me what that was all about?"

"I needed you to shut up for a minute and listen to me. Gray is more dangerous than anyone you've ever tangled with. By a mile. He's a lot more dangerous than me, for example."

"You kissed me to shut me up?"

"You're still not listening! I kissed you to get you to engage your brain."

Alex laughed painfully. "You engaged me, all right. Just not my brain."

Nick's gaze dropped involuntarily to Alex's nether regions. That was a definite swell behind the zipper of Alex's jeans. Well, hell. Now he really was tempted to kiss the guy again and then run away with him. Far, far from here and from Harlan Gray.

Alex was speaking, and Nick dragged his attention

away from Alex's crotch and back to the man's words. "...do hear you. I swear."

"You can't just hear me. I need you to truly grasp what I'm telling you about Harlan Gray. He's possibly the most dangerous man on the planet."

Alex huffed. "I grasped that the first time you said it. And trust me. He's personally not any more dangerous than you are. The only things that make him truly dangerous are his bodyguards and the resources he uses to move around so much with and hide his tracks with. That's what I was trying to tell you earlier. Take those away, and he's just a spy who's gone off the rails. He's just one man—"

Nick slashed a hand through the narrow space between them. "I heard *you* before, too. And I'm telling you this isn't about Gray's resources. It's about his mindset. He's willing to do things you and I are not. He's willing to kill innocent marines who were merely in the wrong place at the wrong time. He won't hesitate to slaughter civilians who get in his way. He thinks nothing of taking hostages, killing children, murdering dozens or hundreds of people at a time to protect himself."

"I get all of that," Alex said carefully. "I believe you. And that's why I have to stop him. I can do it with your help or without. But I need to know which it's going to be. And I have to be able to trust you completely after you give me your answer."

Nick sighed. "Yeah. Trust. That's a hard one for guys like you and me, isn't it?"

The fight went out of Alex, and his belligerent stance relaxed. In fact, he sank back down onto the sofa. Cautiously, Nick sat down beside him, watching the play of emotions across Alex's smooth-skinned facial features.

For a man who held himself so much in check at all

times, a whole lot of feelings were racing across his face right now. So many, in fact, that Nick wasn't sure he could name them all. Frustration, for sure. Worry. Determination.

He had to admire the guy. Alex didn't seem deterred by anything Nick had said about how bad and dangerous Gray was. If anything, it seemed to have hardened Alex's resolve. Reluctant admiration coursed through him. Anyone who knew who and what Harlan Gray was and was still willing to take on the man…? Nick had to give Alex mad props for courage, if nothing else.

Alex's blue-green gaze lifted to his. "It's the right thing to do. Someone has to stop Gray. And for better or worse, it appears the job has fallen to me. I'll die if I have to. If that's what it takes to finish him, so be it."

Nick pinched the bridge of his nose with his right hand. Four aspirin weren't turning out to be enough to control the headache Alex was giving him. "I don't want you to die. That's why I'm volunteering to help you take him down. And yes, if push comes to shove, I can pull the trigger when I've got Gray's face in my sight."

"You're dead certain about that?" Alex pressed. "No pun intended."

"Yes. I am."

"Well, then. I guess you and I are going hunting together," Alex said lightly.

A heavy sense of dread filled him, but something else came with it. Relief. Relief that Gray was finally going to be stopped. Relief that he would be the one to take down his former boss—a man he'd admired and emulated for far too long. Relief that, if Alex died trying to take down Gray, he would undoubtedly die beside Alex, protecting him with his own life, the way he'd protected Gray's for so long. Yep. That felt all kinds of right.

He and Alex would survive this thing together, or they would die together.

He reached over and took Alex's hand in his. For an instant, Alex resisted, but then his arm relaxed and he quit fighting the touch. Nick turned over Alex's hand and ran his thumb over the tough shooter's callus at the base of his thumb.

"The only way you and I are both getting out of this job alive is to work together and trust each other and for both of us to be completely committed to killing Gray. There can't be even one second of hesitation when the time comes to pull the trigger. You hear me? If you get the shot, Alex, take it. Period. Promise me you won't overthink it."

Alex blinked at him, looking startled. Whether that was the result of their holding hands or Nick's sincere plea, he couldn't tell. But Alex laid his other hand gently over Nick's, sandwiching it between Alex's warm, battle-toughened palms.

"Nick. This is not my first rodeo when it comes to eliminating fellow American operators. Of course I'll take the shot. It's what I do. I never hesitate."

Nick stared into Alex's unusually colored eyes, losing himself in their sea-colored depths. "We're agreed, then. I promise not to hesitate, either, and I also promise that I will, indeed, kill him if I get the chance."

"Remember, we have to prove he gave the order to take out those marines. *Then* we can kill him."

"The Medusa photo intel analyst *saw* Gray's guys carry that crate out of the compound in Zagastan. She saw them approach the Hummer with the marines in it, and she saw the Hummer drive away, seconds later. What more proof do you need?" Nick demanded.

Alex said soberly, "There was a glitch in the video

feed from the camera drone. She didn't actually see Gray's guys pull the trigger. And even if she had witnessed them murder those marines, I would still have to get proof that Gray ordered the hit. I won't dispatch him until I have that."

Nick shoved a frustrated hand through his half-dry hair. What was it going to take to convince Alex not to mess around trying to get proof of Gray's guilt first? Gray was going to kill them both long before Alex ever got his precious proof.

Alex said, "If I had been sent to put you down, wouldn't you want me to do my due diligence and assure myself I had the right guy before I pulled the trigger?"

"Innocent until proven guilty, huh?" Nick grumbled.

Alex shrugged. "Sorry. It's how I roll. Even the baddest bad guy gets the benefit of the doubt from me until I'm sure I've got the right person."

"Regardless of the risk that poses to you?" Nick snapped.

"Regardless of the risk," Alex echoed.

And that was why he was falling for this man. Alex's morals were ironclad, and no power on earth would move him off that moral center of his. Nick admired the hell out of that. Truth be told, he trusted Alex like he trusted few others in this world. He used to trust his teammates, but then Gray had bought them off. Nick wondered idly what their honor had been worth. Ten million dollars apiece? A hundred million? More?

Alex jumped up and paced back and forth a couple of times in the small living space. Nick wondered if it was the kiss, or the hand-holding or something else altogether making him so jumpy.

Either way, Alex turned to face him and said, "Do

you think nearly killing one of his guards last night was provocation enough to get Gray to come after us?"

Nick frowned. "Why do you ask?"

"I'm sick and tired of chasing a ghost. I want to provoke him to come for us. In fact, I want him to come after us as hard as he's capable of doing it."

"That's a big ask," Nick responded in alarm. "And no, I doubt he'll care if the guy from last night lives or dies. Either way, with the injuries he sustained, the guy is off Gray's detail for the foreseeable future. He'll cease to exist in Gray's mind."

Alex turned to pace back toward him. "Do you think the injured guy would talk to us?"

"You're assuming he's alive and able to talk. Those are both large assumptions. At a minimum, he fractured his skull when he hit the sidewalk and gave himself a serious concussion. Worst case, he gave himself a brain bleed. For all we know, he's lying in a coma or dead by now."

Alex shrugged. "Have you got a better idea?"

"We could just wait until the auction for the golden statue takes place and pick up Gray's trail there."

Alex argued, "We have no idea when the auction will actually happen, and we have no guarantee Gray will show up for it. Particularly after this evening's fight. Would you expose yourself immediately after your bodyguards got their asses handed to them in a violent confrontation?"

Nick winced. "Fine. You make a good point. He may not show up for the auction, regardless of when it happens."

Alex's gaze narrowed thoughtfully. "Let me make a few phone calls. There's a decent trauma unit in a small private hospital about a half dozen blocks from where we fought Gray's guys. I'll bet that's where they took him."

"The hospital isn't just going to tell you if the guy lived or died. Particularly if it's a snazzy private hospital," Nick objected.

"Oh, I'm not calling the hospital. You forget—I have the combined resources of the CIA and the rest of the United States intelligence network at my disposal."

Nick snorted. "Gee. Must be nice. We did *everything* with Gray off the books. We used to joke around that we took a—" He broke off and made a fast course correction in what he'd been about to say. "We joked around that we even defecated off the books."

Alex grinned as he pulled out his cell phone. "Observe the power of the American intelligence machine."

It took Alex under two minutes to ascertain that Gray's man, named Jed Turner, had indeed been taken to the private hospital last night and, furthermore, that the guy was in stable but serious condition and expected to live. He was still under observation for potential brain swelling on the fifth floor, in the room directly across from the nurses' station.

As Alex pocketed his phone, Nick said reluctantly, "Okay. I'm impressed. You made getting that intel look easy."

"Wanna go see if he's up for a chat now?" Alex asked jovially, well pleased with himself.

"It's after midnight. Visiting hours were over hours ago."

"Since when do rules apply to you or me?" Alex demanded.

"You really do have the bit between your teeth, now, don't you? We're just gonna barge in there, throw our government IDs and our weight around, and talk to Gray's man, huh?"

"I had a little less barging and a little more finesse in mind, but that's the basic idea," Alex replied.

"I guess I'd better have a look in that magic supply closet of yours, then. I can't very well go out in my skivvies."

"I dunno. The nurses might be willing to tell you anything if you showed up like that and shook your junk at them."

"They're nurses. They see junk all the time. They wouldn't be impressed."

Alex threw him a patently skeptical look.

Fine. He knew that women found him attractive. It was just that he didn't usually care what they thought of him. Did he use his looks to his advantage with women on missions? Of course, he did. All spies worth their salt used every tool at their disposal to get the job done. Did he sleep around with women? No. That was an ethical line he drew in the sand for himself.

Alex looked him up and down boldly before obviously losing his nerve and spinning away to stare out the window. The chili pepper lights Alex had strung up yesterday blinked cheerfully, splashing lime-green-and-orange light across his skin.

Nick dragged his gaze away from Alex's athletic physique and forced himself to step into the closet.

Wow. This thing really was stocked with everything a covert operative could ask for. The only thing missing was an arsenal of firearms. But he spied a dozen different kinds of ammunition, and he suspected there was a false wall or hidden compartment somewhere else in the apartment that did include weapons to go with all that ammo.

He rummaged through the folded stack of men's clothing and came up with a pair of charcoal gray jeans and a dark blue cotton sweater that looked as if they would fit him. He pulled them on and headed back out into the living area. As he laced on his shoes, Alex sat at the table, typing rapidly on a laptop computer.

"Whatchya doin'?" Nick asked with interest. He was intrigued by the total focus Alex brought to his tasks.

"Reading up on the Magi Crèche."

"Learn anything new?"

"Not much beyond what Otto told us at the gallery. There are thought to be around fifty pieces to the entire collection. The original set made by the magi is thought to consist of perhaps six or eight figures, probably carved from wood. It's possible they were encased in a metal, likely gold, at a later date. Given that fabulously wealthy Persian rulers commissioned the pieces, speculation is that they're made of precious materials by master artists. My classified intel sources do make one mention of the set."

"Do tell." Nick perked up with interest.

"About two years ago, the CIA picked up a bit of chatter saying the Magi Crèche had been liberated from the Iranian government and might be on its way out of Iran. The rumor hinted that some sort of arms deal was done in return for the crèche, perhaps missile components."

"As in nuclear-missile components?" Nick blurted.

"The report doesn't say. But that's a logical assumption given how frantically Iran is working at building a fleet of nuclear-capable weaponry."

"Ugh." Nick added, "What are the odds Gray saw the same intel report and decided to steal the crèche for himself?"

"I'd say those odds are pretty high."

Nick frowned. "So, what's the end goal here? Are we only interested in Gray, or are we interested in finding and recovering the crèche?"

Alex shrugged. "Stopping Gray is the primary objective. If we happen to recover the crèche in the process, that'll be frosting on the cake."

Nick nodded. "I'm thinking we ask the guy in the hospital if he knows where the rest of the crèche is stored."

"Would Gray share that information with the whole team?" Alex asked in surprise.

Nick laughed. "Not hardly. The actual question we should ask the guy would be something along the lines of is there any place Gray has gone back to a couple of times in the past year."

Alex nodded, catching on immediately. "You think he has stowed the crèche somewhere obscure and had to go back to it to retrieve the gold statue to bring it here to sell?"

"Exactly. The intel analyst who saw the crèche stolen said the crate was big and very heavy. Gray can't exactly haul it around with him, as he goes to a new safe house every night."

Alex asked, "What makes you think the guy in the hospital will tell us where it is?"

Nick shrugged. "We saved his life. He owes us."

Alex winced. "The way I hear it, there's not a whole lot of loyalty among thieves."

"Only one way to find out. We have to ask him."

Chapter 12

Alex tugged at the white lab coat he'd lifted off a hook in a break room two floors down. Nick hunched his shoulders in his jacket beside him. "You remember your name?" Alex asked low as the elevator dinged its arrival on the fifth floor.

"Yeah. I'm Roscoe Turner. Jed's older brother."

"Let me do the talking." Alex added, grinning, "I am, after all, more charming than you."

As the doors slid open, Nick told him under his breath exactly what he could do with his charm. His grin widened even more.

Alex stepped up to the nurses' station. "Hi, I'm Dr. Sylvan from labor and delivery. I was walking through the lobby when this nice man asked me for help finding his brother, a Jed Turner. I'm told he's a patient on this ward?"

The nurse nodded politely. "That's correct. He's right across the hall."

"I know it's breaking the rules, but Mr. Turner has driven all the way from Alabama to see his brother. Maybe he could just peek in for a minute to assure himself that Jed is all right?"

She came around the high desk and said to Nick, "You're his brother?"

"Yes, ma'am." Nick asked anxiously, "Is he okay?"

"Well, he took a pretty bad fall, but he should make a full recovery. If you'd like to see him for a moment, it's time for me to wake him up and check his vitals anyway. Come with me."

"I'll leave you to it, then," Alex said pleasantly, heading for the elevator. "Nice to meet you, Mr. Turner."

"Thanks for your help, Doc," Nick replied in a Southern drawl that made Alex want to laugh.

As soon as the nurse and Nick stepped into the room, Alex reversed direction and ducked fast into the patient room next to the one Gray's man was in. Thankfully, the bed in the room was empty. He heard the nurse's footsteps come back out into the hall, and as he'd hoped, she headed away from the nurses' station, likely doing hourly rounds.

He peeked outside, and watched her enter another patient's room. Quickly, he slipped into the hall and ducked into the room with Nick and Jed.

Nick's former student had a bandage wrapped around his head and looked pale. Bits of brown hair stuck out around the gauze strapping.

Nick was leaning over the bed. He looked up, spied Alex and muttered, "He's sedated. Pretty groggy."

"Perfect."

Nick nodded, and for a bare instant, flashed him a wolflike smile. Then he looked back down at the patient. "Jed, it's Kane. How're you feeling, buddy?"

The man's eyelids fluttered and his blue eyes half-opened. A vague frown crossed his features.

"Nick." A long pause while the guy peered up at him. Then, "Did we fight?"

"I trained you last year in hand-to-hand combat. Remember?"

"Guess so."

"How's your head? The way I hear it, you took a pretty good fall."

Jed's hand lifted weakly off the mattress toward his head and then fell back to the white sheet. "Hurts," he mumbled.

"I'll bet."

Jed seemed to be struggling to retrieve something from his memory, and Alex waited him out along with Nick.

At length, Jed finally mumbled to Nick, "You're gay?"

Alex stared. That was not what he'd expected to come out of the guy's mouth. He glanced up at Nick, who was staring down at the injured man as if Jed had grown a second head.

"What the hell are you talking about?" Nick finally said gruffly.

"Gray said…"

Alex caught Nick's eye roll of genuine frustration and Alex shared the sentiment. Wow. Gray had outed him to his teammates? What a douchebag.

"Not a problem for me," Jed was mumbling. "Do your job. Who cares what you do on your own time?"

Nick smiled gently at Jed, who frowned up at him as if struggling to retrieve some other important tidbit.

Without warning, Jed blurted. "Traitor. He said you were a traitor. Turned in the guys who got arrested in Montana a while back. Did you turn on us, man?"

He traded brief glances with Nick that spoke volumes. Nick was going to be hard to stop from killing Gray if and when they uncovered the man. Alex glanced down at Jed significantly and back up at Nick, who caught the hint. He pasted on a smile and looked down at the groggy man.

"Gray's full of shit." Nick paused to take a deep breath. Then he continued, "I would never betray my own guys. Hell, I trained you myself."

"Then what…tonight…why're you here?"

Nick lied easily, "I was trying to catch up with you and the other guys after you took off out of the art gallery. I came upon you after some kind of fight. You were on the ground and bleeding. You had stopped breathing. I did CPR on you and saved your life. Do you remember that?"

The man's frown deepened as he visibly sorted through blurry snippets of memory, but then his expression eased. "Yeah. Thanks," he sighed.

"Of course. You'd have done the same for me. We're brothers-in-arms." He smiled down at the guy and said smoothly, "I need you to do me a favor. I've gotten separated from the team and need to reconnect with them. After y'all found that tracker on the limo and things heated up the way they have, Gray ordered me to head out and sit on the crate. But before he could text me the location, I lost my damned phone. He's gonna kill me if I don't get to the haul ASAP and make sure it's safe."

Jed nodded faintly and then sucked in a sharp, painful breath after the small head movement. The guy must have the mother of all headaches after hitting the concrete the way he had.

Nick murmured, "I know the town, but I don't know the address of the storage place. Do you have those, buddy?"

"Phone," Jed muttered. "Phone."

"Yeah. My phone was stolen. I've got a replacement

on order, but it won't be here until tomorrow, and I was supposed to leave tonight to check on the statues."

At the mention of statues, some of the tension went out of Jed's body. His eyelids drifted shut.

"Don't fall asleep on me, now," Nick said teasingly. "Where am I supposed to go?"

"Phone," Jed sighed with the last of his consciousness.

His eyes shut. Alex reached out to shake his shoulder lightly. The jostling should have made the man cry out in pain, but he merely moaned a little and went still again.

"Did the nurse put something in his IV when you two came in here?" Alex asked low.

Nick swore under his breath. "Yeah. Must be some sort of sedation and painkiller."

"We're not going to get any more out of him for a few hours," Alex said in disgust. "We can come back in the morning, I suppose. He did seem willing to talk with you, at any rate."

"He must not have recognized us as the guys from the fight."

Alex nodded, his sharp hearing detecting a door closing down the hall. "Time to go. That nurse will finish her rounds soon."

Alex went to the hallway door and watched as the nurse stopped in the hallway beside a door to hang up a clipboard. She moved to another room and disappeared inside. Alex waved for Nick to follow, and they raced down the hall quickly and quietly.

The elevator had left, and there was no time to wait for it to come back. They slipped into the stairwell beside it and Nick closed the door softly.

They jogged down the steps in silence. They ducked out onto the second floor, and Alex returned the lab coat to the break room where he'd found it. No sense causing a ruckus that might cause the night nurse to remember Dr. Sylvan bringing an after-hours visitor to a trauma patient.

They headed out, making sure to turn their faces away from each of the security cameras they encountered on their way. They walked back to the apartment building without speaking, and Alex relished the relative quiet of this time of night. Usually the city was so busy, so bustling and noisy, he could barely hear himself think. But tonight, with shiny Christmas decorations hanging on lamp poles, lights twinkling in store windows and a fine layer of snow coating the ground, it was magically serene.

"I do love this town during the holidays," he murmured.

"You're just a Christmas junkie," Nick teased.

"I like how the holidays bring out the kinder side of people. For a minute we forget to be rotten to one another and we come together to make kids smile and connect with our loved ones. Call me sappy at heart and I'll plead guilty as charged."

He smiled and shrugged, and Nick grinned back, if a little reluctantly, and muttered, "I think it's nice."

"What? Have I converted you into thinking the holidays are nice?"

"No. I think your secret optimism about the decency of the human race is nice. And if it takes all of this schlocky holiday crap to bring it out in you, so be it."

"Be careful, Nick, or I'll turn you into a holiday lover, too."

"Nope. Never."

They got back to the apartment and Nick fell onto the sofa in frustration. "I can't believe Gray outed me to the team. What a jerk."

"That's a nice word for him," Alex said dryly.

"What are we supposed to do now? Jed was no help at all."

Alex flopped down at the kitchen table. And then it hit him. "Phone!" he exclaimed. "Of course!"

"What?"

"Before we resuscitated Jed, we disarmed Gray's men and took their cells. Did you happen to grab Jed's?"

Nick blinked, startled. "Yeah. I did. I stuffed it in my pants' pocket before I started CPR." Understanding dawned in Nick's gaze. If they could get into the phones and poke around in them, they might be able to figure out where Gray was staying. Or at least, they might be able to find the man's trail again.

He loved working with a guy as smart as Nick was. It saved so much explanation and argument to convince someone else that his hunches were worth following. But then, the best operators usually relied heavily on their intuitions and gut feels. Thankfully, Nick had gotten that memo somewhere along the way and was immediately on board with his hunch that they should check out the phones.

Alex pulled out the garbage bag full of their bloody clothes and untied it. He dug around in the crusty garments, stiff with dried blood, and found Nick's slacks. He checked the pockets and came up with a phone. He carried it back to the table.

Nick joined him as he pressed the power button.

"It's password encrypted," Alex announced.

Nick swore under his breath. "By the time we unlock the thing, Gray will have sold his statue and be long gone."

Alex shrugged. "I don't know about that. I know a few things about phone decryption. First thing tomorrow morning, I'll head over to an electronics shop and buy a few things. Then maybe I can get us into Jed's."

"The way he kept saying 'phone,' over and over, I'll lay odds the information we need is in there," Nick said eagerly.

"For now, let's get some rest and hit it again in the morning. There's nothing more we can do tonight."

Their gazes snapped to each other. There was plenty more they *could* do tonight. Just nothing that would advance their efforts to locate Gray.

Never, ever, had he felt this instant a connection with another man. While he was delighted to know that this kind of sympatico existed, why did he have to find Nick in the middle of a mission that very well could be the one that killed them both?

Alex dragged his mind back to the problem at hand. First, they had to find Gray. Then he could explore this thing between him and Nick. But they couldn't indulge in their private desires yet. He couldn't think of anything in the world dumber than stopping, dropping and making out in the middle of a life-threatening operation. He was nothing if not a man of intense self-discipline.

But that didn't mean he had to like it.

They decided that Nick would take the mattress and he would take the couch since he was a few inches shorter than Nick. Not that the stupid sofa fit him, either. After about five minutes trying to figure out how to curl up or stretch out and hang his feet off the end of the thing, he gave up, dragged the sofa's seat cushions onto the floor and stretched out more comfortably.

From the darkness, Nick said, "You can share the mattress with me. I don't bite." There was a momentary pause and he added dryly, "Well, I only bite when invited." An-

other pause. "When there's an established safe word."
A third pause. "And my partner likes it a little rough."

Alex popped to full consciousness, his body abruptly
aroused and his mind racing. So much for him sleeping
anytime soon.

*A little rough, huh? Nick bit? What did he bite? How
hard? Could he bite back?* An urge to nibble his way
across all of Nick's body made him toss and turn long
after Nick's breathing slowed and deepened into sleep.

*A safe word? Heck yeah, he would invite the man to
bite a little—*

He tossed and turned some more. He threw off the
blanket, way too overheated to need it. *Dang it.* He was
going to end up having to go into the bathroom, relieve
the pressure in his groin by hand and then take the cold-
est shower the apartment could offer up.

He did end up taking that shower, and he did eventually fall asleep in the wee hours of the night. But Nick
could stop making any more comments like that around
him at bedtime in the future.

He woke to the smell of something cooking and rolled
off the sofa cushion and onto the hard floor before fully
waking. He stared up at Nick grinning at him from over
by the tiny stove and brandishing a spatula like a sword.

"Whatchya got cookin'?" Alex mumbled.

"Farmer's breakfast, lazy head. It's a thing my Ger-
man nana used to make. She called it *Bauernfrühstück.*
My brother and I called it the everything-but-the-kitchen-
sink meal."

Alex sat up, grinding the bases of his palms into his
eye sockets.

"Didn't sleep well?" Nick asked cheerfully. "You
should've shared the mattress with me."

As if. He wouldn't have gotten a wink of sleep all night if he'd done that. Safe words and biting, indeed.

Sometime in the wee hours of the night, awareness of another feeling crept insidiously into his mind. Fear. It was an unpleasant and unwelcome sensation and he'd spent a long time trying to banish if from his mind.

But the harder he fought it, the more stubbornly the fear lodged itself in his mind. What was he going to do about the problem of Nicholas Kane?

What if Nick and he gave it a go and things didn't work out between them? How was he going to walk away from this man and not look back?

What if Nick walked away from him? How was he supposed to just watch him go?

What if Nick couldn't overcome his hang-ups about dying, or heaven forbid, allowing himself to be a tiny bit happy?

He, of all people, knew better than to expect anyone to change to suit someone else. He couldn't ask it of Nick. It would have to come from inside Nick himself.

Could he stand by and watch this potentially magnificent man self-destruct? Could he let Nick sacrifice himself in the grand gesture Nick seemed to envision as the way he would leave this world?

Alex could see their whole future in his mind's eye, unfolding in snapshots of family and fun and warmth and love. If only Nick could see it, too, and allow himself to reach out and take it all for himself.

Gah. He hated not being in control of this whole situation. He was always in control. And then Nick had blown into his life and turned everything upside down.

He tossed and turned until dawn was starting to creep around the curtains and past the chili pepper lights.

Grouchy, he got up and took yet another shower, this

one hot enough to melt candlewax. He felt vaguely human by the time he emerged. Nick shoved a double mug of coffee into his hand, and he gulped it too quickly, burning his mouth. He didn't care. He took another big swig of the caffeinated goodness.

He finished the coffee just as Nick plated up a concoction of meat, potatoes and chopped vegetables held together by an egg-and-cheese mixture. It was a lot like an omelet but much heartier.

Alex ate quickly, mentally making a shopping list for himself. "Will you be okay here alone while I run out and buy a few things?"

Nick smirked. "I'm just going to do the dishes and watch talk shows all morning. Maybe catch up on my favorite soap opera. Call my girlfriends and talk on the phone."

Alex rolled his eyes and grinned. "Right. Back in about an hour."

It turned out to be more like two hours. The first store didn't have a key component he needed to build a decryption device, and he ended up having to stop by the local FBI field office to requisition the most sensitive part he needed—a motherboard with a high-speed number generator programmed on it. He brought his whole haul back to the apartment and spent the remainder of the morning wiring and soldering. But by noon, he had a crude device ready to try out.

He pulled out one of the other men's phones to test his device on first, in case it fried the content instead of unlocking it. He popped the back off the phone, connected the cell's guts to his crude device and sat back to wait.

"How long will this take?" Nick asked with interest.

"Depends on how long the password is. Anything over six numbers could take a while. With each digit you add in length, the number of possible combinations goes up exponentially."

"Cool. Wanna watch a game show with me?" Nick asked drolly.

Alex frowned. "I don't remember the last time I watched television."

Nick guffawed. "You're missing out, man. With all the streaming services these days, there are more shows than you can shake a stick at."

Alex shrugged. "My work keeps me pretty busy."

"Don't you ever take time off?" Nick asked, sounding a bit incredulous.

"Why would I? My work is important."

"Not even for Christmas?"

Alex rolled his eyes at him. "That's a low blow. This mission is important or I'd be ice skating in Rockefeller Center right now, wearing a bad Christmas sweater and sucking on a candy cane."

"Don't you ever burn out? Get exhausted? Need to rest up and, I don't know, heal?"

"I don't get hurt," Alex replied indignantly. "I'm good at my job."

"I bandaged you up last night. You do, too, get hurt."

"Only since I started running around with you."

Nick snorted. "You mean ever since you decided to tangle with Harlan Gray."

Alex opened his mouth to retort, but the phone in front of him lit up just then. "We're in."

Nick jumped up and came over to stare down at the unlocked device. Alex held it out to him. "You poke around on this one while I hook up Jed's phone."

It didn't take long to get the decryption device set up and it went to work.

Nick asked, "Do you know how to find out if these

phones have GPS tracking on them? I'd love to see where they've been the past few weeks."

"Weeks? They should store location information dating back for months," Alex replied, taking the cell from Nick and typing into it. A screen popped up. "Here we go. This device takes a lat-long location snapshot every few hours. We'll have to enter the latitude and longitude coordinates into a separate map program to find out exactly where it has been, which will be a pain in the butt, but we can definitely track where it has been."

"Sweet," Nick exclaimed.

Alex opened up a simple mapping program and shoved the laptop over to Nick. "You type in the coordinates I give you."

For the next half hour, he read out geographic info while Nick placed virtual pins in an online map. They were just finishing up when Jed's device finally lit up.

"Dang, he had some good encryption on that puppy," Alex commented.

"Wanna map where his phone has been, too, and compare the list of locations to the first one?" Nick suggested.

"Sure. We've got the third guy's locations we can map, as well. Between the three of them, we should get a decent idea of where Gray's been for the past year."

"He'd croak if he knew we could track his movements like this," Nick said in satisfaction.

"Feel free to tell him after we've apprehended him," Alex said, amused.

"Oh, I will. I have a lot to say to him when we catch his sorry ass."

"I'm glad to hear you talking in terms of catching and interrogating him rather than just killing him on sight."

Nick's gaze narrowed. "Forget what I just said. I'm going to go ahead and blow his head off. You can question his corpse all you'd like."

Alex sighed. "I have to do my job first. Then, depending on what we learn, we can kill him."

"I'm amending my earlier statement that whoever gets the shot should take it," Nick said grimly. "I want to be the one to take him out."

"If we have the luxury of choosing, I yield the honor to you," Alex said formally.

Nick's eyebrows sailed up. "Do you mean that?"

"When's the last time I lied to you?" Alex retorted.

"I don't know. When?"

"Never," Alex snapped, offended at the mere idea of lying to Nick.

"Don't get your knickers in a twist. I believe you," Nick said mildly. "You're not a lying kind of guy."

Alex subsided, mollified, and went back to work on decrypting the third cell phone.

It took them several hours, but finally, they had a map on the laptop's screen with sets of red, blue and green pins sprinkled across mainly the East Coast of the United States, one color for each of the three phones they'd plotted.

Alex stared at the dozens of colored dots on the map. "Now we just have to look for a place that makes no sense for Harlan Gray to have visited."

Nick snorted. "As if anything that man does makes sense."

A half hour later, Alex stared down at a hand-written list of nearly sixty cities that all three phones had in common as having visited in the past year. Surely most of them contained overnight safe houses that Gray slept at and then left. There had to be a way to narrow down where he might have stashed a crate full of priceless statues.

"Give me Jed's," Alex said suddenly. "Jed kept repeat-

ing the word *phone*. What if there's other information in
his that we're missing?"

Nick passed it to him, and Alex commenced poking
around.

"Hah! Jed keeps copies of documents from the cloud
on his phone! Bad, bad operational security. But good
for us."

"Can you open the files?" Nick asked eagerly.

"It may take another round of decryption," Alex
warned. He typed the command to open the files and put
his decryption device to work, trying every possible combination of letters, numbers and symbols to open them.

For a while, he watched the device flickering, cycling
through permutations of passwords faster than his eyes
could read them. By now, if it was a six-digit combo, the
phone would've opened. Which meant they were in for
at least several more hours of seven-digit possibilities.

"Guess I'm stuck watching that soap opera with you,"
Alex sighed.

"It's too late for soaps. We've got talk shows or early
news. Unless, of course, you'd like to watch some after-
school cartoons."

"News," Alex declared.

Nick changed the channel, and Alex jolted as an image
of the gold statue from Otto's gallery flashed across the
screen. The reporter was describing how the piece was
thought to come from a priceless collection of statues
depicting the birth of Christ and created by one of the
Three Wise Men, and that it was going to be sold tomorrow night in a highly anticipated auction.

Alex looked over at Nick. "Welp. I guess Otto got his
provenance papers."

Nick replied grimly, "And that means we have an auction to attend."

Chapter 13

The gallery was buzzing with activity when they arrived. People milled around on the sidewalk, wearing tuxedos and formal gowns. A red carpet was rolled out all the way to the curb, and the rich and richer of the art world were out in force, tonight.

News trucks were parked up and down the street. All the major news networks were here to cover the auction of the statue from the Magi Crèche. Everyone who was anyone in the art world wanted to be seen here, and it had the feel of a major gala. Security was tight, and people were being scanned with metal detectors before they entered the building.

Nick led Alex away from the chaos out front, however, and they headed around to the back of the property. It was just as chaotic behind the gallery, with catering trucks, security guards and warehouse crew racing around getting ready for the auction to commence. A hundred other works of art were also on sale tonight, and they all had to be numbered, lined up and transported inside on a tight, smooth schedule.

Crouching beside him in an adjacent alley, Alex murmured, "We'll never get inside unseen."

"We don't have to. We just have to piss off Gray so bad he wants to kill us."

"You think this'll work?" Alex replied.

"If one gambit doesn't work, the other will," Nick muttered. "The one thing Gray can't stand is being embarrassed. He's going to go nuts when our guy inside calls the statue a fake."

"Otto's going to have heart failure," Alex added. "This could ruin him."

"The statue is stolen, and he knows it. He deserves to be ruined," Nick bit out.

"Wow. And I thought I was the one with the rigid moral code."

He glanced over at Alex and shrugged. "You and I do bad and illegal things at the behest of our government, and always for a higher cause of right and good. Men like us had better have a rigid moral code so we never lose sight of why we do what we do."

"Exactly." Alex went still as a pair of black SUVs pulled around behind the warehouse. They had darkly tinted windows and came in fast. Three men jumped out, took a quick look around, and then a fourth stepped out.

"And there's our man now," Nick breathed. "That's Gray in the tuxedo."

"We won't have a shot from this angle when they bring him out," Alex whispered.

Nick looked around at the tight confines of the alley. "We're gonna have to go high."

As Gray and his team disappeared inside, the SUVs

pulled away and turned the corner. Nick commented, "The only place we'll have a shot that the SUVs won't block is that brick building next door to the gallery."

"It's not very tall. It'll be a shallow angle. Hard shot."

"Better than no shot," Nick replied.

"Let me see who's in that building," Alex murmured as he typed on his cell phone. "It holds a hodgepodge of small businesses."

"I've seen enough, here. Let's go find ourselves a perch and get ready," Nick murmured.

The rear door of the brick building was a joke to unlock. They slipped inside the dingy, converted factory. They climbed the metal fire stairs to the top floor and turned left, heading for the office on the end. The cardboard sign taped to the inside of the glass door declared it to be a talent agency. For what, Nick had no idea.

The lock was simple, and the dead bolt above it not much harder to pick. Alex got through both in under a minute. They slipped into an office even more depressing than its exterior.

"No wonder this place has no security," Alex murmured. "There's nothing worth stealing."

Alex said low, "You clear this place, and I'll head across the hall. Find us an egress point. Back in a few."

Nick moved quietly across the room to the pair of corner windows, one facing the gallery and the other facing the alley behind it. He checked quickly for any hidden security measures, even though he agreed with Alex that there was nothing here worth protecting.

A half dozen tall filing cabinets lined one wall, and a battered oak desk took up the middle of the space. Broken slat blinds hung askew over the panes. Perfect. He and Alex would be able to point their weapons past the blinds without disturbing them.

Nick laid the long plastic rifle case on the floor beside the window and flipped the lid open. For Alex, he laid one of two short-range precision rifles inside on the sill facing the warehouse, and he picked up the other. He flipped down the bipod stand attached to the barrel and examined the windowsill facing the warehouse.

Alex opened the office door and announced, "Straight across the hall, I've got the door unlocked, the window opened and two rappelling lines anchored and ready to throw down."

"Cool."

Alex moved over to the window beside him and picked up the rifle.

"Lots of dust on the sills," Nick commented. "Either we clean it off or we'll have to hide the marks from the bipods."

Alex snorted. "Anything recently cleaned in this office would be a huge red flag. How about using a few of these files?" He picked up a handful of manila folders holding what looked at a glance to be résumés and headshots, presumably of actors. Based on the clothing and hairstyles, they were decades old—or auditioning for a period piece from the 1980s. "We can lay them on top of the dust. They may make marks, but it's plausible that whoever works here might lay files on these wide sills from time to time."

"Works for me." Nick carefully placed a couple of the folders on the broad sill, while Alex did the same at the other. They slid the windows open just enough to extend the tips of their rifles, and cold air streamed in. It felt good on Nick's face and dispelled a bit of the stale odor that clung to this place.

The auction started, and the activity calmed down behind the warehouse. The food and waiters were all inside, and the art would be rolling through the warehouse like an assembly line.

Nick said reflectively, "This is weird, having a buddy in a shooting nest."

"I know. Right?" Alex added, "What do you usually think about while you're waiting for a target to show up?"

"Truth?"

"Of course."

"I plan the house I'm going to build when I retire. I design the garden, furnish it, the whole thing."

"What does it look like?" Alex asked.

"It's not fancy. Just a farmhouse. Big porch. Comfortable rooms. Furniture you can live on. The kind of kitchen people want to gather in. You know, sit around and talk while someone cooks."

"Was your childhood home like that?"

Nick snorted. "Hardly. I grew up in a piece-of-crap shack a strong wind would've blown over. Only garden my mom grew was a stand of marijuana out back. Until my older brother discovered it. Then my dad burned it down." He added dryly, "Only time I ever got high. My brother and sister and I all ran out back and breathed in as much of that smoke as we could."

Alex chuckled.

"How about you? What do you think about when you're sitting in a hide?" Nick asked.

"Sometimes I think about the family I'd like to have someday."

"Oh yeah? What does that look like?" Nick asked with interest.

"I picture me and my husband. He's a nice guy. Happy. A homebody. Doesn't know anything about my past and doesn't care. Loves kids. Likes to cook."

Nick winced. He was none of those things. "I've never been around kids, so I can't say if I like them or not."

"Do you put a spouse and some kids in your imaginary farmhouse?" Alex asked.

"Sometimes," he admitted reluctantly.

"What's your perfect spouse like?"

Nick frowned. "I don't know. Hot, I guess."

Alex laughed. "That's it? Your only requirement in a life mate is that they be hot?"

Truthfully, he didn't like to think about a person who would never exist. He blurted, "I don't actually see myself living past my career. I figure I'm gonna die in the harness. Why get all worked up over hopes and dreams that are never going to happen?"

"Note to self—Nick is neither nice nor happy. He's not a homebody, hates cooking and is undecided about kids. He knows everything about me and my job…and only cares if a guy is hot." Alex added wryly, "Yep. You and me—we're a match made in heaven."

Nick frowned. "Yes, but you're hot. From my end of this equation, we'd get along just fine."

Alex laughed lightly. "Sorry. My standards extend beyond how much I enjoy looking at you and the fact that we'd be fantastic in the sack together."

"You like looking at me?"

"C'mon. You know you're a good-looking man. You don't need me to tell you so," Alex retorted.

"And you think we'd be fantastic in bed together?" Nick asked before he could stop the question from slipping out.

"I know it," Alex said firmly.

"What makes you so sure?"

"Because I know what I'm doing, and you're a trainable monkey."

Nick snorted with laughter. "Hah! I have a ton more experience with sex than you. I'm the one who'd be showing you a trick or two."

"Care to place a wager on that?"

Nick actually lifted his eye away from his rubber gun sight to glance over his shoulder at Alex. "Sure, but would I want to win that bet or lose it?"

Alex had also looked up from his weapon. "Depends on whether you prefer to give pleasure or receive it, I suppose."

"I like to do both," he answered frankly. "Where's the fun in sex if your partner isn't having as good a time as you are?"

Alex made no comment. Instead, he reached up to his right ear and pulled out a small, wireless earbud. He held it out toward Nick. "Here. Listen. The auction has started."

Nick popped the device in his ear. A man was speaking. "I have sixteen thousand. Do I have seventeen? Sixteen thousand for the Tiffany earrings. Going once. Going twice. Sold. To bidder number 192."

"Is this the actual auction, like in real time?" Nick asked, startled.

"Yes. There's a wireless feed of it for sellers and remote bidders to log into. I hacked the link before we left the apartment."

"Sweet."

Nick listened as a piece of art was being bid on. It was from some painter he'd never heard of. It sold for just over twenty thousand dollars.

"I thought auctioneers talked really fast," Nick remarked.

Alex replied, "Not at fancy auctions like this one. There's no need to. I expect only a hundred or so pieces will be auctioned off tonight, so there's no hurry to get through it all. Plus, bidders like these here won't get swept up in the excitement of it all and pay more than they intend to for anything. It's probably more effective for the auctioneer to speak normally so everyone can understand the dollar amounts getting thrown around."

"I assume the gold statue will sell last?" Nick asked.

"For sure."

One by one, the other works of art sold. As the sale progressed, the prices climbed higher and higher.

And then it was time. Nick recognized Otto's voice, personally announcing, "And now, the piece we've all been waiting for. Yuri and I are proud to offer for sale a gold statue of a Persian warrior riding a horse. I'm pleased to announce we received papers earlier today confirming this statue to belong to the Magi Crèche."

Over his earbud, Nick heard the collective gasp from the crowd.

Another voice became audible, yelling, "This statue is a fake! The Iranian regime had copies made of the crèche and let them be stolen to hide the fact that the original is still in the hands of the government! I'm one of the artists who was paid to make the copies. I escaped Iran before the government could kill me to silence me…"

The last sentence or two got fainter and harder to hear as the shouter was clearly pulled out of the auction room and struggled against Otto's security men.

An audible buzz of consternation rose from the crowd.

"Was it enough?" Nick asked. "Will Otto suspend the sale?"

Alex shrugged. "We'll find out in the next few seconds."

Otto's voice rose over the crowd noise, calling, "We will be happy to let the buyer examine the provenance

documents and have his or her own independent investi-
gator verify the authenticity of the statue. Of course, we
guarantee the product and will offer a full refund if the
buyer is not satisfied at the findings. Settle down. Settle
down. Let's get the bidding started. Mr. Abdow? If you'd
like to take over and start the auction?"

The auctioneer's smooth voice returned to Nick's ear.
"I'll start the bidding at ten million dollars. I have twenty.
Thirty. Forty. Do I have fifty million?"

Nick listened in awe as the bidding quickly spun up
toward one hundred million dollars. "Dang. Gray sure
knew what to steal to pay for a nice retirement."

"No kidding," Alex muttered. Then, "I've got movement at the back of the warehouse."

"Gray?" Nick bit out. He was staring down at the alley
and couldn't risk moving his weapon too much to peer
over toward the warehouse. He would have only a second or two as it was to make any corrections, take final
aim and pull the trigger.

"Unknown—I recognize one of his guards. Two men
have come out. They're clearing the alley." A pause. "The
vehicle should pull up any second—"

Nick spied two pairs of headlights swing into the far
end of the alley. "Got it. Gray will move fast."

"He'll be moving faster once I shoot at him," Alex
murmured.

"Don't hit him by accident."

"You do know what I do for a living, right?"

Smiling a little, Nick took a long, slow breath, willing
his heart rate to slow. Time to go to work. Another longer, slower breath, with emphasis on drawing out the ex-
halation. His humor drained away. Only the utterly still,
calm presence of Alex beside him registered. And then,
even Alex stopped registering. Everything else ceased

to exist. It was just him, the cold steel against his cheek, the circular view through his gun sight of the alley and the approaching SUV.

"Target acquired," Alex said quietly. He, too, was already into his shooting sequence, controlling heart rate and breathing to make sure his shot was steady. "Ready. Aim."

Nick braced himself for the sound of Alex's rifle firing beside him. They'd decided not to use sound suppressors since the idea was to scare the crap out of Gray and not actually kill him tonight.

Bang.

Bang.

Bang.

Wow. Alex was fast at lining up shots and taking them.

Nick aimed at the SUV's door window and squeezed his trigger. A spiderweb of cracks exploded across the bullet-resistant glass.

He swung the tip of his rifle slightly to the right and lined up the torso of the bodyguard holding the door. He and Alex had debated whether or not to shoot any of the guards and had ultimately decided to use small caliber rounds and aim for the Kevlar vests all the guards would be wearing. It was always a risk to shoot at a human being. They could move at the last second, turning a safe, nonlethal shot into a deadly one.

He and Alex were outstanding snipers, however, and properly provoking Gray took precedence over a small but calculated risk.

Nick squeezed the trigger and watched the man he'd just shot stagger and right himself.

The alley filled with fast-moving bodies. Gray was shoved into the SUV. One man jumped on top of the spymaster and another slammed the door shut behind them, almost catching Gray's feet in the process.

For good measure, Nick swung his weapon left and put two fast rounds into the bullet-resistant windshield. The first shot left no more than a divot, but the second, placed almost exactly on top of the first, caused a rather satisfying spiderweb to blossom across the whole driver's side of the windshield.

There. Gray's men should feel as if they'd been in a full-on shootout now.

"Pack up," Alex said calmly. "Two hostiles incoming."

Nick noted a pair of Gray's men sprinting away from the SUV, both gripping handguns. They were moving *fast*. He would bet they were mighty pissed off someone was taking potshots at their principal.

As he quickly policed his spent shells and put his rifle in the plastic case beside Alex's, he said urgently, "You hung two ropes, right?"

Alex shot back, "Did you remember to put on your rappelling harness?"

He rolled his eyes as he took Alex's rifle and shoved it in the case. Nick scooped up the rifle case and slung it across his back. Alex headed out to deploy their escape ropes, and he hung back for a second.

Just in case their first two gambits to force Gray to follow them didn't work, he had a third one up his sleeve. One that should point Gray squarely at him and not at Alex.

He shouldn't do this. Alex would kill him if he found out—

Don't overthink it.

He had feelings for Alex and didn't want to see the guy die. That was all this was.

Sure it was. He didn't wake up sweating from erotic dreams of him and Alex in bed together. He didn't find the man endlessly fascinating. He didn't respect Alex's skill at his work more than just about anyone else's. The guy didn't make him laugh. Or think about family, friends and what came after this career of his…

"You coming?" Alex called from across the hall.

Nick propped the envelope he'd prepared earlier on the windowsill Alex had shot out of. The name Harlan Gray was printed on it in large letters. Gray's men couldn't fail to see it sitting there.

He followed Alex across the hall, closing and locking the talent agency's door behind him.

"Footprints," Alex whispered urgently.

Nick looked down and saw he was leaving dusty footprints on the linoleum flooring. He rubbed his shoe back and forth across the floor, obscuring the marks. It was a hasty counter-tracking job, but he doubted Gray's men would stick around to do a full forensic analysis of the scene.

Alex was still, listening, and Nick froze beside him. There. He heard running footsteps on the metal stairs they'd used to come up here. Gray's men were inside the building. Which meant the two of them were clear to head outside.

Nick moved swiftly to Alex's side as he sat on the open windowsill and swung his legs over the ledge to dangle outside.

Nick hooked his rappelling harness on to the second rope and gave the anchor point a hard tug as Alex jumped, disappearing from sight. Nick sat on the same metal window frame, swung his legs out and jumped.

He twisted in midair, contorting his body into a jack-knife. His feet impacted the brick wall, and he pushed off with his legs, swinging out and down, letting the rope slide freely through his gloved hands. Three big jumps and one small one, and his feet hit the ground. He yanked on the thin nylon release rope, and both rappelling line and release rope slithered down, hitting him in the head.

There was no time to be fancy. He gathered up the ropes in a messy armful and took off running behind Alex. They reached the end of the alley and ducked around the corner, out of sight of the building.

Alex stopped and methodically started winding rope around his left hand and elbow. Nick did the same, listening hard as he coiled his own. A few small loops around the middle of the larger ones, and the cords were neatly formed into bundles. Nick stuffed his ropes and Alex's into the rucksack Alex wore, and they took off, walking briskly.

They turned the next corner into a darkened industrial area. They ran then, putting some distance between themselves and the alley. They emerged onto a decently lit street with bars and restaurants, where running would attract attention, and they slowed to a walk again. And so it went. They ran when no one was around to see them; they walked when there were other people present.

When they'd satisfied themselves no one had followed them, only then did they head for home.

In the apartment, Nick sat down on the sofa and opened the rifle case at his feet. He passed Alex one weapon and took out the other. Working in silence, they cleaned the firearms.

"So," Alex asked, "did we piss him off enough to come after us?"

If he was ever going to mention the note, now was the moment. But Nick let it pass. No need to tell Alex that he'd written to Gray, telling his former boss he knew where the team who'd stolen the crate were being held. He'd also intimated that the imprisoned men were being subjected to enhanced interrogation and starting to talk about Gray. He offered to tell him where the men were stashed if Gray would cut him in for a share of the cash proceeds from selling the Magi Crèche.

Gray would lose his mind. Not only would he be desperate to silence Nick's old teammates, there was no way he would be willing to cut Nick in on the fortune. Gray never had been any good at sharing his toys.

Aloud, Nick said, "I would say we've definitely got Gray's full attention. Which means we're no longer hunting. We just became the hunted."

Chapter 14

Alex nodded grimly at Nick's quiet pronouncement. It was one thing to theorize about Harlan Gray wanting them dead—it was another thing altogether to realize that had become a reality. He didn't for one second think this was going to be anything but an all-out fight for their lives going forward. Thank goodness he had Nick at his side—

"Um, Alex. Your decryption thing has a red light flashing on it."

"Good. The last phone is finished. Let's see where the guy who ran away from the fight has traveled over the past few months. Maybe with his info we can narrow down our search area some."

In fact, the fourth man's travel data was significantly different from the other men's. While the others had generally journeyed together, no doubt acting as personal security for Gray, the fourth man had traveled alone. A lot.

Specifically, he'd gone to the same place in Upstate

New York three times in the past half year, and each time, he'd stayed there for exactly a month, with exactly a month in between visits. Like a person would if he were pulling alternating shifts keeping watch over something or someone.

Alex commented, "Looks like this guy wasn't part of Harlan's personal cadre until recently."

Nick nodded. "Do you suppose he was guarding the crate of statues?"

"Maybe. Where do his coordinates put him each time he parks for that long?"

Nick typed in his phone for a moment. "Place called Pleasant Falls, New York. It's several hours north of here by car if the roads are clear of snow."

"Good spot to stash a valuable item. Not far from a big city where it can be sold, but not so close that anyone would look for it there," Alex remarked.

"I gather we're heading up that way in the morning?" Nick asked.

"Great minds think alike." Alex searched on the laptop for places to stay near Pleasant Falls. A list of local bed-and-breakfasts in and around the picturesque town popped up. He spotted a sprawling white farmhouse with a big porch called the Pleasant Run Inn. It looked just like the place Nick had described wanting to retire in.

Alex pulled up the availability of rooms at the inn. It only had one room vacant for the next two weeks, but it was the honeymoon suite. It would have a big bed, if nothing else. He booked the room. "I got us a place to stay in Pleasant Falls."

"Cool. I just rented us a car."

Alex asked in alarm, "Did you use a clean alias? One Gray wouldn't know?"

Nick smirked. "I may be hot, but I'm not stupid."

Alex looked around the tiny flat. "I'm gonna miss this place and all its Christmas cheer."

"Should we take the bullets off the Christmas tree?" Nick asked doubtfully.

"Nah. Anyone who comes here will appreciate the décor theme."

"I never did ask. Is this a CIA safe house?"

"Don't ask, and I won't tell," Alex answered cryptically. The people he worked for preferred not to be named, and honestly, he wasn't entirely sure who *they* worked for. He just knew they were the final decision-making authority when it came to sanctioning American assets who needed to be forcibly removed from the field. He didn't ask who they were, and they didn't offer up any information to him. When they gave him an address and told him he could hide there, he took them at their word and asked no questions.

"Are you finally going to agree to share the mattress with me tonight?" Nick asked as he stripped off his shirt and kicked off his shoes.

"If you'll quit undressing any more, I might," Alex retorted. He removed his shoes and set them neatly in front of the sofa, laces loosened and ready to be stepped into fast. He laid out clean jeans, a cotton button-down shirt and clean underwear, as well.

"Are you always that anal-retentive about arranging your clothes?" Nick asked, curious.

"If we have to make a fast getaway, I'm going to do it fully dressed. You're going to end up running down the fire escape in your undershorts because you can't lay your hands on any clothes," Alex replied dryly.

Nick sighed. "I'm usually more careful about such things, but the past few days have been a little nuts."

"You don't say."

Alex was gratified when Nick reached for his shoes and fixed the laces so they'd be easy to don. He even put out his clothes beside Alex's on the sofa. Wow. Was he actually having a positive influence on Nick? Would wonders never cease?

He stretched out beside Nick on the mattress in the dark, unsure of what to expect. They really needed to stay focused on Gray for now.

But that didn't mean he had to like it.

When this thing was over, there was going to be a lot less sleeping going on when the two of them lay side-by-side in a bed like this.

The next morning dawned gray and cold, with snow flurries swirling in the air. Nick left to fetch the rental car and swing by the tailor's to pick up his second suit.

While he was gone, Alex wiped down all the surfaces fingerprints could be lifted from and used a hand-held vacuum to pick up any stray hairs around the place. When Nick texted that he was three minutes out, Alex hoisted their bags and gear, carrying the lot downstairs.

He'd just stepped outside when Nick pulled up and double-parked. Alex loaded everything in the trunk of the car while a cabbie behind them yelled at him in colorful Russian. Amused at hearing Nick called an asshole with ears, he hopped in the passenger side.

Nick pulled away from the curb, grinning.

"You speak Russian?" Alex asked.

"No. Why?"

"I thought you were smiling at the things the cab driver was calling you."

"What did he say?"

"Never mind," Alex said.

Nick continued to smile as he guided the car onto

the entrance ramp for a freeway that would take them north out of the city. "What are you so happy about over there?" Alex demanded. "Nobody likes driving in this congestion."

"We're going on our first road trip together."

"With a vicious killer on our tails."

"Details, schmetails," Nick said jovially.

Alex shook his head. "How long before he comes after us, do you think?"

"Oh, he's already after us. The question is, how soon will he find us?"

"What's your guess?"

"Depends on how many favors he calls in. I rented this car under a new alias that only got built for me a few weeks back. Gray won't attach it to me."

"How can you be sure of that?"

"Because the Medusas created it for me, and Gray doesn't have direct access to anyone who works with them. The military keeps the Medusas tightly compartmentalized and hidden away from regular Special Forces' teams."

"Why's that?"

Nick glanced over at him. "The fewer people who know the United States has women special operators, the more effective the Medusas are in the field."

"I can see that. If nobody's looking for women agents, they could move around freely without arousing suspicion."

"Exactly."

"How long have these women been around?" Alex asked, curious.

"No idea. You'd have to ask them."

"I'd love to meet them someday."

"Maybe you will. They're pretty sharp. More physical

than you can believe and superbly trained. What they lack in brute strength, they make up for with smarts and teamwork. They're fun to run with."

The snow of the past few days had been cleared off the highway and was piled in black, half-melted piles along the shoulder of the road. It looked more like sludge than snow.

But as they cleared the urban sprawl of New York City and headed upstate, the snow piles became taller and whiter and the amount of snow coating the forests along the highway increased markedly.

The north-south line of mountains in the state of New York was divided roughly in half by the Mohawk River, which ran west to east. South of the Mohawk Valley were the Catskill Mountains, and north of the valley rose the Adirondacks. It was to those they headed.

Pleasant Falls lay roughly midway between Albany and Lake Placid, where the mountains started to get tall, and the snow became a thick blanket of white covering everything from trees to building roofs to parked cars.

It took them just under four hours to spot a sign pointing toward Pleasant Falls and Great Neck. As Nick turned west toward the town, on a two-lane road that wound up into the mountains, Alex looked around in delight. "There must be three feet of snow on the ground!"

"Let's hope the roads are plowed all the way to the place you've booked for us."

Alex grinned. "You're a big, strong guy. You can push the car while I sit inside and steer it."

"Hah! I'll steer and you can push!"

"How about we don't get stuck?" Alex suggested.

The road curved through thick forest. The black, bare-branched deciduous trees gave way to stands of fluffy evergreens wearing thick layers of snow that reminded Alex of extravagantly frosted cupcakes.

They crossed over a mountain pass, and the road began to wind down into a narrow valley with a town tucked into it. As they drove down Main Street, Alex looked around in glee.

"Look at all these Christmas decorations! I love this place!"

Nick said grumpily, "This is how I imagine the North Pole—or wherever Santa lives—must look. It's so cheerful and festive I could puke."

Alex laughed, his excitement undimmed by Nick's sour attitude. "Where's that whole going-on-a-road-trip enthusiasm, now? C'mon. Get into the spirit of the holidays. This place is adorable."

"I don't do adorable."

"You like puppies, don't you? Everyone likes puppies. And they're the most adorable things on earth. Or kittens. Or cute little kids. Also adorable. And then there are hand-knit sweaters. Homemade pies. Christmas cookies—"

"Enough already! If I promise to pretend to enjoy myself, will you stop talking about adorable things?" Nick said in what sounded like real desperation. "You sound like that song in the *Sound of Music* about favorite things."

"I love that song!"

Nick rolled his eyes. "Of course you do."

"I'll stop talking about adorable things if you'll give this place a chance to win you over."

"Oh God. You're going to make me drink hot chocolate with little marshmallows and peppermint sticks in it, aren't you?"

"You bet. And we're going Christmas shopping, and looking at lights, and maybe even going caroling."

"I do *not* sing," Nick said forcefully.

"You don't sing, *yet.*"

"You're killing me, here."

"The inn should be just ahead, on the right," Alex said, smiling in spite of himself. They might be different in many ways, but they were alike in all the ways that counted. It was a little crazy how well they fit each other.

The quaint shops gave way to big, old Victorian houses. They were all beautifully restored, colorful and covered in elaborate gingerbread trim.

Alex exclaimed, "This place looks like a postcard!"

"Great. I always did want to die inside a smarmy greeting card," Nick grumbled.

Alex just laughed and didn't try to contain his delight over this town and truth be told, his delight at being here with Nick.

A sign announced that they'd arrived at the Pleasant Run Inn. Nick turned into the driveway, and Alex watched him closely for a reaction as the big white farmhouse with its wraparound porch and welcoming, casual air came into view.

Nick glanced over at him, looking startled. The expression in his eyes went softer than Alex had ever seen it.

"You picked this place for me, didn't you?" Nick murmured.

"I did."

"Fine. I admit it. This is perfect."

Alex shrugged modestly. "I figure if we're gonna die up here, we might as well enjoy ourselves first."

Nick snorted. "And on that optimistic note, the two idiots arrive at their destination."

Alex grinned. "Wait till you see the room I've reserved for us."

They walked inside, and an elderly woman greeted

them with big hugs as if they were her long-lost grandkids. "I'm Jeanette Tucker, and you must be Nick and Alex. I'm so delighted you're here. Your room is ready. Goodness. Look at all those bags. We'd better take the elevator."

"This place has an elevator?" Alex asked.

"My great-grandfather was a close friend of Elisha Otis. He's the fellow who introduced elevators to New York City. Elisha and his wife had a summerhouse just down the street. Mr. Otis installed an elevator here when my great-grandmother had a stroke."

"Nice," Alex commented. It wasn't a huge elevator, and the three of them and their pile of bags had to take turns using it. But in a few minutes, they all had been duly deposited on the second floor in a wide, gracious hallway.

"The honeymoon suite is this way," Jeanette said, leading the way toward the back of the house. "It has a lovely view of the pond and the woods behind the house. It's very peaceful."

Nick's eyebrows all but disappeared in his hairline. Alex grinned at him unapologetically.

Jeanette asked, "How long have you two been married? Are you actually on your honeymoon?"

"What makes you think we're a couple?" Alex blurted, surprised.

"I see how you look at each other. And the way you stand close. It's as if there's a gravitational pull between you. Of course you're a couple. The love between you is plain as day to see. My Edgar and I had it, too."

Alex glanced over at Nick, startled. Nick looked about as disconcerted as him. But neither one of them contradicted her.

In minor shock, he carried his luggage and gear bag after the diminutive woman.

"How many rooms does this place have?" Nick asked, curious.

"I have four guest rooms. The house itself has seven bedrooms if you count the old servants' quarters on the fourth floor. But I use both of those rooms for storage nowadays."

"How many bathrooms?" Alex asked.

"Six. My husband added a few more when we converted this place to an inn so every room would have its own."

"This house is great," Nick said with what sounded like genuine admiration.

"It's too much for me to handle anymore. I really ought to sell it, but I can't bring myself to let go of all the memories."

Nick said gently, "Have you considered hiring a manager to run the place for you?"

She smiled sadly. "Young people nowadays don't want to live in a quiet little backwater like Pleasant Falls. I haven't had any luck finding someone who is interested in the slow pace of life around here, let alone in running an old inn for an old lady."

"I don't know," Nick said warmly. "I think this place is pretty wonderful."

"Do you have children? Grandchildren? Anyone you can leave the place to?" Alex asked.

"I have a daughter who lives in England—she married a doctor over there—and my son is a stockbroker. He lives in New York City and has no desire to come back here. They're good to me, but they have no interest in this old house. Both of them just see dollar signs when they look at it."

Alex ran his fingertips across the glossy surface of a beautiful console table. It looked like old mahogany inlaid with a lighter wood. Maybe maple. It was a gorgeous piece of furniture. In fact, everywhere he looked he saw beautiful antiques, lovingly cared for.

Jeanette opened the door at the end of the hall and threw it wide to reveal a large room with a king-size bed tucked off to the left. To the right, a huge river-stone fireplace rose to the ceiling. A sofa and a pair of chairs clustered in front of it.

"The fireplace burns wood," their hostess said. "There's a fire laid, and you can light it whenever you'd like. I only ask that you be sure to check that the screen is closed anytime you leave a fire unattended. There's plenty of wood in the bin there. Spare towels and blankets are in the armoire, and if you don't like the pillows, I have several different kinds in the hall closet. Let me know if there's anything else you need."

Nick said politely, "When is supper, Miss Jeanette?"

The elderly woman preened a little and then laughed warmly. She seemed to like the moniker. "I'll bet strapping young men like you are hungry all the time. The sideboard in the dining room always has snacks on it. Help yourselves anytime. Breakfast is from eight to ten a.m. every morning, and supper is served promptly at six o'clock. Don't be late, though, or there won't be any food left."

"Yes, ma'am," Nick replied, smiling broadly.

Alex also smiled. There was something truly wonderful about having a grandmotherly woman fussing over them like this. It felt like home. Or at least an idealized version of what he imagined a perfect home would feel like.

Now that he thought about it, his had always had a vague sensed of strained politeness to it. Had that been about him being gay? Had his family really been that tense about it? At least Miss Jeanette didn't seem to be the least bit bothered by the fact.

The woman left and Alex went over to the window. The view of a frozen pond tucked in the trees was as bucolic as the rest of this place.

"The honeymoon suite?" Nick said from behind him.

"It was the only room available. And I figured it would have a big bed we would both fit in."

Nick looked askance at the king-size bed and back at him, his expression dire. "Do you think this is a good idea?"

"I don't think it's a terrible idea," he answered evenly. Although, given how heavily Nick was frowning at the moment, maybe he was wrong about that.

Nick just shook his head.

Alex didn't rise to the bait. They could argue about the sleeping-arrangement issue later. Right now, he wanted to go out and explore.

"I'm going out," Alex announced.

"Let me guess. You spotted some adorable boutique you just have to go check."

Alex answered dryly, "I was thinking more in terms of scoping out places to hide around town, ingress and egress points, good spots for shootouts, and places I don't want to get trapped in. And, of course, establishing our cover. But, sure. If you want to go shopping and check out the local boutiques, I'm up for that, too."

Nick snorted.

"Let me grab my coat," Alex said.

"You might want to grab a sidearm while you're at it," Nick remarked. "From here on out, we need to be ready at all times to get jumped."

"And there went all the joy. Sucked out of the room and replaced with a giant cloud of *bah-humbug*."

"Just keeping it real, man."

"Lighten up. We've got at least a few days to relax and enjoy this place before the boogeyman arrives. Weren't you telling me just last night that I have to learn to let down my hair a little?"

"What hair? You practically have a buzz cut going."

"Says the guy doing his best to imitate a caveman."

"Hah."

"Hah!"

Chapter 15

No way was Nick going to admit to Alex how much he was enjoying walking around Pleasant Falls. The long street through town was lined with dozens of little stores, each one more interesting and adorable than the next. He wasn't much of a shopper, but he got a kick out of watching Alex browse through the eclectic mix of décor, clothes, crafts and tchotchkes being offered for sale.

He was still reeling from Jeanette's declaration that he and Alex loved each other. Did they? Surely not. Except…

Except he felt wildly protective of Alex. And if he stopped to admit it to himself, he felt an underlying panic at the idea of Alex dying at the hands of Gray and his thugs. Was it weird that he didn't much care about dying himself if Alex just made it out of the coming confrontation alive? Was that love?

Or maybe love was the random flashes of the future he and Alex could have together. They could settle down in a place exactly like this. Take over running an inn exactly like Jeanette's. They could have a few kids, fill that big house with laughter, family and friends.

A family of his own. He hardly dared think of it. And certainly not with the threat of Gray hanging over him and Alex. But still. The idea would not get out of his head. Was Jeanette right? Had he found a man he could achieve all his most closely held dreams with? The same dreams whose existence he barely admitted to, even to himself?

The SEALs had always been his family. The guys in his platoon had been like brothers to him, and the married guys' wives had adopted him and the other single guys, inviting them over for home-cooked meals and holiday get-togethers. Sure, it had been fun, but it hadn't been the same as having a family of his own. One with real love, who would be there for him through thick and thin.

Alex found a handmade stuffed toy for his niece, and his whole face lit up at the cute pink lemur. "Natalie's going to love this. She's bonkers for lemurs."

"Aren't lemurs black-and-white?" Nick asked doubtfully.

"This is a magic lemur," Alex said stoutly. He smiled down at the soft toy fondly, and Nick's gut twisted. How nice would it be to have someone look at him like that?

Correction: How nice would it be to have Alex look at him like that?

The thought shocked him. It was just that big old farmhouse playing tricks with his head. It was so identical to the one he pictured retiring in that it was making him think about starting his own family. And Alex just happened to be here with him, staying in the charming inn with him, chattering on about his family, telling stories about funny gifts he and his siblings had gotten for one another over the years.

Still. Jeanette had sounded so sure of herself when she'd declared them to be in love.

It was a Sunday afternoon, and the sidewalks were crowded. As they approached the middle of town and the big town square, families were gathering there in anticipation of some event.

Alex asked a shopkeeper, "What's going on outside?"

"The annual snowball fight is about to get started. You should go join in. It's great fun."

Alex looked over at him with such excitement and hope in his eyes that Nick couldn't resist. He grumbled, "Okay, fine. I'm in. Let's go."

The shopkeeper said helpfully, "You can leave your shopping bags here if you'd like. I'll keep an eye on them for you."

They deposited Alex's bags with the woman and headed outside.

As they stepped into the large, open space, a man with a bullhorn shouted, "Pick your sides, folks, and start making ammunition. Same rules as always. Snowballs must be made only of snow. Don't throw them hard at children, and for you adult kids, if any child under the age of six hits you with one, you are required to execute your best dramatic death fall. As soon as the kiddo laughs, you are allowed to get back up and rejoin the fight. When you get tired of the fun, back up and move to stand on the sidewalk around the square. People who've removed themselves from the fight are off-limits as targets. Of course, if you're on the sidewalk, it's still up to you to dodge errant snowballs. The contest continues until there's no more snow, or until everyone is on the sidewalk."

"Death falls?" Nick muttered to Alex.

"I can't wait to see yours," Alex said back, grinning.

"Personally, I'm planning to clutch my chest, spin around, stagger a little, and then splat face-first in a drift."

Nick grinned. "To see that, I might just nail you with a friendly fire snowball."

"You're not under the age of six," Alex retorted.

"If I act like a five-year-old, will you still die for me?"

Alex rolled his eyes. "That's it. I'm finding some little kid, picking him up and carrying him over to ambush you. Prepare to die, Kane."

"You wish, Creed."

And that was how they ended up on opposite sides of the snowball fight, running around like maniacs, picking up little kids under the armpits and chasing each other around the town square while the kids laughed hysterically and clobbered Nick and Alex with packed snow from a range of about two feet.

The pratfalls were epic, and he and Alex were covered in white by the end of the snowball fight. It stuck to their coats and pants. Their wool gloves were soaking wet and caked in snow, even their hair stuck up in wet spikes thick with the stuff. Alex's scarf looked like a white rope draped over his shoulders, and Nick was pretty sure his boots were both filled with snow.

The fight ended and a mighty cheer went up from all the participants. Nick found Alex, who threw an arm around his waist and dragged him close for a laughing kiss. Their lips were icy cold, but the heat between them changed that fast.

"Thanks for playing with me," Alex murmured against his mouth.

"That was fun."

"I love seeing you laugh," Alex admitted, leaning back to look up at him, his eyes shining.

"Ditto, Creed. Ditto."

"Really? Ditto? That's all you've got? My dude, you need to seriously up your romantic banter game."

"How about this? I can't wait to get you back to that giant bed in our room, get naked and kiss you again."

Alex gulped. He *never* gulped. Last time he could remember gulping, he was about fourteen years old and his first crush had just admitted to having a crush on him, too.

Very belatedly, he mumbled, "Well, okay then. That's better, Kane."

Nick grinned and threw his arm across Alex's shoulder as they headed off the snowball battlefield.

They headed toward the store where they'd stashed Alex's bags, but before they got to it, they encountered a food cart selling hot chocolate and soft pretzels. Nick groaned.

"There's no escaping my holiday cheer," Alex declared. "Deal with it."

They bought steaming cups of hot chocolate and sipped at them as they strolled toward the store. The salty pretzels were the perfect counterpart to the sweetness of the drink. They finished the snack and threw away their cups.

"Admit it. That was tasty," Alex said.

"It was."

"Are you willing to admit that you're having fun getting into the holiday spirit?"

"As long as you don't make me sing, I will so stipulate."

Alex grinned at him and ducked into the store to get his bags. As he came back out onto the sidewalk, Nick asked, "What's next in our holiday tour of Christmas spirit?"

"The shopkeeper told me there's a terrific diner just down the street. Also, every night at seven, the town Christmas tree is lit, followed by caroling on the square."

Nick rolled his eyes. "Of course there is."

"The diner allegedly serves the best burgers and milk-shakes in town. Tell me the last time you had a real short-order burger and a handmade milkshake with real ice cream."

Nick thought back, startled. "I can't remember."

"There you are. To the diner we go."

The place was crowded, and they had to wait for a booth. But when the burgers came, piled high with fixings, the rest of their plates filled with crispy, hand-cut French fries, Nick had to admit that this had been a terrific idea. And the thick, creamy chocolate milkshake abruptly made him remember an outing with his grandmother to an old-fashioned drive-in restaurant.

He mentioned it to Alex, who asked, "How old were you when you went out with her?"

"Six or seven, maybe. It would've been the same year we made the Christmas cookies. She died the next summer."

"Is that the last time you were happy? When she was alive?"

Nick stared across the tiny table at Alex. "What even is that?"

"Really? You don't know what happiness is?" Alex looked around the restaurant full of smiling, talking people. "This is it. Being somewhere nice with someone you love being with, doing something relaxing and fun. Happiness is all the small moments in life that make it good. You try to string as many of them together as you can in between the sucky moments that are also inevitable in life. But when the good ones come, you work hard to make a memory of them for later. That way, when the bad times come, memories of the good times remind you to be patient and wait for happiness to come back around."

"That is possibly the most Pollyanna, saccharine bullshit I've ever heard," Nick declared.

Alex stared at him. "You don't ever think back on good times? You know, to give yourself a little pep talk?"

"No!"

"How do you get through awful missions, then? When you're soaking wet and freezing cold or thirsty and burning hot. You haven't had a bath or slept in days. The bad guys outnumber and outgun you. Who or what do you fight for, then?"

Frowning, he considered Alex's question. "For my teammates, I guess."

"Yeah, but they betrayed you. Who will you fight for, now?"

"I don't know."

"Well, you'd better figure that out, and fast, because we're about to be in a battle for our lives. And when the bullets are flying over our heads is not the time for you to work it out. I'll need you one hundred percent engaged in the fight."

Nick stared at Alex, his mental wheels turning in a direction he should've seen coming but which still stunned him into stillness.

"What?" Alex asked. "You want to say something. What is it?"

"Us. I'll fight for us."

It was Alex's turn to go stock-still. His gaze went wide, then warmed and softened. He reached across the table and laid his hand on top of Nick's scarred, callused hand. He said simply, "I'll fight for you, too."

And there it was. Exactly what Jeanette had seen between them. The irresistible pull, like gravity between two suns orbiting each other. Nick felt it all the way down to his bones. This man was the one.

But he had no idea whatsoever what to do about it.

Was he supposed to say something about it to Alex? Wait for Alex to come to the same conclusion and say something about it to him? Was it a mutual thing? What if Alex didn't feel the same way?

And that was what silenced him. He couldn't bear the idea of baring his soul to Alex and having the man say something awkward like "thank you" or "the timing isn't right for me."

Distracted, he let Alex pay for the meal after extracting a promise from him that Nick would get the next one.

Alex picked up the check and slid out of the booth, grinning. "You do realize we're both on expense accounts from the same government agency, right?"

Nick shrugged. "It's the principle of the thing."

"You're going to want your own checking account even when you're married, aren't you?" Alex tossed out.

Nick stared at Alex's back for a moment before lurching into motion to follow him toward the cash register. Him? Married? A joint checking account? That was possibly the most domestic thing he'd ever heard of. But having thought about it, now it sounded like the most wonderful thing on earth. He absolutely wanted a joint checking account.

What the hell had happened to him? One sweet old lady declared him in love, and the solitary man he'd known and lived inside his head with for his entire life had done an abrupt about-face on everything he'd ever believed having to do with love and relationships.

"C'mon. There's a crowd gathered around the tree at the edge of the square," Alex said eagerly.

Nick allowed himself to be dragged along by the hand, enjoying Alex's unbridled excitement indulgently. What would the people around them think if they knew one of the most lethal men on the planet was beside them, grinning like a little kid as the Christmas tree lights flashed on and sparkled like stars captured in a tree's branches?

A group of men, women and children stepped up beside the tree and began singing "We Wish You a Merry Christmas."

People around them joined in, and before long, most of the crowd was belting out holiday classics.

Nick caved when "Silent Night" started up, singing the solemn carol quietly beside Alex. He reached out to take Alex's hand in his, and they stood there, shoulder to shoulder in the crowd, their voices rising in harmony toward the black sky sprinkled with stars that matched the tree before them.

It was a magical moment.

When the song ended, everyone was quiet for a few breathless seconds, absorbing the beauty of it all.

And then the carolers burst into "Jingle Bells," and the spell was broken.

Nick knew he had a problem. His holiday-hater's heart had done the whole redeemed-Grinch thing and grown several sizes inside his chest today. He loved being here with Alex. He loved all the schlocky Christmas stuff around him. And he loved Alex.

He was *so* screwed.

Chapter 16

Alex smiled over at Nick as the crowd around them began to disperse. No doubt about it—he loved everything about this town and all its silly, romantic holiday rituals. Someday. Someday he would live in a place just like this, heck, maybe this place. And he would immerse himself in family, friendship and every ridiculous, wonderful town tradition.

"A dog," he declared suddenly. "I want a dog."

"Right now?" Nick blurted, sounding surprised.

"No. When I retire and move here."

"What kind of dog?"

"A big friendly one."

"Like a golden retriever?" Nick asked.

"Maybe. But with all this snow, maybe a husky?"

"They're pretty high-maintenance."

Alex shrugged. "What else am I going to have to do with my time besides pamper a high-maintenance dog?"

"Maybe pamper your high-maintenance partner?" Nick suggested.

Alex grinned. "I'll have time for both."

Nick said thoughtfully, "I could see you with a dog. You were great with those kids in the snowball fight."

"So were you!" he exclaimed. Truth be told, he was more than a little surprised at how natural Nick had been, scooping up little kids and chasing him around the town square with them. He would never forget the unfettered joy on Nick's face. It had transformed him from someone dark and dangerous to a much younger, lighter version of himself.

He made a mental note to get Nick to laugh much more often.

Nick said low, "How about we return your gifts to the inn and then go out and do a little reconnaissance?"

"What did you have in mind?"

"Maybe finding wherever Gray has the rest of the crèche stored?"

Alex sighed. Today had been a delightful interlude, but real life called. It was time to buckle down and get back to work. "You're right. The faster we find it, the sooner we can set up surveillance on it."

Nick shrugged. "Actually, I was thinking about stealing it."

"I beg your pardon?"

"Can you think of a better way to infuriate Gray and throw him off-balance?"

Alex stared. "It's bold. Are you sure you want him enraged when he comes for us?"

Nick shrugged. "He's brilliant and calculating when he's calm. I figure he can't be any scarier when he's so mad he can't see straight."

"Have you ever seen him mad?" Alex asked, surprised.

Men like them tended to be icy-cold operators when the chips were down.

"No. I haven't. That's why I think it might be an interesting gambit to infuriate him."

Alex nodded. "I like it. Let's go find that crèche and liberate it."

They had the latitude and longitude coordinates from Gray's man's phone, and it turned out to correspond to a fenced lot full of storage units. The trick would be figuring which one the crèche was in.

"What do you say we set up a hide in those trees above and behind the lot?" Alex suggested.

Nick nodded. "Should we take turns pulling shifts around the clock, or should we both stay here?"

"Let's spend a few hours here together and get a feel for the flow of traffic, and then we can decide."

Nick nodded. He pulled his field knife out of its ankle sheath and commenced hacking at low-hanging pine boughs on trees around them. Alex gathered the cut branches and poked their larger ends into the ground at an angle. The needled boughs all leaned inward, tent-like. When they lay down on the evergreens, they would act like springs and help hold them up off the cold ground slightly. When they'd built up a thick layer, they spread a heavy plastic tarp Alex fetched from the trunk of their car on top.

Alex gestured for Nick to crawl under the low, bushy tree where he'd built the hide. He followed Nick into the cave-like space. It took a little wiggling around and moving branches that were poking him, but before long, he'd settled comfortably on his stomach next to Nick under an insulated tarp.

Nick passed him a set of binoculars, and he scanned the storage lot below. The place was still and deserted.

Alex murmured, "Do you suppose Gray's man stops by to check the unit on a regular basis? Or does he just stand off like us and keep watch over it from a distance?"

"Given the value of the crèche, I'm betting Gray's guy is paranoid as hell about losing it. He'll check it at least once a day, if not more often. Gray's not the kind of man to be forgiving if you lose his billion-dollar retirement plan."

Alex murmured, "I'll bet he varies up the times of day he checks, it, too."

"If we're lucky, he'll check the storage unit after hours, when nobody's around to see him come and go."

"It's what I would do."

"Let's hope you're right," Nick said low.

They settled into silence, waiting patiently for their quarry to show himself. Alex noted that vehicle traffic along the road in front of the storage lot was light and getting lighter as the evening aged. This was the kind of place where everyone went home and was tucked into bed at a reasonable hour.

After about an hour, Nick murmured, "You do realize we could be back at the inn, sitting in front of a nice fire and relaxing, instead of sitting out here, freezing our...toes...off."

Alex laughed ruefully under his breath. "Don't remind me. Those are the sorts of thoughts I try not to have when I'm on a job and trying not to think about how cold my...toes...are."

Nick's shoulder nudged his fondly, and he nudged back. It was nice being out here together, sharing the misery. The companionship did make the time pass faster and, if nothing else, kept him a little warmer.

A few minutes after ten o'clock, a pickup truck slowed on the road and turned off its headlights. Alex's attention riveted on the vehicle. It rolled into the drive and approached the security gate of the storage lot. He felt Nick go utterly relaxed beside him as if he would melt into the ground. He, too, went perfectly still, becoming one with his binoculars, which he trained on the truck as it pulled into the lot, its lights still off.

The truck drove between rows of storage units and stopped in front of one in the middle. A man climbed out of the truck and lifted the combination lock securing the unit.

Alex strained to see the numbers the guy dialed in. He thought the first number was a few numbers above zero. The second number was approximately halfway around the dial, and the last was maybe ten digits to the right of the second one. It wasn't a lot to go on, but it was better than nothing by a long shot. And maybe Nick had seen more detail. Not that he was going to break silence to ask him right now.

The man removed the lock from the hasp and pushed the door up. The metallic noise was loud in the crystalline silence of the night. He disappeared inside the unit.

Alex started counting in his head. *One potato. Two potato. Three potato...*

The guy came outside in under a minute. Sloppy. Alex doubted he'd even checked nails, bolts, locks or whatever it was that secured the crate.

The man closed and secured the door and climbed into his truck. He drove through the gate, turned on his lights, steered onto the road and drove off.

"Did you recognize him?" Alex asked quietly.

"No."

"Do you think it was one of Gray's guys?"

"Who else would go into a unit, carry nothing in, take nothing out and leave that fast?"

"Fair point."

"I caught the first number of the combination, but then his arm moved, and I didn't see the rest," Nick said.

"Perfect. I got a good idea of how the latter numbers related to the first number, but didn't see the first one specifically."

"Cool. Wanna go break in and have a look inside that unit?" Nick asked.

Alex's gaze narrowed thoughtfully. "I do. But did you notice how cursory his inspection of the crate was?"

"Well, yeah. He was inside about sixty seconds total. Why?"

Alex asked, "What if we steal the crèche?"

"You're sure you're okay with that? It's one thing to talk about it. It's another thing altogether to commit a felony, Mr. Law-and-Order."

"We could return them to their rightful owners. Then it would be repatriation, not theft."

"To the government of Iran?" Nick asked doubtfully.

"Okay, so maybe we should give them to the Smithsonian instead."

Nick nodded briskly in agreement. "Do you want to let Gray know we've stolen his toys, or do you want to let him think the statues are still in the storage unit?"

"I could go either way on that. If we make the theft obvious, he'll show up here within a few hours of the next check on the statues. Can we be ready to take on Gray and his whole team that quickly?"

Nick scrunched up his face. "We could use some reinforcements before we tangle with Gray's entire team."

"We could wait to steal the statues until we're ready to pull the trigger," Alex said reasonably.

Nick glanced down at the quiet storage units. "Thing is, Gray's gotta be spooked. He knows we tracked his car.

We hospitalized one of his guys and demolished three more of them in a fight. We shot at him in the alley. It's possible he'll move the crèche without warning. I say we go in now, take the statues but hide the theft. Then we finish getting ready for a shootout at the OK Corral."

Alex nodded. "It's an aggressive plan. I doubt Gray will see it coming. He's got to be used to everyone being scared stiff of him."

"He is."

"The gear bag in the trunk of the car has wire cutters in it. I'll start snipping through the back fence while you rewire the security system."

Nick pushed to his feet and held a hand down to Alex. He took the proffered hand and rose to his full height in front of Nick, their fists clasped between them.

"In case we die in the next twenty-four hours, I've really enjoyed working with you," Alex murmured. "You're a good man."

Nick stared at him in the thick shadows, but even with his night vision fully adjusted, Alex couldn't make out the expression in his eyes.

"Is that all?" Nick said low, his voice rough.

"Is what all?"

"Is that all you feel for me? Professional respect?"

He stared back at Nick. Was he ready to make a grand declaration of his feelings for this man? In the middle of a mission that was about to go red-hot? It was a terrible idea. They both needed to focus intensely on the fight to come.

"Hell no, that's not all I feel for you," Alex blurted.

"Care to elaborate on that?" Nick said gruffly.

"Not here. Not now, when we've got a job to do."

"Then, when?"

In desperation, Alex answered, "When we get back to the inn."

"I'm holding you to that."

His stomach leaped and twisted nervously. Did he even know how he felt about Nick? Did he have the words to express it, not to mention the courage? What if Nick didn't feel the same way? Would Nick do what Alex's family had done and say all the right things, smile politely and then stab him in the back?

It would kill him if Nick betrayed him. He hadn't felt this way about any man, ever. If he had stripped down naked and rolled around in the snow, he couldn't feel any more exposed. His entire being felt raw. Hypersensitized. Every tiny snowflake that hit his face felt like a needle piercing his skin. Every whiff of breeze felt like a knife slicing through him.

"Well, are you coming or not?" Nick said from a few yards away.

He lurched into motion, following Nick toward where their car was hidden, a hundred feet down the road, behind some bushes. Operating mechanically, he obscured their footprints, being sure that no compressed tracks were left under the layer of snow he swept over their path.

Nick popped open the trunk and unzipped the gear bag. Alex took the handgun Nick passed him, checked the safety, cleared the chamber, popped in a magazine of ammunition and slipped the weapon in the pocket of his coat.

He took the wire cutters as Nick murmured, "I'll meet you at the unit when I'm done disabling the alarm."

Alex pressed the earbud more securely into his ear. "Let me know if you run into any problems."

"Will do."

They headed out to perform their respective tasks.

Alex found a likely spot in the fence, hidden from the front of the lot by a row of storage units. He wished he had a big set of cutters with handles as long as his arm. He would be through this barrier in a matter of seconds. As it was, he had to use both hands to cut through each wire, and it was a painful and tedious process.

He finally rolled back a three-foot-wide by two-foot-tall section of the hurricane fencing and secured it with a length of trip wire.

He lay down on his belly and eased through the gap, being careful not to catch his clothing on any of the sharp ends of the cut wire. He made his way to the correct row and ran down it on the balls of his feet, being careful to hug the building and move only on the bare concrete under the small overhang.

When he reached the unit, he commenced checking the cheap aluminum garage door for alarms. Gray's man hadn't disabled anything from the outside before entering the space, and he'd been inside such a short time Alex doubted he had fiddled with an interior electronic alarm. But there were still plenty of low-tech ways to trap a space to tell if anyone had been in there.

He checked all around the perimeter of the door for hairs or pieces of tape tucked in an inconspicuous place, near a hinge or down near the ground.

The door was clean.

Surely Gray's men weren't that sloppy.

Although, if the guy had been coming here once or twice a day for months and never had a problem, maybe he really had gotten that complacent. Alex mentally tsked. The spotlights at each end of the row abruptly went dark.

Thank you, Nick.

He pressed his ear to the door to listen for any beeps warning of a power interruption to a security system.

All was quiet.

Had Gray really parked upward of a billion dollars' worth of art in a storage unit with no additional protections on it whatsoever?

Maybe that was the point. By not placing any security here at all, Gray was relying on the sheer obscurity of this place and the lack of attention being drawn to it to protect the crèche.

He had to give the man credit for being ballsy. Seriously so.

Satisfied the door wasn't trapped, he pulled out a two-inch-long Cyalume stick and bent it sharply to break the tiny glass divider inside. As the chemicals at each end of the tube mixed, it commenced glowing lime green. He popped the stick into his mouth.

Then he lifted the combination lock and opened his mouth just enough to see the numbers on its face. He tried to release it a few times, with no success.

He said low, "What's the first number?"

"Six. I'll be there in two."

That should give him just enough time to get this lock opened. He dialed in a six and then turned the dial about halfway to the number thirty. He did a full revolution and then stopped at the number forty. He gave a tug. No joy.

He tried again. Six. Thirty-six. Forty-six.

Six. Thirty-eight. Forty-eight.

Click.

Chapter 17

Nick closed the electrical box. It had been a trick to bypass the security system without cutting any wires. But when they were finished here tonight, he needed to reactivate the system and leave no one the wiser that he and Alex had broken in.

He slipped outside the office, eyeing the patch of snow between him and the storage units. He mapped a path using existing footprints and tire tracks and carefully picked his way across. When he reached the units, he slipped under the eaves where there was no snow and ran down the row to the dark shadow standing in front of Gray's unit.

"Any security on the garage door?" he asked Alex.

"None. And I have the lock open."

"Nice."

Alex said low, "Egress point is at the end of the next row. Turn left and go about twenty feet. It's at ground level and tied open."

"Roger that. I'll take the right side. You take the left."

Alex nodded in understanding and reached for the door handle down near the ground. "Ready?"

Nick nodded. "Ready."

Alex slid up the door. The sound was deafening, but there was no help for the metal-on-metal screech.

Nick slipped inside fast, shining his flashlight on the wall just inside the door. Nothing but cinder block. He flashed the light around the small space. He saw no sign of any alarm in here. On the off chance that there might be a microphone hidden in here, he hand-signaled an all clear to Alex, who gave back the same gesture.

Alex pulled out a handheld device and methodically swept it up and down over the walls, looking for electronic signals of any kind. An audio bug, a camera, a radio communication—even the slightest electrical current would register on Alex's meter.

Just in case, Nick took up a position in the doorway, weapon drawn, waiting for any response to the sound of the door opening. He scanned up and down the narrow alley. All was still and quiet.

"Clear," Alex said low from behind him.

Nick eased inside the unit and pulled the door down behind him. "Seriously? He's got no security at all around this stuff?"

Alex replied, "I think that's the point. He's relying on the utter lack of protection to protect it."

"Let's have a look at the crate, then."

It was some six feet long and four feet high. It was perhaps three feet deep from front to back. *At last.* He'd finally found the thing that his team had stolen all those months ago. Raging curiosity to look inside tore through him.

Alex had already run his nifty meter all over the crate,

but Nick did a visual inspection now, looking for wires, sensor pads, even tiny strips of foil between the lid and sides to indicate that the thing was trapped in any way.

"Do you see anything?" Alex asked from behind the crate.

"Not a darned thing. And that's freaking me out a little," Nick confessed.

"Me, too. Still. We've got to open it sometime."

"Maybe you should go stand by the door, just to be safe," Nick suggested.

"We're in this together. If you go down, I'm going down with you," Alex replied with an intensity that sent little shivers of delight down Nick's spine.

"Here goes." He reached for the hasp on the trunk and pulled it open. He lifted the lid a millimeter and propped the lid there by resting it on the tips of two ballpoint pens. He inspected the narrow opening, using his flashlight to look for anything attached to the inside of the lid or hinges.

"I can't believe I'm saying this, but it's all clear."

Alex nodded. "Then, let's open this sucker all the way."

Together, they lifted the heavy lid. Alex opened his mouth and dim green light illuminated the interior of the crate. Inside were dozens of individual cartons tucked into wooden packing shavings.

The boxes looked mostly made of wood, but as he took a closer look, they were elaborately decorated. Some were inlaid with precious metals. Others were crusted with jewels. Some were blackened with age, while others sparkled in the Cyalume lighting.

"Shall we open one?" Alex asked.

"Sure. You pick."

Alex reached for the nearest box and pulled it out carefully. He set it on the floor in front of the crate, and he and Nick knelt in front of it. The thing was flattish and square, only about a foot tall but twice that wide. Alex lifted the lid, and a magnificent gold statue of a man lay in a satin nest before them. The man had a long beard and carried a tall staff with a shepherd's hook atop it. His robes were covered in jewels that formed an elaborate swirling pattern all over the garment.

"I'm guessing another Wise Man," Alex murmured.

"Do we want to take the whole nine yards or just the statues?" Nick murmured.

Alex glanced up at him. "I'm thinking just the statues. The storage boxes are probably where the bulk of the weight comes from. I tried to lift the corner of the crate when I was checking it out, and I don't think the two of us could carry the whole thing out of here."

Nick nodded. "Besides, if Gray's man opens the crate to look inside, we'll want him to see everything where it belongs. I doubt Gray's guy routinely opens anything to actually check on the statues."

"We're going to have to get their cases back in the places they came from, though," Alex said. To that end, Nick watched him snap several quick photos of the interior of the large crate. Good idea. They'd have pictures to check their replaced storage boxes against.

"Let's do this in an orderly fashion," Nick murmured.

"Right. I'll pass the top layer of cartons out, and we can lay them on the floor exactly as they were packed inside the box. We can do that with each layer of cases until we reach the bottom of the crate."

Working together, it didn't take them long to unload the entire thing. In all, there were forty-two smaller boxes inside the larger crate.

Nick looked over at Alex. "Okay. Are you ready to see what the birth of Christ really looked like?"

Alex's chest rose in a visible deep breath. "Let's do this."

They started with the top layer, opening each box carefully and lifting out the statue inside. Working quickly, Alex passed them to him one at a time and then used a knife to cut out some or all of the padding inside. In most of the cases, silk fabric lined the box, and Nick took both statue and raggedly cut length of silk from Alex. Gently, Nick wrapped each figurine and then tucked it into one of the two large storage sacks he'd brought along.

Nick tried not to gawk at each statue as Alex handed it to him, but it was hard not to. Most of them were fully as exquisite as the golden horse and rider that had been auctioned off.

As they reached the final and bottom layer of boxes, though, the quality of the workmanship became less refined, the materials less gaudy. These must be the very first pieces added to the crèche. They'd probably been made by the mystics of the order that originally owned the crèche, and not by wealthy Persian kings.

Alex reached for the last box. It was larger than all the others and made of blackened, cracked wood. It had simple iron bands around it instead of gold and jewels. "I'll bet this is it," he breathed.

Nick glanced up sharply from stowing the previous statue. "You mean the original pieces? The ones carved by the Magi?"

Alex nodded. "We should open this one together."

Nick moved over to kneel beside him. "I've never been a religious man, but I'm nervous."

"I know. Right?"

The hinges on the box were made of leather nailed

into the back of the case and the back of the lid. It had undoubtedly been replaced over the centuries, for it was in reasonably good shape. Still, he and Alex lifted the lid with exceeding care.

The first thing he saw were bits of straw, turned gray with age and brittle. Very gently, Alex scooped aside the gray straw to reveal rough fabric that looked fully two thousand years old. It, too, was gray with age and looked fragile.

"I think that's linen," Alex said breathlessly.

"That would track with biblical fabrics, wouldn't it?" Nick replied in a hush.

"Uh-huh."

"Go ahead. Unfold it." He watched with rapt attention as Alex very gently lifted a fold of the fabric. Another fold. One final fold.

Nick stared down. There, nested in more ancient straw, was the Nativity. The first and only *original* Nativity.

"Wow," Alex breathed.

Wow, indeed. The Nativity was carved from wood, the individual figures smaller than he'd expected. A sheep was probably three inches tall, a donkey maybe four inches tall. A bearded man of middle age, wearing a plain robe, was no more than six inches tall. But the detail was incredible. His face looked weary. Worried. But also protective.

"Is that Joseph?" Nick asked, reaching out reverently to point at the figure.

"I think so. Will you look at Mary? She almost seems alive."

Nick looked at the figure on the opposite end of the crate, a young woman carved in the same incredible detail as Joseph. He said in awe, "She looks so young."

"And tired. Like a new mother," Alex added in wonder.

At last, Nick let his gaze slide to the baby in the center of the box. Something profound moved within him. This depiction of Christ had been made by a man who'd actually gazed on the human face of the Baby Jesus.

The figure of the infant was tiny. Wrapped in a bit of frayed, decaying linen and tucked into one end of a long, low box. The rest of the box held what looked like ancient hay. It was mostly crumbled to dust, but bits of the stalks remained and formed a small pile below where the baby lay.

"The manger doesn't have any legs," Alex said. "It's more like a watering trough."

"Weren't mangers used to feed animals? I should think it would look like a feed trough."

Alex shrugged. "My parents' nativity scene had a little cross-legged thing about the size of a bassinet that depicted the manger. Our Baby Jesus fit in it just about right."

"Welp. Future nativities are going to have to change that," Nick said with light humor.

"I'm afraid to touch the figures," Alex said low. "They're too holy for a guy like me to handle."

He knew the feeling. "Maybe we should just take the whole box. It was packed at the very bottom of the crate. If we put all the other boxes back, we should be able to disguise its absence."

Alex nodded and carefully closed the lid. Nick lifted the heavy wooden box, which weighed a good forty pounds, and carried it over to the sacks. He moved all the other statues over to the second bag, clearing the first just to carry this priceless treasure.

"All right," Alex said briskly. "Let's repack this puppy."

They commenced the challenging job of replacing all the storage containers, now empty, back in their original positions. There was a bit of trouble when they realized they would have to put something else in place of the large nativity box to hold up the ones that had been resting upon it. They experimented with various bits from their gear bag until they hit upon standing both of the binocular cases upright in the bottom of the crate and placing a clipboard across them. The improvised platform was just the right height and strong enough to take the weight of the next layer of storage boxes.

After that, the work of repacking the crate went quickly. They closed the container and headed for the door. Alex bent down to lift it and froze, his hand on the handle by the floor.

"What?" Nick asked quickly.

"Powder. There's powder on the floor, and our footprints are all over the place."

Nick looked down in shock. It was an old spy trick and as simple as they came. On one's way out of a room, a spy sprinkled a fine layer of something like baby powder on the floor and then checked later to see if it had been disturbed.

Alex moved quickly to the back of the unit and dropped to his knees, where he commenced using his neck scarf to wipe the floor clean. Nick left the bags of figures by the door and joined him, unwinding his own scarf and wiping down the faint footprints they'd left all over the floor in the baby powder.

When they'd wiped their way over to the garage door, Alex carefully wiped off the bottoms of his boots while Nick rummaged in various coat pockets until he found a small container of white styptic powder. It was a coagulant sprinkled on superficial wounds to stop them from bleeding. It was the closest thing they had to baby powder.

He watched as Alex worked carefully, sprinkling a

fine layer of the stuff across the floor. Because they hadn't noticed it when they came in, they had no way of knowing where or how much baby powder Gray's man had put down before he'd left the unit the last time. They would just have to hope they got it close enough to the same that the guy didn't notice any discrepancies.

As Alex reached him by the door, Nick pulled the metal panel up about halfway, and they slipped underneath it.

"You get out of here. I'll meet you at the car after I reset the office alarm," Nick murmured.

Alex nodded and took off, cradling the bag with the original Magi Crèche against his chest. Nick headed for the office with the other sack.

It didn't take him long to reactivate the alarm system. As soon as the lights blinked on outside, he sprinted down the row of storage units, turned left and ran hard for the fence, searching as he went for a low hole.

There.

He screeched to halt on his knees and pushed the bulky bag through the hole. Dang it. The bag caught on a wire. He fought grimly to untangle the canvas from a protruding wire. *C'mon, c'mon, c'mon.*

He heard a car approaching on the road. Dammit. It was slowing down. He glanced over his shoulder. It was turning into the parking lot, and its lights were off.

Not good.

Reactivating the alarm had sent a signal to someone that there had been a power interruption.

The bag finally popped free. He shoved it the rest of the way through the fence and crawled frantically after it. His hips had barely cleared the hole when he rolled over on his back, yanked his legs clear and untied the section of fencing. He shoved it down, tucking the edge into the snow. Working fast, he used the length of wire Alex had tied it up with to fasten it down. It didn't want to lie flat, but he had no more time to fix it. A man was getting out of his car and walking toward the office.

Please don't find any evidence of my work and warn Gray.

Nick low-crawled away from the fence, into the woods, pulling himself along on his elbows and taking freezing facefuls of snow that went down the collar of his coat and melted on his chest. He stopped periodically to use a tree branch to mess up his tracks in the snow. He couldn't hide that some critter had come through here, but he could hide the fact that it had been a human.

Finally, the storage lot disappeared into the trees behind him. He pushed upright, slung the bag over his shoulder and took off running through the forest, paralleling the road.

He ought to be about to where the car was hidden, now. He swerved down the steep hillside and charged toward the road as he heard a siren wail in the distance. Crap. They had to get clear of here before the police arrived.

He burst out of the trees practically on top of the hood of the car. He rolled around the side of it and threw open the passenger door. He jumped in and Alex pulled onto the road before he even had his door all the way shut. He turned around and lifted the big bag into the back seat, setting it down as gently as he could as the car jerked and righted itself.

"Sit down," Alex bit out. "Here they come."

Nick slammed his butt in the seat and dragged the seatbelt across his chest as Alex rounded a bend in the road. A police cruiser raced past them in the opposite direction.

"Silent alarm?" Alex bit out.

"I think the return of power sent some sort of message to the owner of the storage lot that there'd been a power outage. I'm guessing he and the cop will walk up and down the rows of units, make sure nothing is out of place and go back to bed."

"I hope you're right. Otherwise, this town just became a very bad place for us to be."

Nick looked over at Alex's profile, lit in the dim glow from the dashboard. "I expect Gray to come soon. Very soon."

Chapter 18

It took all of Alex's considerable discipline to keep the car down to the speed limit and drive sedately back to the inn. He parked in front of the rambling house and glanced over at Nick. "We've got to keep up appearances for now. And we have to find a place well away from all these civilians to confront Gray."

Nick nodded, his eyes more worried than Alex had ever seen them. "For now, let's just get back to the room without arousing Jeanette's suspicion. She's a sharp lady."

"Leave the crèche here or take it with us?" Alex bit out.

"Leave it. She would ask what was in the bags."

He nodded and climbed out of the car. He took a hard look around the front yard for anything out of the ordinary. All was quiet.

A small lamp glowed in the foyer, and they moved swiftly up the stairs and down the hall to their room. Alex opened their door quietly and they slipped inside. Only when it had closed behind Nick did Alex let out his breath. They'd done it. They'd stolen the Magi Crèche from Harlan Gray.

Nick paced a lap around the room and ended up stopping in front of the fireplace to light the fire already laid there. Alex joined him, sinking down on the sofa in front of the hearth.

Nick finished tending the fledgling flames and joined him on the couch.

"Now what?" Alex asked.

"Now we have a lot to do quickly. We need to get more firepower, and I'm telling you, we need to call in reinforcements."

"We also need to find a place away from Pleasant Falls and figure out how to draw Gray to it. I don't want a giant shootout in the middle of this nice little town."

Nick nodded grimly. "I'm thinking a place up in the woods would be good. With lots of cover. Remote. Hard to get to."

"I saw a pair of snowmobiles in Jeanette's garage earlier. If those work, maybe we could borrow them. Scout out a good place," Alex suggested.

Nick pulled out his cell phone and Alex said in quick alarm, "Who are you calling?"

"The Medusas."

"You think they'll give us support?"

"I know they will." When he disconnected the call, Nick said merely, "They're coming."

The fire popped loudly just then, and Alex jumped. Nick grinned. "A little tense, are you? Does that mean you're finally taking the threat of Gray seriously?"

Alex huffed. "I've always taken him seriously. I'm just a little on edge after stealing a priceless holy relic."

"We liberated it and will make sure it gets into the

right hands. We didn't steal anything. We have no intention of keeping it for ourselves and no plan to profit off of it."

Alex shrugged, conceding the point.

"Any chance you would consider calling in a few more fixers like yourself to help us out?" Nick asked.

"You really are terrified of Gray, aren't you?"

It was Nick's turn to huff. "Yeah. What of it?"

"Okay. If you're that scared, I'll call for my own backup." Alex took out his cell and dialed a phone number he'd only used a handful of times in his entire career. It was an emergency contact who would immediately relay his requirement for life-or-death assistance to the appropriate people in his chain of command. He said the code phrase to indicate he needed the whole cavalry to come to the rescue, and the woman at the other end dispassionately replied that she had received his message. But despite her apparent disinterest, he knew it would cause a flurry of panicked activity back at headquarters.

"Who will they send to help you?" Nick asked, curious.

"Guys from the Special Operations Group, if I had to guess."

Nick nodded. "That's where Gray pulls his team from. Sharp operators over at SOG."

Alex should hope so. Only the finest of SEALs, Delta operators and similar types were invited to join the CIA Special Operations Group. It was a small unit of arguably the most lethal human beings on the planet.

Nick said, "In the morning, we need to find a gun dealer and stock up."

Alex replied, "I brought a whole bag of weapons from the safe house in New York City. But we could probably use more ammo, and maybe some low-grade explosives."

"I knew there had to be a cache of arms somewhere in that place!" Nick exclaimed. "There was all that ammo in the closet and no firearms to go with it."

Alex grinned. "I was sure I was going to come back there sometime and find the walls torn open, the weapons' closet emptied and you gone."

"Nah. I would never have run away from a guy as sexy as you."

Alex's belly tightened involuntarily. Cripes, the effect this man had on him. He'd never been around another person who made him react from the core out.

"Speaking of which," Nick said grimly, "you said earlier that you would explain your feelings for me when we got back here. Thoroughly. And in detail. So, start talking."

Alex didn't know where to look. At Nick? At the fire? Out the window? Maybe at a spot over Nick's head?

Well, hell.

"You go first," he tried lamely.

"Nope. You go first this time," Nick said firmly.

Alex's brows came together in a frown. An urge to pick a fight and dodge this whole conversation surged through him, but he shoved it down. That would be childish and unfair to both of them. Nick had asked him an honest question and the man deserved an honest answer.

"Here's the thing," Alex said slowly. "This isn't the right time to have this conversation."

"Agreed," Nick said evenly. A pause. "But we're having it anyway. Continue."

"I've never had a conversation like this. On or off the job," Alex tried.

"Noted. I forgive you in advance for being awkward or for sticking your foot in your mouth."

He scowled at Nick. "Not helpful."

"How about this? I promise to hear you out without comment."

Alex considered that for a moment. "Better."

"Okay. Ground rules laid. Start talking."

Alex huffed. "This isn't an interrogation, for crying out loud."

Nick just looked at him expectantly.

"I think you're a great guy. Furthermore, I think you're a hell of a fine operator. One of the best." Alex searched for more words. These were not his weapons of choice in life. He used his brain and his hands and his training and let them do the talking for him. "I have…feelings… for you. Do I know what they all are? No. Do I want to figure that out? Yes. Can I describe them all to you thoroughly and in detail? No."

"Try."

He stared at Nick, who, to Alex's vast frustration, was giving no hint at all of what he thought of Alex's declaration of feelings.

"I suck at this," Alex grumbled.

Nick merely arched an eyebrow at him in a silent dare to carry on.

Alex opened his mouth. Closed it. The words were right there, hovering on the tip of his tongue. But he hadn't said them to anybody, ever, as an adult, and certainly not as a gay man to another man.

He'd told his parents and sisters he loved them, when he was younger. And they'd said it back to him. Blithely, while betraying his love behind his back. His gut clenched anxiously. What if Nick did the same thing? What if he laid his heart bare and Nick stomped on it—

"Stop," Nick said sharply.

Alex looked up, startled. "Stop what?"

"You just spun up inside your head and went all tight

and closed down on me. Stop overthinking everything for once, will you?"

"But you insisted that I tell you what I feel—"

"There are more ways than with words to do that, you beautiful, brilliant moron."

Alex stared at him in total incomprehension. And then it hit him.

"Oh."

Nick stared back intently. "Yeah. Oh."

The ball was firmly in his court. Nick had batted it back to him and was now silently asking him what he planned to do about it.

All his doubts coiled inside him, tying his heart in knots, while nervousness wrapped around him from the outside in thick, paralyzing loops. He felt trapped. Suffocated. Bound into complete immobility.

This was his life. He'd always been snared by his own insecurities. It was why he was good at his work. He had no life of his own. No feelings of his own. No family. No friends. Nothing that gave him cause to break free of these emotional bonds.

Until now.

He lifted his gaze to Nick in anguish. "I don't know how to do this." He took a deep, unsteady breath, and added low, "Help me, Nick."

Nick surged forward, moving across the sofa until their knees banged together. He stood up, dragging Alex to his feet by the shoulders. "You've got to get out of your head, Alex. That's the only place you're imprisoned."

"I don't know how to do that."

Nick's arms went around him and pulled him close against the hard length of his body. "Good thing for you, I do."

And then Nick was kissing him, his mouth hot and demanding and hungry. Nick kissed his face and throat, his eyes and temples. And his mouth. Oh, how Nick kissed his mouth.

He kissed Nick back feverishly. It was clumsy and fully as awkward as he'd feared it would be, but Nick didn't seem to care.

They stripped off Alex's utility vest and set it aside. Then his turtleneck sweater went over his head and momentarily got stuck on his face. They laughed a little as they finally tugged it free. Nick's hands reached for Alex's belt, and Alex sucked in a sharp breath.

Nick looked up quickly. "You say the word, and I'll stop. No questions asked."

Alex exhaled slowly, his stomach touching the backs of Nick's fingers. "Don't stop."

His belt slithered free of its loops and fell to the floor. He reached for Nick's utility vest and helped Nick shrug out of it. They unzipped their boots and kicked free of them, and then there was a moment of simultaneous, one-footed hopping as they fought to free their clingy, wet, wool socks from their feet.

Wearing just their cargo pants, they came together once more. Nick put his palms on Alex's chest, and Alex shivered as those callused hands eased across his skin, leaving a trail of goose bumps and utter destruction in their wake.

He couldn't resist. He reached out and plunged his fingers into the thick dark hair on Nick's chest. It was silky in contrast to the rock-hard muscles beneath. He trailed his hands lower, tracing the washboard ridges of Nick's stomach that contracted under his touch. Alex slipped his hands around Nick's lean waist as Nick did the same to him.

Nick grabbed his glutes in both hands and tugged him

closer until their zippers brushed together suggestively. Alex groaned a little as the metal teeth rubbed against his burgeoning erection.

Nick released him abruptly and stepped back. A protest rose in Alex's throat but never found voice because Nick reached for the offending zipper and tugged it down. He slipped his hands inside the waistband of Alex's pants and pushed the canvas fabric down.

Oh, clever man. Nick had also snagged Alex's underwear, and the spandex trunks peeled down his body, as well. His erection sprang loose all at once, and freed from the constriction of his clothing, filled so hard and fast the sensation all but drove him to his knees.

But Nick beat him to it, sinking down in front of Alex. Before he'd barely registered that, Nick's wet, hot, slippery mouth had taken him in. Nick sucked once, twice, and Alex's legs nearly gave out. He groaned long and low in the back of his throat.

"Gotta stop that if you want me to last more than a few seconds," Alex managed to gasp.

Nick chuckled and rose to his feet, reaching for his own zipper.

"Let me do that," Alex managed to croak. He pushed Nick's hands aside and pulled the zipper down slowly, inch by inch, vividly aware of the bulge behind his knuckles. He could feel Nick's erection jumping and jerking behind his hands, and Alex all but came then and there. Only an act of supreme self-control stopped his own body from exploding, he was so turned on.

He pushed Nick's pants down, and Nick kicked them off his feet. Alex reached for Nick's underwear and drew it down his body, as well, holding his breath as Nick's erection came free and announced itself loud and proud.

Alex wrapped his fist around the heated organ, loving the feel of it throbbing in his hand. He gave a light, experimental tug, and Nick stepped forward, groaning under his breath. Leading him by it, Alex backed toward the bed, where Jeanette had thoughtfully turned down the covers earlier.

As the backs of Alex's thighs bumped into the high mattress, Nick surged forward, knocking him backward onto the bed. Alex had barely hit the sheets before Nick was there, following him down.

One of Nick's thighs landed between his, and Nick's hands landed on either side of his head. He looked up in the flickering firelight as Nick stared down at him, lowering himself slowly, slowly in a reverse push-up.

Their legs tangled together. Then their bellies touched. Then their chests. And finally, Nick's entire body weight eased down onto him.

It felt so good Alex felt an urge to sob with pleasure. And he was not a sobbing kind of guy.

Nick kissed him slowly this time. Leisurely. They got to know each other's mouths and preferences as they kissed lightly, then deeply, with tongue and without, light nips and deep, drugging kisses. And all the while, their erections pressed against each other's groins, promising pleasure, lust and explosive, mind-blowing release.

Nick, resting his weight on an elbow above Alex, shoved his hands through Alex's short hair, pulling his head back and exposing his neck. Alex gave his throat to Nick freely, loving the heat of Nick's mouth on his skin.

"Um, Nick?"

"Mmm-hmm?"

"Don't we need to have a conversation about who's doing what?"

Nick slid his free hand down Alex's front, past his belly button, followed the line of hair downward, and wrapped around Alex's swollen flesh, pumping up and down its length once. Twice.

"I want to do all the things with you. I want to be inside you, and I want you inside me," Nick growled. "I want not to know where I end and you begin. So, you pick which way this is going to go first. But before tomorrow morning, we're doing it all."

Alex's toes literally curled in delight at that prospect. He realized Nick was staring down at him expectantly and that his fist had gone still. He was waiting for an answer.

Words. He had to use his words again. "Uh, I think, uh, I'd like to stay just like this, but with you making love to me first."

"You've got it."

He purely loved Nick's matter-of-fact response. He didn't make a big deal out of it, didn't make Alex feel weird for asking to bottom first. He just nodded, and oh thank goodness, his fist started to move again on Alex's engorged flesh.

Nick's second thigh joined his first one, and he pushed Alex's legs farther apart. Nick leaned over, laying across Alex's left thigh and hip for a moment, opening the drawer in the nightstand and taking something out. He rose to his knees, and Alex heard foil tearing.

"You had a condom already stowed in the bed stand just in case?" he exclaimed.

Nick looked down at him indignantly. "I'm shocked you didn't think ahead, Mr. Creed. Since when don't you contingency plan for all possibilities?"

His mouth opened and closed. "I admit it. I fell down on the job."

Nick finished rolling a condom onto his own penis and reached out to grasp Alex's. "Nothing feels fallen to me around here."

Alex rolled his eyes.

But then Nick opened a squeeze tube, and his slippery fingers were abruptly moving around Alex's most private parts. It felt so good he thought for a second that he might faint.

Alex reached down to grip Nick's erection, not so much as to give pleasure but simply to stay anchored in reality. Velvet over granite was the impression that flashed through his mind.

And then Nick took over guiding himself to Alex's eager body.

"You ready for me?" Nick asked. "Because my dude, I'm gonna fill you *all* the way."

Alex panted a little as he felt the stretching pressure. It wasn't quite painful, but that was because Nick went very, very slow and gave him all the time he needed to adapt. And then the worst of it was passed, and he nodded. Nick drove forward steadily then, filling him until he could hardly breathe. When Nick was seated to the hilt, their bellies pressed together, Alex's erection trapped deliciously between them, he stared up at Nick in wonder.

"We good?" Nick asked. His voice sounded gratifyingly strained.

"Uh-huh."

"Thank goodness. I don't think I could've stayed still one more second." Nick began to move inside him, slowly at first, but then with gathering force and speed. And with each thrust, Alex rose to meet him. Higher and higher they drove each other, their bodies straining together, desire clawing inside both of them in search of release.

Alex stared up at Nick, who stared back. The raw intimacy of staring into each other's eyes—into each other's souls—was intense and lifted the sex out of the realm of the physical and into the realm of magic.

Making love with Nick stripped away everything he hid behind, all the composure, all the self-control, all the overthinking, the insecurity, the uptightness. And with each layer that fell away, Alex felt more and more exposed, more emotional. More alive.

It was as if he'd been living in a fog bank for so long he'd forgotten what the sun looked like. But as they burned away the last vestiges of the mist, Nick burned as brightly as the sun. They burned together.

Nick drove into him harder and harder, faster and faster, and Alex drove back. Their bodies slapped together, and the friction became a raging wildfire they'd lost all control of.

When Alex thought he couldn't take one more second of it, Nick's hands slipped under him to grab his hips. Alex grabbed Nick, as well, and hung on for dear life. One last, mighty thrust, and Nick's entire body tensed, arched into him at the same time Alex arched up against Nick, and both of their bodies spasmed for long, long seconds. It went on and on until Alex actually did black out a little, overcome by an excess of pleasure so intense he could hardly absorb it all.

He blinked back into his body and began to register sensations. The glorious weight of Nick's body on top of his. Drugging waves of pleasure coursing through him. Skin on skin. Their legs tangled together. His breath light and fast.

Alex realized the ropes binding him had, indeed fallen away. He finally had not only the right words but the freedom to say them.

"I love you, Nick."

Chapter 19

Nick's entire being went still from the inside out. He stared down at Alex in the half dark of the firelight. His hair was uncharacteristically chaotic, but there was nothing the slightest bit chaotic about Alex's steady, warm eyes, staring back at him solemnly. Alex loved him? It wasn't just the delirium of great sex talking?

"Really?" he heard himself asking in a hoarse voice he didn't recognize as his own.

"Um, yeah. You don't have to feel the same way or say it back—" Alex started.

Swiftly, Nick leaned down and kissed the man into silence. Then, when Alex had gone still beneath him, he lifted his mouth away from Alex's far enough to say, "I love you, too, you giant goofball."

"I'm not a goofball!"

"Are, too. But you're my goofball," Nick said fondly.

"You're such a jerk."

"But I'm your jerk," Nick replied more seriously. They stared at each other in wonder, as if they both were struggling a little to absorb the enormity of what had just happened between them.

Alex twined his fingers in Nick's hair and tugged. "Yeah," Alex sighed against his lips. "You're my jerk."

Nick rolled to one side, and Alex rolled with him, their limbs still entwined and Alex's head lying on his shoulder.

A single thought came to Nick. *If I die this second, I will die a happy man.*

Whoa. *Happy* was a word he couldn't remember ever applying to himself. But there it was. Alexander Creed made him happy in ways he'd never imagined possible. He relaxed in the dark and listened to Alex's breathing calm and settle into sleep, and it was one of the nicest things he'd ever heard. As Alex slumbered beside him, relaxed and warm, it soothed and lulled Nick, as well.

He vaguely registered the dark cloud of Harlan Gray on the horizon, but the calm of being with Alex held. Tomorrow would be soon enough to deal with that problem. For tonight, he and Alex had each other. And it was the best moment of his life.

Who knew that making love with a man that he actually loved had made all the difference in the world? He might be an old dog, but it appeared he was capable of learning new tricks after all.

Love. Not a word, not a thing he'd ever expected to find. But here it was, in all its magnificence and glory. And he was fully okay with that.

Nick woke slowly, registering with vague displeasure that the sun was shining around the edges of the heavy curtains. Sometime in the night, between bouts of mind-shattering sex, Alex had gotten up and closed the velvet blinds. True to his prediction, they had done all the things in all the combinations, alternately napping and waking through the night to make love again.

Both of them were inordinately fit men with extreme stamina. It had made for a very long night with very little sleep. But there was no doubt about it. They were a perfect match. Not only did they have similar strengths but also similar creativity. Alex had surprised him like no other lover he'd ever had, and he was pretty sure he'd surprised Alex a few times, too.

Nick stretched lazily, loathe to end their tryst. Oh my. A number of muscles expressed protest. Score another point for Alex. Not many of his lovers over the years had worked him out to the point of actual muscle fatigue. He finally forced himself to open his other eye and noted that the bed beside him was empty, the covers thrown back.

The shower went on in the adjoining bathroom, and he grinned to himself. Had he, perchance, made Alex a wee bit sore as well? The good news was the shower was plenty large enough for two adults. In fact, large enough for two adults to make love in...

The house either had a large water heater or a continuous water-heating system, for they ran the water for almost a solid hour, first making love under it, and then taking turns letting the hot spray pound their muscles into relaxation.

At last, Nick had to admit it was time to get on with their day. And they had a big one ahead of them. After a large breakfast of tall stacks of pancakes and enough bacon to feed a football team, he and Alex headed out to the shed where the snowmobiles were stored. Jeannette had told them the machines hadn't been ridden in over a year, but that if they could get them running, they were free to take them out.

It took a quick tune-up and an oil change, but in about an hour, the two machines roared to life.

Jeanette had mentioned over breakfast that local skiers had built and maintained small emergency shacks in the nearby mountains. Apparently, they were stocked with firewood, water, canned food and blankets, perfect for the lost or stranded skier. Nick and Alex were hoping to find one in reasonably good repair and stock it for their own purposes.

They loaded gear bags onto the backs of the machines and headed out. The recent snow was blindingly white, and the ride into the back country was beautiful. They found what they thought was an old ski trail, and they followed it slowly, ducking under branches that encroached upon their path.

It ran for perhaps a mile before coming to a ramshackle structure that must have been one of the old ski shacks. Nick turned off his snowmobile and climbed off it to take a closer look.

Alex did the same, commenting, "It's in pretty rough shape."

"It looks as if a lot of the original wood siding is lying around on the ground under the snow, though. If we brought out nails and hammers, we should be able to repair a lot of it. And this siding is inch-thick oak. It would stop a bullet."

"We need to check out possible approaches to this spot," Alex said. "Make sure the general public isn't likely to stumble on to it."

They spent the next hour doing just that and concluded that they had, indeed, found the perfect place to ambush Gray.

"How are we going to draw him up here?" Nick asked.

"Easy." Alex grinned. "We bring the crèche up here. He'll turn over every rock in the Adirondacks looking for it."

"But it's *priceless*. And you want to use it as bait?" Nick squawked.

"Have you got any better ideas?"

"We could use ourselves as bait."

Alex frowned. "If he thinks we don't have the crèche with us, he won't come after us. The moment he figures out we've stolen the crèche, that will become his sole obsession. He'll find that to the exclusion of all else. Once he has it back, and only then, will he turn his attention to hunting us down and killing us slowly and painfully."

Nick sighed. "I agree. But I hate the idea of using the crèche as bait."

"So do I. But we have to stop Gray."

Nick stared at Alex, who stared back grimly. At length, Nick said, "Fine. We use the crèche. We bring it up here."

"We should set up a defensive perimeter around it. Layers of traps and alarm systems. Then we'll need to find a good spot and set up a hide for ourselves."

Nick nodded. "We should build a series of them around the shack that we can retreat to as he and his men try to overrun our position."

Alex frowned. "You think we'll need to retreat?"

"I think we'd be idiots not to plan for it."

It was a game of anticipating what Gray's men would do and then thinking about how to outfox each move they might make. When they'd outlined a network of spots to build sniper hides in, they marked each location on their GPSes and headed back to the inn.

They grabbed a late lunch and loaded up with the supplies they needed to repair the shack and the ammo they

needed to stock in each hiding spot. Lastly, they strapped
the bags with the crèche statues to the backs of the snowmobiles. They told Jeanette they would be camping tonight and headed out.

They used the last of the daylight to repair the cabin.
Thankfully, it didn't have to be pretty. It just had to repel
bullets and have enough slits for them to shoot through.
They laid planks in the rafters to form a rough ceiling
and tucked the bags containing the precious statues on
top of that, where they should be clear of gunfire.

Heading out in the rapidly falling twilight, they went
to work setting up sniper hides. They used hollow logs
and dug holes under rocks to stash ammunition, tarps
and even first-aid kits. Finally, they retired to the shack
to catch some sleep and take turns standing watch.

As Alex hunkered down in his bedroll and Nick settled in to observe the surrounding forest, Alex asked,
"How long do you suppose it'll take for Gray to find us?"

"I expect him here in the next day or so. Catch some
sleep, goofball."

"Love you, too, jerk face."

Nick smiled indulgently as Alex closed his eyes and
promptly fell asleep. They hadn't had time to talk today
about last night, but there wasn't much to say. It had been
perfect, and they were meant to be together. At least that
was how he felt, and he was pretty darned sure Alex felt
the exact same way. He sure *hoped* Alex felt the same.

As stars wheeled slowly overhead and the long hours
of the night passed in a majestically slow march, his
thoughts turned to the house he mentally constructed
when he was bored.

Except tonight, it looked exactly like the Pleasant Run
Inn. He was living there with Alex. They'd built little
guest quarters out back for Jeanette to retire in, and there

were kids in the house. A whole bunch of them. They would run the inn and go to town snowball fights and sing Christmas carols and drink hot chocolate with silly little marshmallows in it—

A movement outside caught his eye, yanking his attention back to the forest around him.

It was nearly 3:00 a.m. Almost time to hand the watch off to Alex and catch some sleep himself.

He stared at the spot where he'd seen a shadow flicker that shouldn't have flickered. Had the movement been down near the ground, he would've written it off as a raccoon or a fox. It had been about five feet off the ground, though. It had been too big for a bird or a squirrel…

He used his foot to kick Alex's boot lightly through his sleeping bag. "Incoming," he breathed.

Too soon! They weren't ready! They hadn't run practice scenarios. Hadn't finalized an order that they would use the hides in. They hadn't even decided who would take the north side of the shack and who would take the south side.

Truth was, neither of them needed to practice a thing. He just wasn't ready to have this idyllic time with Alex come to a violent end.

Alex rolled out of his sleeping bag, gripped an assault rifle across his chest and pulled night optical devices over his eyes. He moved quickly to the opposite wall of the shack and took up a waiting-and-watching position, peering out at the forest through a slit in the wall.

The biggest problem with Gray hitting them now was they had no backup. The Medusas had replied that they would make all due haste to the area and contact Nick when they arrived. Alex hadn't heard anything at all in response to his urgent request for help.

Crap, crap, crap. Gray had outmaneuvered them. He'd somehow correctly anticipated what Nick and Alex would do. Worse, he'd used his superior resources and private army to move faster and get here before he and Alex got help.

"Clear over here," Alex said just loud enough into his throat-mounted microphone to be heard in Nick's military-grade earphones.

"Negative on heat sources over here," Nick replied into his throat mike. "But I definitely saw a hostile due west of us, about fifty feet out."

"They'll know we're in here, then. They'll have picked up our heat signatures," Alex said matter-of-factly.

"Dammit," Nick bit out. "We should've assumed he'd get here tonight and disguised our heat signatures."

"The idea was for them to find us," Alex reminded him quietly.

"I don't want you to die!" he burst out under his breath.

"Bless your heart, darlin', but I don't want to die, either," Alex drawled.

"I'm serious."

"So am I," Alex retorted. "And I don't want you to die."

Nick huffed. "Is there any way I can talk you into jumping on one of the snowmobiles and heading back to town to call in reinforcements?"

"Not on your life," Alex snapped. "If they know only one man is in here, they'd rush you the second I'm gone and overrun your position. We're in this together, Nick. All the way to the end."

Nick closed his eyes in agony. They'd only just found each other. They'd had so little time together. He wasn't ready for this! He needed more time with Alex. They had so much more living and loving to do before the end.

Because the end was going to be just that. The *end*. Death. For both of them. He *had* to find a way to get Alex out of here.

"I appreciate your loyalty, Alex. Really. But maybe I only saw a scout. It's possible he has gone back to join the rest of Gray's team and let them know he's spotted a couple of skiers in a shack they might want to check out in the morning."

"Or," Alex said coolly, "he's moved over the crest of the ridge so we can't see him and is waiting for the rest of Gray's team to join him before they make their move."

"In that case, do you want to get out of here? Head out the back door to the first hide we set up?"

"Given that they haven't already attacked us, I think we should," Alex answered.

Nick nodded. Moving efficiently, he donned his utility vest, which he'd loaded up earlier with all the ammunition he could cram into it. He picked up a spare assault rifle and slung it across his back, checked the handgun in his pocket, the knife in its ankle sheath and tightened his optical device around his head.

Then he rigged the first of their traps. The remote firing devices he'd attached to a pair of assault rifles on tripod stands pointed outward. When Gray's men hit the trip wires attached to them, the weapons would shoot into the woods. He and Alex didn't care if the flying bullets hit any of Gray's men. They just needed Gray and his team to shoot back and give away their positions by their muzzle flashes.

Alex finished tucking a pair of heat packs into the neck openings of each of their insulated sleeping bags, simulating their faces poking out. Alex moved to the low trapdoor they'd cut into the back wall earlier.

Nick watched him ease outside with quick stealth that Nick took a moment to admire. And then he followed Alex.

The moon had set hours ago, but it was a clear, starry

night with just enough ambient lighting to cause a faint glow to rise from the snow. Their white arctic suits blended in with the surroundings, however, and he raced after Alex, crouching low.

He reached the first hide and eased down behind a giant, downed tree trunk. Nick turned up the magnification on his NODs and scanned the woods around them carefully. All clear. But someone else was out here. He could feel it.

Alex hand signaled, "We're not alone. No contact." Meaning, Alex was convinced someone was out here, too, but hadn't yet seen him.

He signaled back, "Affirmative."

The tense standoff lasted for another hour of complete silence and no movement out there. Whoever was watching the shack was probably still in position and unaware that the two of them had slipped outside. But that would change when the heat packs Alex had left in their sleeping bags wore out in another hour or so and began to cool down.

Then, Nick suspected, all hell was going to break loose.

Only one thing was on his mind now. He had to find a way to get Alex out of this confrontation alive. Even if it meant sacrificing his own life.

Chapter 20

Alex scanned the trees around their position for the hundredth time. By now, he was familiar with every branch, every mound of snow, every dead leaf still clinging to a branch overhead.

Any minute, Gray's whole team would arrive and charge the ski shack. Certainty of that rippled across Alex's skin, making the fine hairs on his arms stand up.

He had to find a way to get Nick out of this alive. Nick had finally allowed himself to love again. He was finally starting to get past the betrayals of his childhood, starting to think about having a family of his own. He had to get a chance to fill that hole in his heart.

By rote, Alex ran through the litany of people he'd killed over the years. Far too many of them had been Americans, men and women just like him who'd had a moment of weakness. They'd given in to temptation, and he'd come for them. How many of those people could've made restitution, could've learned their lesson if given a second chance, could've returned to the ranks of productive operatives for the US government if he'd given them the chance?

But no. He was the Judge. He'd deemed them guilty, sentenced them to death and executed the sentence. How many families had he destroyed? How many widows and orphans had been left in his wake? He was the one who needed to die out here. Not Nick. Nick was just a soldier doing his job, a guy trying to right a great wrong perpetrated by his buddies. Nick was one of the good ones.

But he was not. He'd amassed a ton of lethal karma debts in his career, and the time had come for him to pay up.

Alex breathed, "When they realize we're not in the shack, you drop back to the second hide, and I'll hold this position as long as I can. I'll join you once you're set up to cover my retreat."

In theory it was a solid plan. Of course, he had no intention of joining Nick at all. He had a large enough block of C-4 in his pocket to make a crater with a fifty-foot radius around himself and incinerate everything inside it. Including himself. And the crèche. He did feel bad about that. But neither one of them could afford to get weighed down hauling out the heavy bag of statues, and he was willing to destroy any piece of art, no matter how rare and valuable, to save Nick.

If he could just draw Gray and his team close enough, he could take them all out at once.

And Nick would live.

Peace settled over Alex. He'd found true love at last. Nick knew everything about him and thought he was perfect just the way he was. And that was enough for him. It was more than he'd ever expected to find in this lifetime.

"Here they come," Nick breathed.

Alex tensed. He joined Nick in peering over the log. Up the hill, the shack lay still and silent. And then, without warning, the two booby-trapped weapons Nick had set up inside the shack began to fire out into the woods.

An answering barrage erupted from the woods on the other side of the shack. At least they'd gotten the direction that Gray and his team would approach from correct. Alex counted fast. Six weapons were firing at the cabin. He marked their positions and sighted in on the one closest to him. Using the heat-painting feature of his optical devices, he tried to spot the human behind the gun, but the guy had complete cover from a tree.

Swearing under his breath, Alex moved on to the next firing position. One by one, he checked each weapon discharging at the shack, and not one shooter had exposed himself to return fire. Alarm skittered through him. These guys were good. Fully as good as Nick has warned him they would be.

Instinct warned him to turn around and scan down the exposed hill behind them, and he was barely in time to spot the man creeping toward them in stealthy silence. Alex swung his weapon up and double-tapped two shots into the chest of the guy, who tumbled backward down the steep slope.

Alex touched Nick's shoulder twice and then scrambled after the hostile to verify the kill. But when he got to where the man had fallen, there was no body. Gray's man must've been wearing body armor. Crap. But then, he and Nick were also sporting the stuff. Military grade, capable of withstanding point-blank assault-weapon fire.

He ran back up the hill to Nick. Under the noise of the barrage Gray's men were still peppering the shack with, he muttered in Nick's ear, "We have to go. This spot is compromised."

Nick nodded and slid back from the log. Alex took off running down the slope a second time, angling across it toward the next hide they'd set up for themselves. Unfortunately, they were going to have to fight uphill, with Gray's men holding the high ground above them.

Alex flopped down behind a huge boulder that was actually an outcropping of the hill itself. Quickly he scanned the forest behind them while Nick set up his weapon on a bipod stand and scanned in front of the rock.

"Clear," Nick breathed.

"Clear."

The gunfire was tailing off above them. Gray's men would be approaching the shack now. They'd mainly be hunting whoever'd shot at them, and he doubted they would find the crèche. He also doubted Gray was out here in person, running around in the woods like a common foot soldier. It was beneath the great spymaster.

Nick had suggested Gray would send in an advance team to keep them busy while Gray's main force assembled. Time to start picking off the foot soldiers.

"I'll be back," Alex murmured. "Going on a hunting expedition."

Nick nodded, his eye never leaving the rubber sight of his weapon.

Alex moved out into the trees silently. This was what he did best. He was a predator. He moved around toward the far side of the cabin, certain there was at least one more roaming hunter out here besides the one he'd shot.

There. He spied a brief, slow movement. Maybe a hand reaching up to adjust a sight on a rifle. It wasn't much. But it was enough. Moving at glacial speed, he lifted his own weapon. *Bingo.* A heat signature lit up on the ground.

Cognizant of the body armor, he aimed for the target's neck. It was a hellishly hard shot, but well within his capability. He exhaled slowly, emptied his mind and became one with his weapon. He squeezed the trigger and watched as the target went limp and still on the ground.

Splash one.

Now to find the man he'd shot before. He figured the guy must've retreated back toward the main force of Gray's troops to assess his injuries and recover his cool, if nothing else. He headed in that direction.

He'd almost given up on finding the guy when he spied a figure creeping slowly across the hillside toward Nick's current position.

Oh no he didn't. That guy didn't get to sneak up on *his* man, thank you very much.

With cold precision, Alex raised his rifle, lined up the neck shot and took it. The man's legs went limp and he dropped like a stone.

Splash two.

Alex eased closer to the cabin, watching where he went through his rifle sight. There. Gray's men had found the trapdoor, and one was coming out it now. He didn't have a shot at the guy that wouldn't hit body armor, but he didn't need to kill him. He just needed to make him run. Gray's other men would follow behind.

Alex aimed at the man's side and put two bullets into the guy's ribs in quick succession. The impacts would hurt like hell, even through body armor.

Sure enough, the man cried out, jumped up and took off running into the woods. Three more foot soldiers piled out fast and took off behind him. For good measure, Alex shot one of them in the back. He staggered and nearly went down but found his balance and scrambled into the trees.

Alex risked transmitting to Nick, "They've got body armor and helmets. Neck shots work. Two down. Four incoming to you. I'm hunting the last two." He figured that of the six who'd been shooting at the shack, only four had gone inside, which left two more out here. He didn't think the two he'd already killed were part of that original six-man fire team.

Nick clicked his mike to acknowledge the information.

Alex looked side to side. Which way to go? Since the two guys he'd killed had both circled left around the shack, he decided to circle right in search of the other two hunter-killers prowling around out here.

He came upon the first man no more than a hundred yards beyond the shack. He was positioned to take out anybody who returned to the cabin after his guys cleared out of it.

Alex snorted. As if he or Nick would ever be dumb enough to come back to a location that had already been compromised. It took him a while to circle around behind the guy, and he prayed the men headed toward Nick continued straight down the hill into Nick's kill zone.

He'd hoped to have these two hunters taken care of by now so he could head back toward Nick and cover him from any rear attacks. The last guy had to be out here, somewhere. *C'mon, where are you? Show yourselves.*

There. He spotted a shape in front of him. A shot at the back of the neck wasn't as sure a kill as a throat shot, but it was the only shot he had. His weapon was a large enough caliber to bust through vertebrae and kill his target.

Alex lined up his shot and took it. The man slumped forward over his rifle, motionless.

Off to his left, an abrupt barrage of gunfire announced that the team had found Nick, or they had stumbled into his line of fire. Either way, it was *on* over there.

A quick movement no more than fifty yards in front of him startled Alex mightily. A *third* hunter had broken cover to run for the shootout.

Alex took off running after the guy and was horrified when Gray's man unleashed a barrage of automatic weapon fire at Nick.

A mistake, that. Nobody was taking out *his* man.

Alex stopped moving to calculate the guy's path of motion and exhaled, waiting for him to run into his sights. As Gray's man flashed into his viewfinder, Alex pulled the trigger, quickly adjusted left a hair and fired again.

He took off running without waiting to see if he'd taken out the guy. Killing a moving target was exponentially more difficult than killing a stationary one, and he assumed the shooter was still alive. As he charged toward where he'd dropped him, he raised his weapon again, readying it.

The hunter was lying down, but rolled toward him and shot just wide of Alex's face as he crashed out of the brush. Alex actually felt the heat of a bullet passing by his cheek. Ducking, Alex shot fast, putting two rounds into the guy, who went still. Dang. That had been a close call.

Now to get to Nick.

You'd better be alive, you beautiful bastard. You have children to conceive and raise.

Chapter 21

Nick picked off two of the four people rushing his position before they had any idea he was just below them on the hillside. But the two remaining guys split up and ran from him at right angles. Not good. They were going to circle around behind him and flank him.

He had to fall back. Now. No matter that Alex hadn't rejoined him. If he stayed, Alex would find a corpse when he got here. And before he died, he had to make sure Alex was safe.

Nick grabbed his weapon, the last magazine of ammo, and took off running down the hill at top speed. He hurdled over the log that was their next hide and flopped to the ground with his back against the cold wood.

"At hide three," he breathed into his mouthpiece.

He watched left and right, his gaze swiveling back and forth, waiting for one or both of the remaining hostiles to circle behind this spot to kill him. He might only take out one of them before going down himself, but at least that would leave Alex with even odds.

He spied a single figure at the bottom of the hill, much lower than he would've expected the pair chasing him to have gone. But, hey. Each to their own. If the guy wanted to have to come uphill to approach him, so be it.

He lined the guy up in his sights and then jolted. He knew that quick, graceful way of moving. He jerked his muzzle up and away from Alex.

"I have you in sight," he breathed.

"Well, hell," Alex replied in disgust.

Nick smiled briefly. Didn't like being seen, huh? "Two hunters flanking me."

"I'm sliding east," Alex breathed.

Nick had complete faith that Alex would find his man and take him out, so he turned his attention solely to the western approach to this position. Which was probably why he spotted the most subtle of movement slightly above him on the hill.

Because of the guy's body armor, Nick had to wait for the man to come closer to get a shot. In the meantime, he lay down, minimizing his own body signature as much as possible behind the log.

The hunter stopped and crouched for a long time. Probably was scanning the area around him. Then, as the guy finally stood up and turned toward him, Nick got a shot. He took it, and the hostile dropped.

"West down," he breathed.

Alex didn't even click his mike in response. He must be right on top of his target and not be able to shift or reply at all.

Nick scanned the whole hillside and saw no movement. Holding his breath, he waited for Alex to report in.

Bang. Bang.

"East down," Alex said quietly.

Thank goodness. He exhaled carefully.

"That everyone?" Nick asked.

"I think so." Alex added, "Coming in over your right shoulder."

A shape dropped to the ground beside him, startling him badly. He hadn't heard Alex approach at all. "Holy—" He broke off. "Glad to see you're alive."

"Ditto, Kane."

"Really? Ditto? Is that all you've got?"

"If we get out of this alive," Alex muttered, "I'm crawling back into that huge bed with you and not getting out of it for a week."

"Deal."

"Ready to clear the hill with me?" Alex asked low, but still managing to sound pleased with himself.

He scowled at Alex for a moment. "Let's go."

"Nice shooting, by the way."

"You, too."

Their gazes met, and they exchanged short smiles.

It took them until about an hour after sunrise to assure themselves that no more of Gray's advance team remained on the hillside. They disarmed the corpses, took the radios and phones, and moved off into the woods to wait and see who showed up next.

Nick caught a couple hours of sleep, and Alex even caught a nap in the late morning. They spent the afternoon doing the preparations they'd hoped to do before anyone showed up, and repositioned nearly to the top of the mountain. They would hold the high ground this time.

As the sun dipped into the west and slipped behind the mountains, Nick braced himself for the main attack. By now, Gray knew that none of his advance team had reported back in.

Tonight, Gray would throw everything he had at them.

Chapter 22

Alex looked down the hill through a long-range scope. The black, bare skeletons of the trees only partially obscured the view. He could see the ski shack was badly shot up after last night's attack, with hundreds of bullet holes in the wooden walls. They'd patched it up with more lengths of old siding they'd nailed across the worst of the holes today to make it look fortified. It should be where Gray's army started its search.

They hoped.

The crèche was still tucked up high in the rafters of the shack, well above where Gray's men had been firing at the structure last night. Hopefully, it would continue to stay safe in its hiding spot.

They had briefly debated trying to carry it down the hill this morning and put it somewhere safe, but they hadn't had the time to spare, and they couldn't guarantee that Gray's men wouldn't have spotted them coming down off the mountain and attacked on the spot.

As darkness fell gently around them, Alex glanced over at Nick. "You ready for this?"

"As ready as I'll ever be. I've trained my whole life for this moment. You ready?"

Alex smiled. "I hunt guys like Gray for lunch."

"You made tracking them look easy last night," Nick commented.

"I got a good shock when I went to confirm my first kill and the guy was gone," Alex admitted. "And I had a very close call with a guy who leaped out of hiding when you started firing at the kill team coming down the hill. He might've gotten the jump on me had you not distracted him."

Nick winced. "I take no pleasure from men I probably trained nearly killing you."

"I'm glad I've had some time to work with you so I had an idea of the skill level these guys brought to the table. To be honest, I'd have underestimated them if I didn't already know you."

Nick smiled over at him. "Have I told you today that I love you?"

"You have not."

"Well, I do."

Alex savored the warmth spreading outward from his chest. "When this is over, how do you feel about buying the Pleasant Run Inn from Jeanette and running it ourselves?"

"Funny you should ask. I was thinking last night about building her a little guesthouse out back so she could stay where her family was raised. I figure we'll need her help learning the ropes of running an inn."

"Really?" Alex blurted.

"Really. I love the idea. We can have our wedding beside the pond. Or maybe in the drawing room. Whatever you want," Nick said.

Alex stared. "Our wedding? Was that a proposal, Nicholas Kane?"

"That was a pre-proposal. I'll do it right when we get off this damned hill. With a ring and roses and champagne and the whole sappy nine yards."

Alex stared incredulously until Nick said a little defensively, "What?"

"When did you become a romantic at heart?"

"Guess I always was one. It just took you coming along to reveal it."

Alex leaned over and grabbed Nick's shirt, dragging him close for a kiss. "That was my pre-acceptance of your pre-proposal."

He started to move back to his weapon, but Nick grabbed his shirt this time and dragged him close for a long, sexy kiss that had him thinking about how soon they could get off this mountain and get back to their room at the inn.

"Shouldn't someone be watching the cabin?" he mumbled against Nick's lips.

"Party pooper."

"Let's get this mess cleaned up so we can get on with our lives," Alex said firmly.

"One cleaning job, coming up."

They went back to watching the cabin.

Alex said thoughtfully, "Last night, I was prepared to die to protect you."

Nick snorted. "I spent last night trying to figure out how to die in a way that would get you off this hill alive."

"How about we agree to both get off this mountain alive?" Alex said soberly.

Nick took his eyes off the binoculars to stare at him a long time. "I'll try if you'll try."

Alex met his dark stare. "I will if you will."

"Okay, then. We both stay alive. We fight to the end. No grand sacrifices in the name of saving the other guy. We live together or die firing the last rounds in our weapons at the bastards."

Resolve hardened in Alex's chest. They would find a way to do this. They would defeat Gray and his men somehow. And then they'd go get that inn and that storybook life they both deserved. Well, Nick deserved it. He was just grateful to be the man Nick had chosen to live the fairy tale with.

It was midnight when Gray's army arrived on tracked snow vehicles that roared up the mountain and rolled straight up to the shack. The rear tailgate of one vehicle dropped, and a Gatling gun opened fire on the cabin, literally shredding the walls as he and Nick looked on in horror.

"I only count four men," Alex murmured in confusion.

Without warning, Nick swore violently and rolled onto his back, taking his gun with him. Instinctively, Alex ducked as a drone overhead unleashed a volley of gunfire on their position, exploding the log where his head had just been. He and Nick scrambled under the cover of a tree and then took off running through the forest, zigzagging back and forth.

Alex noted vaguely that Nick wasn't heading for their next designated shooter's nest. Instead, he was veering off to the south, away from the cabin, toward a rock wall they'd found late this morning. What was he doing?

Grimly, Alex followed, his mind raging with questions over what Nick had in mind. But he had no breath to ask, and Nick surely had no breath to answer.

They burst out of the trees and the rock outcropping rose some thirty feet over their heads.

"Find an overhang and get under it," Nick said tersely. "I'm climbing this rock."

"Why?" Alex demanded.

"Gotta take out the drone. And I should be able to get a phone signal on top of it. We need help now. Or we're dead."

"I'm coming with you," Alex declared.

"No—"

"We agreed."

Nick grabbed him and kissed him hard, effectively silencing him. "Fine. Shut up and climb. But you live for me. You hear?"

Alex smiled a little as he grabbed a handhold and pulled himself onto the rock face. They hadn't scoped out this wall, and free-climbing it at night was suicidally dangerous, but they had no choice. He heard the distinctive whine of the drone somewhere nearby. They had to get a clear shot, and soon.

Alex used every bit of his speed and coordination to pull himself on top of the wall in little more than a minute. He rolled onto his back, pointing his rifle toward the sky and scanning fast.

There.

He aimed at the drone, made the corrections for shooting upward and pulled the trigger. A miss. He aimed again. This time, a puff of smoke rose from the attack drone, and it spiraled down out of the sky just as Nick reached the plateau beside him.

"Dang, you're fast," Nick panted.

"Make the call."

Nick pulled out his cell phone. Alex listened in as Nick said urgently, "If you have any resources to blank out satellite coverage of Upstate New York, now's the time to pull in that favor. We're in big trouble up here."

A male voice answered tersely, but Alex couldn't make out the words.

Nick busted out in a big smile and said, "That's the best news I've had in weeks. We'll meet you down there."

He pocketed his phone and Alex said, "Well?"

"The Medusas are here. And apparently, a few of your friends have arrived, as well. They're inbound to the coordinates of the cabin as we speak. They've formed a cordon at the bottom of the hill and will be herding Gray and his men up toward us in the next few minutes."

"We're inside that cordon?" Alex asked.

"Correct."

"How do you feel about heading for hide twelve and giving Gray a personal welcome to the love shack?"

Nick grinned. "I love that plan. Let's go."

Hide twelve was the last one they'd built and directly above the cabin on top of a good-sized rock outcropping. Although it had no cover overhead, it had the perfect vantage point to take out anyone approaching the shack's front door—or at least the remnants of it, hanging askew in the door frame.

He and Nick moved cautiously through the woods as they made their way down the mountain, but the Medusas and their reinforcements were making no effort to move quietly below them as they closed the net around the cabin and Gray's army. If anything, they were being noisy intentionally, beating the bushes to drive Gray's men toward the place.

Alex stretched out on the cold, rough rock, pressing his cheek against his rifle. "How many men do you guess Gray brought with him?" he murmured off-mike to Nick.

"No idea. Up to twenty, maybe."

"Dang. Do you suppose he's in the area?"

"Gunnar Torsten—he's the commander of the Medusas—said a surveillance satellite was appropriated and pointed at Upstate New York about an hour ago. He got it shut down right before I called him. My guess is Gray was sitting offsite somewhere nearby, watching a satellite feed."

"So, Gray's blind," Alex replied, nodding in satisfaction. "Will he come in person to supervise our murder?"

"No. But he'll come in person to retrieve the crèche," Nick answered grimly.

Without warning, a dozen commandos burst into the clearing around the cabin and took up positions. But instead of pointing at the shack, they pointed outward, away from it, defending it.

"What's up with that?" Alex muttered.

"I don't know—" Nick broke off. "Aww, hell. Gray's already inside the cabin."

"He has the crèche!" Alex exclaimed under his breath, lifting his rifle.

"Not yet," Nick bit out. "If we give away our position before the Medusas get here, Gray's men will kill us before we get help."

Alex subsided, unhappy. Nick was right, but Gray had the crèche. His gut rebelled at the precious relic being in such a monster's hands.

They didn't have long to wait, however. Another line of figures lit up in the heat-seeking optical functions of their rifle sights. A male voice called over a megaphone, "You're surrounded, Gray. Come out with your hands behind your head. Tell your men to lay down their weapons and surrender."

Gray's men didn't move a muscle.

The line of Medusas and whoever was with them

closed in a little more. They all took up firing stances, behind trees or rocks. Gray's soldiers were completely exposed in the tiny clearing around the cabin. If they didn't surrender, they were all going to die, cut down in cold blood.

"Tell them to surrender!" Alex whispered urgently to Nick. "They might listen to you since they know you."

"How? I don't have a megaphone."

"No, but we have those phones we took off his guys last night. Can you call them?"

"I don't know if they've changed the group-chat phone number or not," Nick said doubtfully.

"Try. I've seen enough death for one lifetime," Alex begged.

Nick nodded grimly at him. "I'll try." He dug around in the thigh pocket of his pants and came up with one of the confiscated cell phones. He dialed a number from memory. Nick laid it on the ground between them with the Speaker function turned on.

A gruff voice said, "Who is this?"

"Nicholas Kane. It's over, Gray. Your men are outnumbered three to one by people as skilled as they are. There's no way out of that cabin alive."

Gray swore colorfully. "You have no idea how good my men are."

"Yeah, Harlan, I do. I trained a lot of them. But I'm out here with military Special Forces operators and a whole bunch of CIA fixers. You know. The guys sent out to kill men like you when they go rogue. And right now, they're poised to take out not only you but every one of your men. You're done."

"You stole it, didn't you?" Gray accused.

"You mean the crèche? We liberated it from you to

return it to the people who ought to have it. Unlike you, we're not thieves."

Gray swore in a steady stream then, ranting about how nobody would've ever seen it if not for him. He was a hero for finding it and stealing it. Because of him, the whole world was going to see it.

He failed to mention that he was going to become rich selling off the pieces first.

"You're not listening to me, Harlan," Nick said patiently. "It's over. You don't get to sell any more pieces of the crèche. You're not going to get rich, and you're not going to walk out of that shack alive if you don't surrender."

That finally seemed to break through to Gray. The other end of the call was silent for a long time. Then he said simply, "If I can't have it, then nobody else can have it."

The line went dead.

Oh, no. No no no. Not good. Gray was not the kind of man who made empty threats.

Alex jumped to his feet and shouted frantically down the hill at Gray's men, "Get away from the cabin! Run! He's going to blow it—"

Ka-BOOM!

Alex was knocked backward violently by the explosion and nearly all the way off the rock he and Nick were perched upon.

Alex hit his head hard, and even though he had on a helmet, he was dazed by the blow. He stared up at the sky, unsure of where he was and why he was lying on his back.

"Alex. Alex! Can you hear me? Are you okay, baby? Talk to me."

"Don't call me baby," he mumbled, barely hearing his own voice. Dang, that explosion had been loud.

He stared up at Nick in dismay. "He blew himself up, didn't he? Did they run? Did his men get away?"

"Some of them. About half stayed by the shack. They're gone," Nick said soberly.

"And the crèche? Did he throw it out?"

Nick shook his head.

"Oh man," Alex said softly. He felt as if he'd just been punched in the gut.

Nick said in dismay, "You and I are the last people who ever saw the crèche. I guess we'll have to tell the world what it looked like."

"Or maybe we should just keep that to ourselves and let people imagine it the way they want it to have been," Alex said quietly.

"Maybe. That's a decision for later. Right now, I want to get you to a medic to look at your noggin. You hit it pretty hard, there, when you tried to save Gray's men. What were you thinking, standing up and shouting at them like that? They could've shot you—"

He reached up and pressed his fingers against Nick's lips. "I was doing what you would've done. I was trying to save lives, for once."

"What are you talking about?"

"You've always been in the business of saving lives, and I've always been in the business of taking them. I wanted to be like you."

"You giant goofball. You are exactly like me! You've saved countless lives. We just went about it different ways."

Nick held a hand down to him and Alex reached up and took it. He let Nick drag him to his feet and pull him into a surprisingly gentle kiss.

And that was how a group of a half dozen women in full tactical gear managed to surround them and break out into cheers and catcalls as Nick kissed his lights out. Of course, he kissed Nick back just as passionately.

"Hey, you two," a man geared up like the women called out. "Get a room, will ya?"

Against his mouth, Nick muttered, "That's Gunnar and his Medusas."

"Suppose he'd be your best man at our wedding?" Alex muttered back.

"I'll ask him. Tomorrow. After we've gone back to our room and I've properly proposed to you."

"Maybe I'll propose to you, first," Alex declared.

Simultaneously, they said, "Will you marry me?"

"I said it first," Alex said quickly.

"It was a tie!" Nick exclaimed. "And we fought to a stalemate!"

"Fine. What's your answer?" Alex challenged.

"Yes!" they said again exactly simultaneously.

"I'm okay with a tie," Alex said, gazing up at Nick. "As long as it's a knot tied with you."

"That's the hokiest thing I've ever heard," Nick declared, grinning ear to ear.

"Then, I guess you're marrying a hokey man, aren't you?"

"Guess I am."

And they sealed the deal with another kiss, the first of a lifetime full of them.

* * * * *

**WE HOPE YOU ENJOYED
THIS BOOK FROM**

◆ HARLEQUIN
**ROMANTIC
SUSPENSE**

Danger. Passion. Drama.

These heart-racing page-turners will keep you guessing to the very end. Experience the thrill of unexpected plot twists and irresistible chemistry.

4 NEW BOOKS AVAILABLE EVERY MONTH!

#2207 TO TRUST A COLTON COWBOY
The Coltons of Colorado • by Dana Nussio

Jasper Colton could never act on his crush—not only is Kayla St. James his employee, but his father's corruption sent her dad to prison. And yet he can't help but step in when she's dealing with a stalker. As the threats escalate, the two of them find their attraction hard to resist.

#2208 IN THE ARMS OF THE LAW
To Serve and Seduce • by Deborah Fletcher Mello

Attorney Ellington Black will sacrifice everything for his family. But when his brother is charged with murder, Special Agent Angela Stanfield puts his loyalty to the test. As her investigation puts her in danger—and points to a different killer than his brother—Ellington finds himself in the role of protector...and desire turns to love!

#2209 HOTSHOT HEROES UNDER THREAT
Hotshot Heroes • by Lisa Childs

Hotshot firefighter Patrick McRooney goes undercover to find the saboteur on his brother-in-law's elite Hotshot team, but as his investigation gets closer to the truth—and he gets closer to Henrietta Rowlins—threats are made. And Patrick isn't the only one they're targeting...

#2210 TEXAS LAW: UNDERCOVER JUSTICE
Texas Law • by Jennifer D. Bokal

Clare Chambers is a woman on the run and Isaac Patton is undercover, trying to find a hit man. When a body is found in the small town of Mercy, Texas, the two have to work together to catch a killer before Clare becomes the next victim.

The whole desperate plan began simply as a last-ditch attempt to save his life. He never intended for anyone to get hurt. That day, not long after Thanksgiving, he walked into the bank full of hope. It was the first time he'd ever asked for a loan. It was also the first time he'd ever seen executive loan officer Carla Richmond.

When he tapped at her open doorway, she looked up from that big desk of hers. He thought she was too young and pretty with her big blue eyes and all that curly chestnut-brown hair to make the decision as to whether he lived or died.

She had a great smile as she got to her feet to offer him a seat.

He felt so out of place in her plush office that he stood in the doorway nervously kneading the brim of his worn baseball cap for a moment before stepping in. As he did, her blue-eyed gaze took in his ill-fitting clothing hanging on his rangy body, his bad haircut, his large, weathered hands.

He told himself that she'd already made up her mind before he even sat down. She didn't give men like him a second look—let alone money. Like his father always said, bankers never gave dough to poor people who actually needed it. They just helped their rich friends.

Right away Carla Richmond made him feel small with her questions about his employment record, what he had for collateral, why he needed the money and how he planned to repay it. He'd recently lost one crappy job and was in the process of starting another temporary one, and all he had to show for the years he'd worked hard labor since high school was an old pickup and a pile of bills.

He took the forms she handed him and thanked her, knowing he wasn't going to bother filling them in. On the way out of her office, he balled them up and dropped them in the trash. All the way to his pickup, he mentally kicked himself for being such a fool. What had he expected?

No one was going to give him money, even to save his life—especially some woman in a suit behind a big desk in an air-conditioned office. It didn't matter that she didn't have a clue how desperate he really was. All she'd seen when she'd looked at him was a loser. To think that he'd bought a new pair of jeans with the last of his cash and borrowed a too-large button-up shirt from a former coworker for this meeting.

After climbing into his truck, he sat for a moment, too scared and sick at heart to start the engine. The worst part was the thought of going home and telling Jesse. The way his luck was going, she would walk out on him. Not that he could blame her, since his gambling had gotten them into this mess.

He thought about blowing off work, since his new job was only temporary anyway, and going straight to the bar. Then he reminded himself that he'd spent the last of his money on the jeans. He couldn't even afford a beer. His own fault, he reminded himself. He'd only made things worse when he'd gone to a loan shark for cash and then stupidly gambled the money, thinking he could make back what he owed and then some when he won. He'd been so sure his luck had changed for the better when he'd met Jesse.

Last time the two thugs had come to collect the interest on the loan, they'd left him bleeding in the dirt outside his rented house. They would be back any day.

With a curse, he started the pickup. A cloud of exhaust blew out the back as he headed home to face Jesse with the bad news. Asking for a loan had been a long shot, but still he couldn't help thinking about the disappointment he'd see in her eyes when he told her. They'd planned to go out tonight for an expensive dinner with the loan money to celebrate.

As he drove home, his humiliation began to fester like a sore that just wouldn't heal. Had he known even then how this was going to end? Or was he still telling himself he was just a nice guy who'd made some mistakes, had some bad luck and gotten involved with the wrong people?

Don't miss
Christmas Ransom *by B.J. Daniels,*
available December 2022 wherever
Harlequin books and ebooks are sold.

Harlequin.com

HARLEQUIN
PLUS

Announcing a **BRAND-NEW**
multimedia subscription service
for romance fans like you!

Read, Watch and Play.

Experience the easiest way to get
the romance content you crave.

Start your **FREE 7 DAY TRIAL** at
<u>www.harlequinplus.com/freetrial</u>.